THE TIMELESS VIGILANTE

THE TIMELESS VIGILANTE

THE FIRST BEAUFONT™
BOOK ONE

SARAH NOFFKE

MICHAEL ANDERLE

LMBPN® Publishing
2375 E. Tropicana Avenue, Suite 8-305
Las Vegas, Nevada 89119 USA

Version 1.00, April 2024
eBook ISBN: 979-8-88878-748-9
Print ISBN: 979-8-88878-928-5

THE TIMELESS VIGILANTE TEAM

Thanks to the JIT Readers

Jackey Hankard-Brodie
Dave Hicks
Daryl McDaniel
Deb Mader
Veronica Stephan-Miller
Diane L. Smith
Jeff Goode
Christopher Gilliard
Dorothy Lloyd
Jan Hunnicutt
Angel LaVey

For my family, Craig and Lydia.
Familia Est Sempiternum.

— Sarah

To Family, Friends and
Those Who Love
to Read.
May We All Enjoy Grace
to Live the Life We Are
Called.

— Michael

CHAPTER ONE

THERE'S A NEW SHERIFF IN TOWN

<u>**Commissioner's Office, Los Angeles Police Department Headquarters, Los Angeles, California, United States**</u>

Burdens were made to be carried, however heavy they were. Peter Stevenson knew that better than most. As the Commissioner for Los Angeles, he had felt the weight of the city's problems breaking his back for over five years. The job never got any easier but as a diehard public service officer, the stress was always worth it.

Reaching for his trusty bottle of antacids on his desk, Peter caught sight of something stir in the shadows in the open doorway. He paused. Someone was there, lurking in the darkness. It was late. The cleaning crew had already gone home. Most nights, Peter stayed past the janitorial staff—working long into the early morning hours.

Something flashed on the other side of Peter's office. A blur of movement assaulted his vision. The Commissioner pushed back, tensing and defenseless as the hooded figure took a position in front of his desk.

Although Peter couldn't see the visitor's face, he recognized the man dressed in armor. He sighed, grabbing at his chest, willing his heart to slow after the scare. "You nearly gave me a heart attack," Peter said through a measured breath. "What are you doing here?"

The man stayed in the shadows, his face obscured, but Peter pictured his crooked smile when he laughed, enjoying having frightened the overworked Police Chief. He hadn't seen the man often, but each time was marked by adrenaline, since he often showed up uninvited and with a hint of a threat.

"You're so easy to scare," the man said, still laughing coldly. "That's why you're being replaced."

Peter stood at once, shaking even more now. "You can't get rid of me. We had a deal."

"You *had* a deal with the old leader," the man stated, defiantly. He reached out, drawing his finger over the front of Peter's desk, like checking for dust. He held up his gloved hand, inspecting it. "They've been replaced, just like you."

"By who?" Peter asked, wishing he'd taken his antacids, his chest tightening with tension.

The man chuckled again, throwing back his head slightly, not displacing the hood covering his face. "By me."

"Well, you can't get rid of me," Peter argued, shaking his head. "I don't work for you. I simply had an arrangement."

"Don't you see, you've always worked for us," the man said coldly. "We put you in power and kept you there. Now I'm in charge and I've decided that you're being replaced."

"I'll fight this. I'll fight you," Peter said, vibrating with sudden anxiety. He would go to the mayor. He'd go over everyone's head. He'd go to the House of Fourteen, the organization that governed magic in this world. They were the most powerful agency. He'd ensure that he didn't lose this job—the one thing that meant everything to him.

"There is no fighting this," the man said, withdrawing something from behind his back.

"I can't be fired!" Peter yelled, his face flushing red with anger.

"Oh, you're not being fired," the man said, lifting his hand up, but the darkness concealing what he was holding. "Like I said, you're being replaced. We all know the bureaucracy of electing a new Commissioner is ridiculous and cumbersome. But when the role is suddenly vacant, it's much faster and easier to fill."

An ambient light caught the shine of the gun. A soundless scream flew from Peter's mouth. The Commissioner of Los Angeles had seen a lot in his day, but he'd never seen his life flash before his eyes.

"You can't do this," Peter croaked, looking around suddenly for a way to defend himself. For a way to call for help. He stumbled back, hitting his rolling chair.

The man stepped forward, his crooked teeth showing when he smiled. "Of course I can. There's a new sheriff in town."

CHAPTER TWO

THE GIRL IN THE SHADOWS

<u>**Back Alleyways of West Hollywood, California, United States**</u>

This showdown between Vinny's gang and his rival, Maurice's, had been a long time coming. The fights in the streets were numerous, each gang member taking a shot when they could. It was time that the leaders fought—ending this battle— proving once and for all who ruled the streets of Los Angeles. Vinny knew it would be him.

Facing the large man in the alleyway, Vinny felt the familiar thrill of adrenaline as it filled his veins. Maurice might be larger than Vinny, but that didn't matter. This fight would be won by the quickest hand. It would be secured by the first man to pull his gun and fire with the truest aim.

Eyeing the men flanking Maurice, Vinny counted the many figures dressed in black. There were three of them and three men standing at Vinny's back. When this fight was over, there would be fewer. But because the gang leader was so confident that he'd win, he didn't worry that he'd lose all his men.

Behind Maurice and his goons, people passed by the narrow alleyway on their way home or off to the bars and restaurants.

The shootout would no doubt take down innocent people, but that wasn't Vinny's problem.

They were fighting under the streetlamps in a back alleyway. That was one way they'd lessened stray bullets. But he'd mostly chosen this place for the duel so they didn't get the attention of the police, rather than to protect the innocent. If a few who weren't gang members took a bullet, then what did Vinny care? He had to show Maurice who was boss, once and for all.

"This ends tonight," Vinny said, his voice clear and loud, his hand flexing next to his gun on his hip.

Maurice laughed, showing a row of silver teeth. "Where do you want to be buried?"

Vinny's eyes flicked up when the streetlamp over them sputtered, making him nearly pull his gun prematurely. That wasn't the rule, though. Vinny was many despicable things, but he played by the rules. He wouldn't pull his gun until the countdown.

"We agree that whoever wins this, rules the streets of Los Angeles. Their gang members show the winner allegiance, right?" Vinny asked, looking around at the other men surrounding the man before him.

Another laugh from Maurice. "Yeah, your gang is about to work for me, being my footstools."

Tired of Maurice's usual smack talking and ready to put a cap in this guy once and for all, Vinny was ready to call for the countdown. Before he could, the streetlamp flickered overhead. Went out completely, raining sparks down on the gangs below, like there had been an electrical fire.

Something dropped down from the sky between Vinny and Maurice. A crouched figure stood. In the dark, Vinny could only make out the outline of a small person before they sprang into action. Before anyone could react, before anyone could fire, before the shouts rang out, a boot whacked Vinny hard across the face.

He hit the pavement with a thud, never remembering being assaulted so hard and abruptly. Rolling to the side, he watched a slender, hooded figure in black knock out Maurice, kicking him hard across the face. Behind him, Vinny's men fled, their footsteps sounding like true betrayal to him.

One of the gang members rushed forward, but the strange intruder spun around, thrusting their boot into his stomach, knocking him into the men behind them. They fell like dominos. Picking up a trashcan, the invader threw it down on the cluster of tangled men on the pavement.

In a blur, the assailant defended themself from the last man standing, one who had been hiding to the side. Easily, the hooded figure wrapped their arms around the man's neck, twisted forward and threw him over their back, hard to the concrete, knocking them out at once.

Vinny made to stand, but a boot pushed him down again, pressing hard into his back.

"If you want to kill each other, then do it," the voice of a woman said. "But don't do it where innocent people can get hurt. If this happens again, then next time, I won't leave any of you alive. Got it?"

With his face pressed hard into the smelly pavement, Vinny could only manage a grunt that he hoped sounded like yes.

The woman picked up her foot, stepping back into the shadows. Vinny lifted up, catching sight of the stranger who had taken down five men at once and scared away the cowards he called gang members. She was beautiful in the ambient light from the neighboring streets, her hood having fallen back to reveal a long blonde braid over her shoulder. She was dressed like straight out of the medieval era in an armored top laced up in the front and a half skirt and boots. Her porcelain skin made her seem fragile, although the way she'd kicked all their asses contradicted that observation.

"Who are you?" Vinny asked through a mouthful of blood,

knowing that he'd never seen anyone like this before. "W-W-What are you?"

"I'm Gen Beaufont," the woman said, glaring down at him. "I'm a medieval warrior, meant to fix this world."

And just as fast as the vigilante had appeared, she vanished, leaving no trace and all who had witnessed her prowess, cowering in fear.

CHAPTER THREE

THE PSYCHIC DRAGON

Genevieve Beaufont hadn't gone by that name since she left 1426 London, England. That had only been a few weeks ago, but still the woman she used to be felt a world away. Gen had no idea when she followed two women through a portal that she'd traversed six hundred years into the future. She had no idea the women were her relatives from modern-day Los Angeles. She had no idea where Los Angeles was or that there was another continent on the other side of the world. And the list of things that Gen didn't know had only gotten longer since being dropped and stuck in the twenty-first century.

Gen Beaufont could never go home. Her curiosity had always gotten her in trouble. This time, it had gotten her stranded in a brand-new era. Thankfully, the universe hadn't totally left her abandoned. For one, she had her modern-day family—the Beaufonts. They were leaders in the House of Fourteen, comprised of the most powerful magicians in the world, which ironically was the magical governing agency that Gen and her father, William, had founded. They also held many other roles as magicians in the present time, like leaders of the dragonriders.

That was the other part of Gen's life that didn't suck. She had her dragon egg, her most prized object that she stole in the 1400s and buried. She'd found the dragon's egg in the forest—the animal within the shell speaking to her in her mind. He'd told her that he was the first dragon egg ever spawned. Not knowing what a dragon was, Gen was very confused. Then he told her, telepathically, that she had to hide him because the world wasn't ready for a female dragonrider and she was meant for him.

Afraid of trusting a disembodied voice in her head, but also of losing him, Gen did as she was told. And so, the egg stayed buried in London until last week, when the dragon called to her and she dug him up. A lot had changed in Gen's life, except for one thing —her dragon was still hiding away in his shell, unwilling to hatch even now.

Gen strode into the living room of the condominium that belonged to her relatives from the future, a pair of siblings, Clark and Liv Beaufont. They were her relatives, twenty-something generations in the future.

And their residence? Well, it looked like a shiny white box with angular surfaces and hardly a lick of color anywhere. But plastered across the walls of the dining room was the family motto that Gen's father William had coined and which had been passed down through the years. The words read: *Familia Est Sempiternum*. And that simple phrase meant: Family is forever.

Gen paused in front of the dining room table. She lowered her chin and regarded the shimmering, huge dragon egg with slight annoyance.

"So, you were right," she said out loud, although that wasn't necessary since he spoke in her head. It just made her feel a little less crazy if she was speaking rather than having a back and forth with a dragon, telepathically.

Of course I was right, the dragon said in his deep voice in

Gen's head. *I clearly heard the gang members due to their ill will and violent intent toward each other. Those kinds of emotions broadcast thoughts louder than anything else.*

"Right," Gen said, having learned after digging up her dragon's egg that he couldn't just hear her thoughts, but those of others, although not consistently. The dragon apparently was also psychic and also promised to have other abilities that he would one day reveal to her.

So, you seemed to have had an easy time of breaking up that showdown, which would have been a blood bath in the streets, the dragon whose name Gen didn't know yet stated. She apparently would know his name upon meeting him, but only if she was in fact his one true rider. It was the final test to their bonding and sealed their connection.

"It would have been a bit easier if I had some help," Gen said, glaring down at the massive egg covered in shiny purple-like scales, giving the dragon a pointed look that he could sense, even if he couldn't see. However, Gen also knew that he saw through her eyes, through something called scrying, so he got extra glimpses of her world, meaning he would have seen the whole fight with the gang members in the streets of Los Angeles.

"I mean you," Gen continued. "You could have been there to help."

I was busy, the dragon said blankly.

"Doing what?" Gen challenged, sticking her hands on her hips.

Being.

"Being what?" Gen asked.

Being remarkable.

Gen sighed. "When are you going to hatch? And don't say, when you're ready. You've been in that shell for over six hundred years. I think you've incubated long enough."

When I feel like it, he replied.

"I think you're afraid."

Afraid of what? the dragon questioned.

"You're the very first dragon egg ever spawned and now you're the last to ever hatch, since all two thousand have hatched already—all but you, Mr. Two thousand and one."

I prefer to go by Number One, not Two Thousand and One, the dragon stated matter-of-factly.

"So, the way I see it is you're worried that when you finally hatch, you'll be a runt and everyone will be like, the first dragon isn't that impressive."

I don't have stunted growth, the dragon argued. *I will hatch when the time is right. When the environment is.*

"Can you give me a clue of when that will be?" Gen asked. "I don't want to be asleep or fighting bad guys alone and miss your big hatching. I mean, I'd take you to these fights. However, bringing an egg along isn't really that helpful. You're about as effective as rolling a stone at villains."

Bowling ball, the dragon stated.

"Say what?"

In modern times, where you find yourself, there's a game where people roll a heavy ball at pins to knock them down. That's the better reference. I'd be like bringing a bowling ball to a fight.

"How come you've been in that shell for all your life, and you know more about the world than me?" she questioned.

I listen, he answered. *I pick up on things. I'm in touch with the social consciousness. Oh, and I'm psychic.*

"Like you knew when those bad guys were about to have a showdown in the streets of Los Angeles," she stated. "Imagine how effective we could be if you broke out of your shell and helped me out."

I'm busy...

Gen sighed, looking around at the place full of white shiny surfaces and things she didn't understand. "Okay, well, fine. Just don't leave me waiting much longer."

Like you left me buried for six hundred years?

"That passed for me within seconds, but sorry, I'm sure that was lonely," Gen offered, sympathetically.

It made me a good listener, the dragon stated in her head. *Now go and get something to eat. I hear your stomach growling.*

Gen nodded, turning for the kitchen. "I'll try, but I don't really know how anything works here."

Just don't put your finger in an electric socket and you'll be fine, the dragon offered.

Gen frowned at the egg. "What's a… Never mind. I'll figure it out on my own."

CHAPTER FOUR

THE RELUCTANT HATCHLING

<u>Dining Room, Beaufont Residence, West Hollywood, California, United States</u>

"I say we threaten to toss him over the balcony railing," Liv Beaufont said, nodding at the large purple dragon egg sitting on the dining room table, like a centerpiece.

Gen smirked, having made a similar threat to encourage her dragon's egg to hatch. "He says that he'd just bounce off the cement and roll."

Liv grinned across the table at Gen. She looked very similar to the medieval warrior with her long blonde hair, blue eyes and strong build. It made sense though because they were blood-related, just twenty-something generations apart. Liv was one of the two women who Gen had followed through what she thought was a portal across space. It turned out it was a time gate.

Liv, who worked as Father Time's assistant, had been in 1426, fixing some holes in time, and then Gen had spotted the imposters and followed them. That was the short story of how the woman who was born in 1406 was sitting at a breakfast table in the twenty-first century in West Hollywood.

Ironically, Olivia Beaufont, who only went by Liv, similar to how Gen didn't go by the name her father gave her, Genevieve, was a current warrior for the House of Fourteen. Gen and her father had created the magical governing agency with six other magician families. She was the first warrior, the role of the ones who were meant to police magic out in the world. Their counterparts, the councilors, were like her father, William Beaufont. They were the thinkers of the House of Fourteen and analyzed and assigned the cases, ensuring that magic was balanced and right in the world.

Apparently, a lot had changed in the world since William and his daughter created the House of Fourteen. Thankfully, the magical governing agency was still in power and doing the job that her father and she built all those centuries ago. That was something, but for Gen, understanding the changes of the modern world would take much time and probably be very comedic to her relatives, as well as her dragon, who strangely understood the world better than her, although hiding in his egg still.

"I don't think bullying the dragon out of his egg is the right approach," Clark Beaufont said, turning a page in the book he was studying, taking a sip of his steaming coffee at the same time. "From what I've read, a dragon knows the perfect time to hatch based on their purpose and their rider's maturity. It's about finding the sweet spot between time and development."

Clark Beaufont, the only male in the current Beaufont family, reminded Gen a lot of her father, who she already missed sorely. It was hard knowing that she could never get back to her time and see her father. It was easier knowing that she still had family and a mission.

Not just that, but Gen had a mission and opportunity in the twenty-first century. She realized now that she was always meant for this time period. That was why despite everything that Liv and Father Time did to put Gen back in her timeline, it didn't work. This warrior was made for the modern world.

Back in 1426, her father insisted that Gen fight for justice. However, Gen was a rebel who wanted to ride a dragon. She didn't know what that meant, but over time she learned and now that's all she wanted. To be the rebellious type soaring over the sky. In the modern era, that was allowed for women. Back in the medieval time, it wasn't an option.

Gen looked across the table at Clark, the guy who was like her cousin in the future. His blond hair and blue eyes reminded her of William Beaufont, the biggest influence in her life. He might have wanted her, Gen, to be something that she wasn't, but that's only because he didn't know that she had a dragon's egg. He simply didn't know what was possible. And it wouldn't have been allowed for Gen. Not until Sophia Beaufont came along six hundred years later were women allowed to be dragonriders. Everything happened for a reason and those reasons were at play in Gen's life currently.

"Many a dragon has hatched well before they bonded with a rider," Liv argued. "I think that Rufus is just being stubborn."

Gen laughed, looking at her plate of waffles with uncertainty. "His name isn't Rufus, although I can't tell you what it is."

"You won't know what it is until he hatches," Sophia Beaufont advised beside her sister and brother at the breakfast table. This woman was the first actual female dragonrider, although she looked more like a princess with her dainty features and small build and Beaufont blonde hair and blue eyes. However, there was a fierceness in Sophia's eyes that no sane man would challenge, thinking he'd survive. "But I assure you, that you'll simply know it—at your heart."

Sophia had been the first female dragonrider, the first in a hundred years. There had been one thousand and one dragon eggs spawned in the beginning. Then Sophia came along and another thousand spawned. That was the end. All those eggs had hatched—all but Gen's dragon's. He was the very last. But dragons lived thousands of years, so the fact that he and his rider would be here for a long time was something. But also, made Gen antsy for her dragon to hatch so that their life together could start.

"That's bizarre to know someone's name without them telling you," Gen said, looking at the shimmering purple egg, wishing that she could read her dragon's mind the way he could read hers. Gen mused, amazed by this new life and everything that was a part of it.

"Is the waffle okay?" Clark asked, giving Gen a look of concern. "I'm sure the food here is strange to you. I can make you whatever you like."

"The food must be weird," Liv acknowledged. "Are you mostly used to boiled potatoes and roasted turkey legs? Do you know how to use a fork?"

Gen chuckled, grateful for the teasing.

"Don't be so rude," Clark admonished, glaring at his sister across the table.

"She's right actually," Gen admitted. "Forks weren't really common in the 1400s in London. But I'm a master at observing and have figured it out watching you all." She pointed to the siblings all daintily holding forks.

"You are a master at adapting," Clark said with a sincere smile.

"I think you should lean into this medieval thing." Liv dropped her fork and picked up her waffle, tearing into it with her teeth. "Don't conform to our ways. Instead, you should make us savages."

Again Gen laughed. "I'm sure that I'm going to slip up and do a lot to embarrass myself. But I have to think of my father, William Beaufont and how he'd want to represent the family. I've already got a hot temper, so I think it's best if I at least try and have a little decorum."

Liv took another bite of her waffle, using her hands. "Decorum is overrated. You're going to be a dragonrider and they are the most rough and tumble amongst us."

"That's actually very true. What I think you should do is come to the Gullington," Sophia began, picking at her waffle. "That's the home of the dragons. We have experts there in Scotland who can advise. They'll know if there's a problem. They can probably advise on the timeframe. You can be trained as a dragonrider and more while you wait."

Gen nodded, kicking her own waffle around with her fork. "That sounds smart." She'd heard about this Dragon Elite, the organization of angel dragonriders who presided over the arbitrations of the world's government. They were the supreme source of order over the world's affairs. They were different from the Rogue Riders, the other organization of demon dragonriders who presided over the criminal world, keeping it at bay. Both were considered valuable and neither bad, but they served a different purpose. Like yin and yang. Like black and white.

"Well, I think you'll fit in really well in the Gullington," Sophia offered. "How about we take your dragon's egg there for a change of pace? I'm sure you're getting bored hanging around here while these two work." She thumbed in the direction of Liv and Clark.

"I don't think she's bored," Clark said, leaning forward, giving Gen a pointed look. "Last night, there was a strange report about a lone woman who broke up a gang fight before it could take down civilians. And it was right down the street from here. You wouldn't know anything about that, would you?"

Gen hid her grin. "What's a gang? What's a civilian? I don't know what you're talking about."

Liv threw her head back, laughing. "I love her so much. She's ignorant when she needs to be and then educated when she decides. We will never know the truth with this one."

Clark regarded his sister with annoyance. "She's your relative, for sure."

Gen patted him on the forearm. "You are much more like my father, the first councilor for the House of Fourteen. He abided by rules and wanted the rest of the world to follow suit. I, on the other hand, well, I was like Liv here. I wanted to break the world and make it anew."

Liv laughed again. "Damn it, if you're not just me from the past."

Gen nodded, smiling at Sophia. "But yes, I think the Gullington sounds old-world and more up my alley. I don't understand electricity and modern conveniences. Take me to Scotland."

"Okay, but just so you know, it's somewhat modernized, just more stuck," Sophia advised. "But yes, I think it could help you to know when your dragon is going to hatch."

All four Beaufonts looked to the center of the table at the large dragon egg. Gen wanted to meet her dragon. That's what she needed to make this strange new life feel complete. But she knew her dragon was waiting until she was ready. So she just needed to do everything to get there. Then they could start their life together, tearing up the bad guys and making the world a better place—finally.

CHAPTER FIVE

THE HEARTBEAT OF THE HIGHLANDS

<u>The Gullington, Scotland, United Kingdom</u>

Emerging from the swirling portal, Gen found herself enveloped by the rugged embrace of the Scottish Highlands. The rolling green hills were a stark contrast to the metallic sheen and incessant drone of Los Angeles. The air was crisp and invigorating, filling her lungs with a freshness reminiscent of an England she once knew, yet untouched by the soot and clamor of 1426 London.

Before her stretched vast expanses of undulating hills like waves spreading towards distant mountains which pierced the sky with their stoic presence. Rock formations stood majestically like guards across the landscape. They cast long, dark shadows against the heather. Hidden amongst these natural fortresses were caves, their mouths agape promising shelter or perhaps the entrance to worlds unseen. A loch lay nestled in the valley below, its surface a mirror to the changing moods of the sky.

It wasn't just the sights that captivated Gen, it was the scent of wet earth mingled with the hint of wild thyme and the peaty perfume of distant fires. The mix of smells painted a picture more vivid than any she had ever known. The sounds, too, were a solace to her soul after the loud and incessant mechanical noises of Los Angeles. The melodic call of a distant bird, the rustle of grass underfoot and the soft murmur of the loch lapping at its banks were all welcoming sounds from a world Gen thought she'd lost forever.

Yet, amidst this familiarity, a sense of strangeness tugged at her mind. Something unseen pulsed in the distance, its rhythm steady and compelling, like the heartbeat of the land itself. Gen wasn't afraid of this unknown entity that she felt before her, but rather extremely curious.

There, in the wilds of Scotland, Gen found not the disorienting sense of her arrival in Los Angeles, but a connection to the earth that felt as ancient as her soul. The contrast was profound. Moments prior, Gen had been in a world where nature was mastered and muted. Now to step back in time to where wildlife was revered made her feel a sense of home that she'd thought she'd lost forever.

Sophia, the picture of elegance and poise, stood patiently beside Gen, allowing her a peaceful moment to get to know the land. Gen knew that this was her relative, but she thought that in any life and with any arrangement she would like the dragonrider beside her. She was pure goodness, not too overwhelming in personality and not too bland.

Liv and Clark, who had stayed in Los Angeles, were the extremes to this, leaving the younger sister, Sophia, to have found her place in the middle. Gen also quite adored Liv and Clark because their personalities uniquely matched them to their roles as warrior and councilor, respectively.

"This is known as the Expanse," Sophia began, finally breaking the silence, waving at the hills, mountains and loch in the distance. "The dragons live in the Caves there." She pointed to the opening in the rock formations.

Suddenly, Gen couldn't look away as she held her dragon's egg close to her chest. She longed to see a dragon in the flesh since she'd only ever heard of these majestic creatures and later saw artistic renditions of them. The first dragonrider was announced in 1420, the same year that she found her egg. However, the dragon in the egg she held now insisted that he was the first egg spawned and since then, Mother Nature had confirmed this for Gen.

She still couldn't believe she lived in a world where Mother Nature, who went by Mama Jamba, and Father Time, who went by Papa Creola, were close family friends to the Beaufonts. As Gen regarded the magnificent land before her, she had a feeling things were about to get a lot stranger.

Sophia pointed to the untouched hills where Gen sensed something pulsing like a person. "And over there in the distance—"

"Is a castle," Gen interrupted Sophia.

The other woman grinned at her in surprise. "How did you know? Did your dragon tell you?" She indicated to the large purple egg in Gen's arms.

She shook her head. "No, I just sensed it. But why can't we see this castle?"

"It's protected by the Barrier, which keeps the Dragon Elite hidden from enemies or fans." Sophia laughed, encouraging Gen to follow her forward. "We only need to cross the Barrier and then you can see the Expanse for what it really is."

True to her word, after a few steps, a huge and majestic castle appeared. It nearly made Gen halt in her tracks, feeling so struck by an image she associated with her old life, which was only a few weeks ago. But still, the rustic look of the castle reminded Gen of her time traveling the hillsides of England and even a few trips through Scotland.

"It's…not…right." Gen finally got out the words, not sure exactly what she was trying to say or why they came out that way.

Sophia actually nodded to this. "You're very intuitive and see that which most don't. The Castle, like the Gullington, is not a place as much as it is a person. It's created and run by a man, who is hardly that—more a demi-god. The Castle is his heart." She nodded at the loch in the distance. "The Pond is his blood. The Expanse is his mind. And every fleeting part of him affects the way the Gullington behaves. The winds change by this man's breath."

"That's magical," Gen said in awe.

Sophia winked at her. "It was a gift from Mama Jamba. She wanted the Dragon Elite to have a home that took care of us the same way that the noblest and most loyal soldier would. Quiet is that man. His intentions mind the flock." She motioned to the sheep in the distance. "And his moods, well, they make things ever changing. The Gullington is now your home, since you're a dragonrider, so get ready for some crazy antics. If Quiet likes you, then your room in the Castle will be exactly to your liking. If he doesn't, which I couldn't see being the case, then you'll probably get tossed out of bed by an invisible force regularly."

Gen chuckled, again astounded by this world. "I can't wait to meet this god-like man named Quiet."

"You won't have to wait long," Sophia said, pointing her head to the front of the Castle. "He and our dragon expert are already waiting to greet us." She glanced up to the rock formation and grinned as the head of the first dragon Gen had ever set eyes upon peeked out of the cave opening. "Oh, and Lunis, my dragon, is here and excited to meet you."

Gen held up the egg. "And my dragon too."

Sophia shook her head, continuing forward. "The dragons all know each other, having been connected through the chi of the dragon from the very beginning. They've never met since they've always been one."

CHAPTER SIX

THE DRAGON'S NOBLE SALUTE

<u>The Expanse, The Gullington, Scotland, United Kingdom</u>

Gen's gaze lifted to the mouth of the towering caves set high upon the craggy face of the mountain. There, against the stark contrast of the weathered stone, was the head and neck of a creature so magnificent, so utterly beyond the realm of her understanding, that for a moment, she forgot to breathe. The giant blue dragon was covered in shimmering scales like sapphires in the sunlight. Lunis surveyed the world below with eyes that sparkled with the wisdom of the ages.

Then, with a grace that contradicted its immense size, the dragon dove forward, like doing a free fall. Quickly after clearing the cave, he unfurled his wings—a breathtaking span that caught the morning light and splintered it into a thousand dazzling hues. The air thrummed with power as the dragon flapped his wings. The sheer force of the movements sent a gust that whipped through Gen's hair and tugged at her clothes, a physical testament to the creature's might.

As Lunis sailed through the sky, his flight was a dance of elegance and strength, each beat of his wings propelling him closer to where the two women stood on the Expanse. The land itself seemed to hold its breath, the usual whispers of the wind and calls of distant birds falling silent in awe of the spectacle unfolding.

The dragon's approach was heralded by the shadow it cast, a moving darkness that played across the green tapestry of the hills. Lunis landed in a masterful display of power and control, the ground beneath his feet barely whispering a protest despite the dragon's colossal weight.

Then, in a gesture that was as unexpected as it was breathtaking, the dragon bowed before Gen, his great head lowered in a noble salute. The moment was surreal, a blend of fear, wonder and an unspoken bond that tugged at the core of her being. Here, in this wild corner of the world, Gen stood face-to-face with a creature of legend, a being of majesty and mystery that had stepped right out of the pages of the fairy tales.

The experience was exhilarating, a vivid splash of magic against the canvas of reality, making Gen's heart race with a mix of excitement and a touch of whimsy. In this encounter, the impossible became possible, and Gen knew that her journey in this new world had taken a turn into the realms of the extraordinary.

When Lunis lifted his head, Gen was surprised to see the blue dragon smiling. It was such a strange, unexpected gesture on his face and yet, he looked about like a pirate, thinking of the punch line to a joke. His wise eyes danced with amusement, looking between her and the large purple egg in her arms.

"He's heavy, isn't he?" the dragon asked, winking at Gen.

Not at all expecting this after that greeting, Gen cut her eyes to Sophia, giving her a look of confusion.

The dragonrider sighed heavily. "Could you have started with hello instead of calling her dragon fat?"

"I'm not calling him fat," Lunis replied, folding his large wings into his body neatly. "I'm simply implying that her arms are probably quite tired. That egg is about as big as her." Shaking this off, Lunis glanced back at Gen. "And I'm sorry. I meant to say, hello, dear majesty, first warrior and Founder for the House of Fourteen, time traveler and ancient ancestor of the Beaufonts." He then cut his gaze back at Sophia and stuck out his tongue. "How was that?"

Sophia laughed, shaking her head and looking at Gen. "If you were expecting the sage-like dragon experience, you're not getting it with Lunis. He tells dad jokes and makes insults. It's his thing as the first dragon of the new generation. He likes to be as ridiculous as possible."

"*You're* ridiculous," Lunis fired back.

"Well, nice to meet you," Gen said, lifting the egg that was quite heavy in her arms. "And he's okay, but I look forward to setting him down."

"Go ahead," Sophia encouraged, motioning to the two figures striding over from the Castle. "Mahkah and Quiet are joining us."

"Okay." Gen slid the large purple egg onto the grass in front of Lunis, who eyed it with intrigue.

He then bowed his head slightly. "And hello to you, Old Man."

Gen laughed. "So you can talk to him? You two know each other?"

"We all know each other," Lunis said. "But you have to know his name instinctively to fully bond with him, so I can't give you any spoilers. Each rider must get to know their dragon on their own."

"Well, I'm just hoping that you all can tell me when he's going to hatch," Gen said with a sigh. "I'm hoping it will be this century."

"I think it will be soon," Lunis said, a new seriousness to his voice.

Gen was about to press for more information but right then, the two men from the Castle neared. One was tall, slender and stoic. He had dark, tan skin and his long black hair pulled back in a long braid, much like how Gen wore hers. The other, well, he was a short, round gnome with rosy cheeks and bright blue eyes.

"Oh, you must be Quiet," Gen said, stepping forward and curtseying slightly to the tall man wearing a serious expression.

"Actually, I'm Mahkah, the expert on dragons," the man said, pointing to himself and then to the gnome, several feet shorter than him. "This is Quiet. This is his Gullington which gives him a distinct knowledge of dragons, being the one who looks after their home and has for over five hundred years."

"Oh," Gen said in sudden surprise and embarrassment. She hadn't expected that the unassuming gnome with the chubby cheeks and a burlap hat covering his round head was the demigod who Sophia had described as being all of the land and castle where they stood presently. "My apologies. Well, I'm Genevieve Beaufont but please call me Gen."

"We've heard much about you, Gen," Mahkah said, bowing slightly. "And of your dragon, the first egg ever spawned."

The gnome muttered something, but Gen didn't make it out, either because his voice was so low or his words incoherent, she couldn't tell. However, Mahkah and Sophia both nodded to him, like they perfectly understood what he said.

"It is very exciting that we will have another dragonrider and the first egg ever," Sophia said, smiling at Gen. "We simply have to wait until your dragon hatches."

"And you said that would be soon?" Gen asked, looking at Lunis quizzically.

"Yes, I think so," Lunis said in a suddenly refined voice.

"Well, when? What can I do?" Gen questioned.

"Why don't you try telling him a few jokes," Lunis offered.

Sophia groaned. "Oh, no. Not this… She's brand new to our world. Give her a break, would you?"

"What do you mean?" Gen asked, confused, looking between Sophia and her dragon. "Why would I tell my dragon's egg a few jokes?"

"To see if you can crack him up," Lunis said and then roared with laughter, throwing his head back and vibrating the ground with the noise.

Sophia sighed. "Sorry, Gen. My dragon is special. I told you, he tells dad jokes. They never, ever stop. Not for decades."

Gen smiled, chuckling softly. "I like a good joke. But I'm not sure that will work on my dragon. Do you all have any ideas? He says he will hatch when he's ready, when I am and when the environment is."

"How about you give us a moment to inspect the egg," Mahkah offered, thoughtfully, the picture of calmness. "Then we can give you a full assessment and hopefully some answers."

"That's a good idea," Sophia said, motioning to the Castle. "And in the meantime, I'll introduce Gen to the leader of the Dragon Elite, Hiker Wallce."

Quiet muttered something, again inaudible under his breath.

Sophia nodded, a grim expression on her face. "I know. I'll deal with the wrath of that man. It's sort of my full-time hobby at this point."

"What wrath?" Gen asked, looking between the gnome and Sophia, wishing she knew what was going on. "Is something wrong?"

"Just that I've been keeping secrets," Sophia answered, tugging Gen toward the Castle. "Come on, this will be fun. Let's go to Hiker Wallace's office. I love watching that man get angry."

CHAPTER SEVEN

THE TALE OF TWO SISTERS

**<u>Hiker Wallace's Office, The Castle, The Gullington, Scotland,
United Kingdom</u>**

When Sophia led Gen into the Castle, she hurried her
upstairs, giving her a guilty look. Gen didn't ask any questions, as
she was taken to a second-floor office which apparently belonged
to this Hiker Wallace. However, Gen's silence was mostly because
she was overwhelmed by the grandness and whimsy of the
Castle's interior. It was unlike anything that Gen had seen and
then also, ironically, very much like the places she'd grown up. It
had the bones of a medieval castle, but the flare of the modern
world.

Gen had stepped through the towering front door, its stained-
glass window of angels casting a kaleidoscope of colors across
the stone floor in a silent welcome. The grandeur of the
entryway unfolded before her with its exposed beams. They were
a testament to the craftsmanship of her time, intricately carved
with old charm.

A grand staircase swept upwards, inviting exploration leading
to an open loft. Paintings adorned the walls, each a portal to a

moment frozen in time. Overhead, a rustic chandelier dangled, its light flickering like stars caught in a net of iron.

A coat of arms stood on the second-floor landing, bold and proud. It seemed to guard the artworks of dragons and their riders. Portraits of people long past gazed down, their eyes alight with the echoes of their achievements, inviting her into their ranks.

She felt a surge of familiarity, the architecture and adornments a mirror to the life she'd been ripped from. And yet here, her old world was touched with a whimsy that danced on the edge of magic and was very inviting.

Every detail, from the warmth of the hearth to the scent of aged wood and the soft glow of candlelight, spoke of old-world elegance that seemed to infuse the very air with anticipation. This was a place where the past met the present, where stories were not just told but lived, and where every corner held the promise of discovery.

Gen, with her warrior's heart and medieval soul, felt an overwhelming sense of belonging. It was as if the castle itself had extended an invitation to step into its embrace and become part of its ongoing story. She didn't know for sure, but she wanted to believe that even after her brief meeting with Quiet, that he liked her. That he, as the bones and living breath of this place, was saying that he welcomed her.

Sophia breezed into a regal office, the back wall lined with hundreds of volumes of old books. On the far side, there was a bank of windows that overlooked the Pond and Expanse in the distance, framing them perfectly. And to the left, sitting with his head down and attention on a set of papers on his desk, was a large, hulking man.

Gen guessed this was Hiker Wallace, the one Sophia hinted at having a bad attitude. He had blond hair to his shoulders and a beard to match, but she couldn't make out much more about him.

His head was bowed low and his eyes focused on the paper before him.

Without looking up, the man said, "Is this about the Commissioner of Los Angeles?" Hiker had a thick Scottish accent that made Gen think she was still in the 15th century.

Sophia halted suddenly, giving Gen a look of uncertainty. "No, sir. This is about something…else…"

With an annoyed sigh, Hiker glanced up, his mustache vibrating from the gesture. His eyes screwed up with confusion at the sight of Gen. "And who is that?"

"This is…well, sir, it's a funny story," Sophia began, actually looking a bit nervous for once.

Hiker grunted, narrowing his light-colored eyes at Sophia. He pressed his hand down on his armored tunic, growling low. "You and I almost never find the same things funny."

"True," Sophia chirped, pretending to laugh. "But isn't that because you don't find most things funny?"

Hiker didn't seem to think this warranted a reply and simply glared at her.

Sophia motioned to the chair in front of Hiker's desk, encouraging Gen to take it. Not wanting to be rude, Gen did as instructed, sliding into the high-backed, intricately carved chair, just as Sophia did the same thing beside her.

"You see, sir," Sophia began. "This is Gen and I couldn't tell you about her, well, because at first I didn't know because my sister Liv hadn't shared with me about the snafu in time travel. And then I did find out, but I was planning the right time to share this information with you and lo and behold, today's your lucky day."

Hiker lowered his chin, giving Sophia a pointed look that accurately spoke of his bad mood. The dragonrider was right, this man didn't seem like the cheerful type. "Get to the point. Why have you brought this actor from medieval Times into the Castle? How did you even get her in here?"

He looked Gen over. She was still wearing her warrior clothes from back in the day because mostly it was all she had and it was what she felt comfortable wearing. Liv and the other Beaufont women had of course offered for her to have some of their clothes but she didn't feel right about it. Therefore, Gen was wearing an armored top with cross stitching in the front, a half skirt, several belts strapped across her chest and hips and knee-high boots. It was the kind of things that medieval warrior women wore in her day. But since she was the only one, it was really only something worn by her.

Sophia cleared her throat. "She's not an actor. She's from the 15th century. And you will know her as Genevieve Beaufont, the first warrior and Founder for the House of Fourteen. She came through a time travel gate, following my sister and my niece, Rose, when they were repairing holes in the space-time continuum. But she's stuck here in this time." Sophia said all of this in quick succession, not even pausing to breathe between sentences.

If Sophia was worried that Hiker was going to be mad, then she was in for a surprise. The leader of the Dragon Elite put his head in his hand, resting on his elbow on his desk and regarded her with mild annoyance. "This sounds like a real pain in the rear end for Papa Creola. I bet that man wants to murder the Beaufonts. Genevieve Beaufont was a pretty big deal and if she's here, then she's not in the 15th century creating the history that we desperately need her to establish. She's the very foundation of the governing world of magic. So please, tell me, why is it that you've brought your colossal problem to me?"

Sophia held up a finger, pausing the man seated before her. "I'm getting to that. But good news, sir. Apparently, Liv, Rose and Father Time learned that Gen here was never supposed to go back. This is her timeframe."

He shook his head. "Of course, it's not. I know my history. Hell, I lived that history. I've been alive for close to six hundred years. I met Genevieve Beaufont and she was the cornerstone of the magical world."

"That's nice to hear," Gen said proudly, now knowing the truth of what happened and feeling an overwhelming sense of gratitude to her sister, Elizabeth, for her courage.

Hiker cut his eyes to her. "It is and you look younger than I remember. But it's nice to meet you again. Now get out and back in your own time before you make ours disintegrate."

Gen couldn't help but laugh. "We haven't met. Not until just now anyway."

"Of course we did," Hiker argued, growing even more annoyed. "Your son, Oscar Beaufont was one of my riders."

"Oscar," Gen said, fondly. "That's a nice name she chose."

Hiker's eyes widened with annoyance. He jerked his head to look at Sophia. "What in the bloody hell is going on here?"

Sophia let out a long breath. "Gen never went back to her timeline—ever. She simply went missing in 1426. So her father, William Beaufont, who had just founded the House of Fourteen with his daughter, became worried when the first warrior went missing. He thought that her absence would put his leadership in jeopardy. So even though he was upset about the mystery of losing Gen, he had her twin sister, Elizabeth replace her."

Hiker seemed to think for a moment. Shook his head. Narrowed his eyes. "No, Elizabeth is the one who went missing. I know my history. It was a mystery and William never quit looking for his daughter..." His voice trailed away as his eyes widened with understanding. "He never found her, because she came through a time gate to the modern world... You're Genevieve Beaufont, aren't you?"

She nodded. "I prefer to go by Gen. But yes. My sister Elizabeth would have taken my role, pretending to be me. My father wouldn't have been able to explain to the Founding families how the first warrior for the House of Fourteen just disappeared. It would have tarnished his reputation when he had just established himself as a leader over the magical world."

Hiker pushed back in his chair, seeming overwhelmed. "Wow, this is a lot to process. But at least you being here won't unravel the fabric of time." Hiker brought his distant gaze up, looking straight at Sophia. "So although this is fascinating family history and more, why have you brought this first of the Beaufonts here to me?"

"That's the part most relevant to us as dragonriders," Sophia began with a tense smile. "Gen found a dragon egg in the 15th century and buried it."

"Oh, did she?" Hiker laughed. "And now she wants to know what happened to it, then?" He glanced at Gen. "Well, they've all been found. They've all hatched. Sorry, Missy. You're a couple decades too late."

Gen's face remained neutral. "Actually, last week, I dug up the dragon's egg I buried."

Hiker scowled. "That's impossible. There were only ever two thousand dragon eggs. They've all since hatched."

Sophia shook her head. "There were two thousand and one eggs. And Gen, my long-lost ancestor, found the very first one. And she has it now—unhatched."

CHAPTER EIGHT

WELCOME TO THE DRAGON ELITE

**<u>Hiker Wallace's Office, The Castle, The Gullington, Scotland,
United Kingdom</u>**

"For the love of the angels! When were you going to tell me
this?" Hiker pushed up to his feet, glaring down at Sophia,
hostility brimming in the man. He was simply huge with large
shoulders and wearing an armored top and thick kilt. He looked
like the stuff of legends with his many medallions around his
neck and holster on his hip. Gen could definitely see him riding
atop a dragon, slaying bad guys. Unfortunately for her and
Sophia, he looked ready to slaughter them.

"I'm telling you now, sir," Sophia began in a low voice, like
trying to disarm him with her soft tone. "I only found out about
the dragon's egg recently and I've been trying to help Gen to
navigate in this brand new and disorienting time. It's been a lot
for her and the dragon's egg wasn't really a concern until I got
her settled."

"And are you settled?" Hiker asked, looking at Gen at once, his
tone oozing with mock concern. "How are you feeling? How has
the transition been?"

Gen, a little confused by this change in tone, shrugged. "It's been a lot, but I'm managing."

"Great, now how in the bloody hell didn't I know that there's an unhatched dragon's egg?" Hiker boomed, throwing his hands into the air. His voice echoed all around the office as his face flushed red with anger.

Sophia rolled her eyes, looking at Gen. "That was his attempt at sarcasm, pretending to care how you are adjusting when he feels like he has the bigger issue."

"Mama Jamba said there were only two thousand eggs!" Hiker yelled, still not realizing that was unnecessary. He glared directly at Gen. "That's Mother Nature, for your information. She created, well, just about everything. But most importantly, she created the dragon eggs and she said there were only two thousand."

"I know who she is and she lied," Gen stated. "She said she was waiting for me and couldn't give you a spoiler."

He threw his hands into the air, tossing back his head. "Of course she did. That woman loves to keep things from me." He lowered his chin. "How did you find the first dragon egg? And why did you bury it?"

"Well, the dragon called to me in the woods—"

"She's magnetized to this egg!" Hiker interrupted, gazing at Sophia like this was a cruel joke.

"Yes, sir," Sophia replied.

"Yes, and he told me that he was the first dragon's egg ever spawned," Gen stated.

"What was the year?" Hiker asked.

"1420," Gen answered.

Hiker nodded. "The year that the first rider magnetized to a dragon."

Gen nodded too. "Yes, and that's when I learned what dragons were. Before that, I just thought I was going crazy, talking to this egg that called itself a dragon. No one knew what those were. But he told me to bury him because otherwise we would have been separated. For starters, my father wanted me to be a warrior for the House of Fourteen. And secondly, women weren't dragonriders in the 15th century. I was barely allowed to be a warrior. My dragon knew that and said our time wasn't yet…"

Hiker's eyes widened as he regarded Sophia with astonishment. "This dragon, this first of the dragons, he knew that women wouldn't be dragonriders until you came along? Is that what you're trying to explain to me?"

"It seems so," Sophia answered. "The dragon knew that Gen would be pulled into the future. And you know better than anyone that she wouldn't have been allowed to be a dragonrider, even if she could talk to her dragon telepathically."

He nodded in understanding. "It was a different time then. Your sister, Elizabeth, the one who pretended to be you, she was only accepted as a warrior by most because she didn't fight."

"That's because she didn't like fighting," Gen stated. "I was the rebel who liked to put bad men in headlocks, which was why my father made me a warrior, but now we know how that turned out."

"Headlocks, you say?" Hiker asked, appraising her with a new sense of intrigue.

"She's badass, sir," Sophia gushed, smiling at Gen. "She's going to make an excellent member of the Dragon Elite. And she has the first dragon's egg ever. And it will be the very last to hatch. How cool is that?"

"How many times do I have to tell you that cool means cold, not neat?" Hiker asked, then seeming to think of something, he tilted his head to the side in confusion. "Why doesn't Gen talk strangely if she's been here for only a wee bit?"

"She's outfitted with a communication device from Papa Creola," Sophia explained. "It translates our vernacular for her and then also her Old English for us. It's completely seamless. And she can understand what I mean when I say, 'cool.'"

"Oh, it's similar to the chi of the dragon that allows dragonriders to understand and speak any language then," Hiker said, nodding in understanding.

"Yes, that's where Father Time got the idea from," Sophia stated. "Maybe you could get one of the devices, sir. I know you've been in the modern era for centuries and you still talk like a Viking."

His eyes fluttered with annoyance. "I wasn't dropped into the modern world when I was twenty-years old. I have lived well over five hundred years and some things are ingrained in me. I've had to evolve the Dragon Elite over centuries and it hasn't always been easy."

"But I've helped, haven't I, sir?" Sophia asked, batting her eyelashes up at the man.

Hiker glared at her, before giving his attention to Gen. "When Sophia showed up, she was the first female dragonrider," Hiker explained. "That was a new situation for me. For centuries, I'd only ever led men as riders. Not only that, but the dragonriders were pretty much dormant, in hibernation. That was due to a war between mortals and magicians. The Dragon Elite had been rendered ineffective because mortals couldn't see magic."

"And if you can't see a dragon, then they can't arbitrate over nations, creating world peace and fixing negotiations," Sophia added, filling in the blanks.

Hiker nodded. "The few dragonriders I had left and I were pretty much locked down at the Gullington for a couple hundred years." He glared at Sophia. "Then the war ended and mortals could see dragons and magic once again."

He thumbed in Sophia's direction. "Next, this one bounces in and shakes everything up, telling us that we must go rule over the modern world once more. I allowed us to evolve and have tried my best to fill the ranks as all the dragon eggs hatched and magnetized to riders. It wasn't simple since dragonriders aren't the easiest group to organize and train."

Hiker sighed, looking tired suddenly. "We've finally ironed out all the kinks. I didn't think we'd have any big changes for another couple centuries. I mistakenly thought I'd get a break. But now all of a sudden, you, Gen Beaufont, have shown up with a new egg. Just when we thought all dragon eggs had hatched. And then you inform me that you stole the very first one and hid it away until now… Why are the Beaufonts always a big headache for me?"

"Sir, you had like two hundred years off," Sophia dared to tease.

He glared at the small dragonrider, flaring his nostrils. "I haven't had a day off since then, not from the time when you showed up. And now I've got a thief from the medieval era to try and corral."

Before Gen could tell this huge man off, Quiet appeared in the doorway. The small gnome looked so unassuming as he beckoned the leader of the Dragon Elite toward him.

"I'll be right back." Hiker stalked across the office, disappearing out into the corridor at once.

"So do we like him? Or not?" Gen asked, giving Sophia an amused expression.

"We do," Sophia said with a giggle. "He's a grumpy Viking, as I like to call him. He's stubborn and rigid, which plays off nicely from my cheery and easygoing disposition. We make an excellent team. Like good cop and bad cop."

"What's a cop?" Gen asked.

Sophia shook her head. "I'm sorry, I forget just how big your knowledge gap is in this modern world. I guess the communication device doesn't decode everything, does it? But Hiker is similar to you and your lack of modern knowledge because he spent so much of his time locked up in the Castle, so maybe you two will be good for each other."

"Maybe…" Gen said, not so sure she could work with

someone who was so stern without giving him a bloody nose regularly.

"I figured out what your dragon is. Quiet just told me," Hiker grumbled, interrupting the conversation as he thundered back into the office.

"A dragon, I'm hoping," Gen said, tensing. "That's what he told me. Is he not one? Is he a dinosaur? A platypus? What is he?"

Hiker started pacing the open space of the office, a well-worn tread across the old wooden floors. He'd definitely made that path many a time while he pulled on his beard, like now. "I can't say."

"What?" Gen questioned, bolting forward, looking between the man and Sophia. "Why not?"

"You have to figure it out on your own when he hatches," Hiker explained. "It's part of his namesake, which you must instinctively know. If I tell you, then I compromise your bonds."

Gen sat back, annoyed. "Are all things a riddle in this place?"

Sophia nodded. "I'm afraid so…"

"Well, does Quiet know when the egg is going to hatch?" Gen asked, her chest vibrating with anticipation.

Hiker nodded. "Yes, it will be in three days, on the morning of the new moon. That gives you just enough time to prepare, doing the standard Dragon Elite trainings. Sophia will take the lead on that." He turned to his second-in-command. "Run her through the combat and mental exercises. Get her equipped with proper armor and a weapon. Ensure that she's ready when her dragon hatches so that they can start rider training promptly."

Gen's heart raced, making her feel it might explode. She coughed on a breath. "I can't believe this is happening…"

Hiker looked directly at her, a serious expression in his wise, timeless eyes. "Believe it. You're one of us now. Welcome to the Dragon Elite."

CHAPTER NINE

THE HOUSEKEEPER'S TALE

<u>Dining Hall, The Castle, The Gullington, Scotland, United Kingdom</u>

The long table in the dining hall of the Castle was set with plates, cutlery, napkins and goblets for at least two dozen people. However, only Gen, Quiet and Mahkah sat at the far end. There were several covered dishes sitting in the middle of the table, but Gen didn't make for them, even though the savory aromas were very inviting.

Quiet was seated, ironically very silent, simply glaring at his empty plate, like willing food to magically appear. Mahkah seemed nervous, checking over his shoulder at the large double doors of the dining hall, looking for Sophia. She'd had to stay back in Hiker's office to have a meeting with him—apparently about this Commissioner of Los Angeles. The three sat quite awkwardly, none of them very good at small talk.

They were stationed in the huge dining hall which was as grand as every part of the Castle that Gen had seen thus far. The ceiling was over thirty feet high with wrought-iron chandeliers. The old stone walls were adorned with armor and weapons, each with a story to tell from the history books. The room seemed to hold the ghost of festive dinners and parties through the centuries, but currently the huge space was still and mostly unoccupied.

"Oh, good, you're all sitting around in uncomfortable silence. I'm more than happy to join you and make things even more tense. I love a good awkward moment," a woman said, breezing in through the large doors. She had a thick Irish accent and long red hair that flowed down her slender back. Over her bony frame, she wore a beautiful blue dress that brushed the stone floors as she made her way for the far side of the table, where the three sat.

The woman who Gen realized at once was an elf, based on her pointy ears and features, paused beside her, smiling elegantly. "You must be the reason that my husband is stomping around and raving mad. I'm so very happy to make your acquaintance. You've started off on the right note, in my book."

Gen blinked at the strange woman who seemed a little wacky but then also very refined. It was a bizarre combination. "Your husband is Hiker Wallace? And you're glad that I've made him angry?"

"Very much so," the woman said, pulling out the chair next to Gen and taking a seat. "It's not a hard job to make that man mad, but you seem really well equipped for it. I haven't seen him this angry…well, since S. Beaufont showed up." She threw her head back, laughing. "He was expecting a Shawn or a Steven when he heard an S. Beaufont was joining the Dragon Elite. There hadn't been a rider in a century. And in pops this sweet and beautiful woman named Sophia. He nearly lost his mind. It was devilishly brilliant to watch."

Gen glanced across the table at Mahkah and then Quiet, her expression begging the question on her mind, which was, "What the hell is going on here?"

Quiet glanced up from his plate, looking straight at the

woman. He muttered something, but again Gen couldn't make it out.

The woman laughed. "Oh, I remember how you rearranged his office, downsizing him due to his bad attitude. That was also incredibly entertaining to watch."

Mahkah cleared his throat, offering Gen a polite smile. "This is Ainsley and as she said, she's Hiker's wife and lives here at the Gullington."

"Oh, are you a dragonrider?" Gen asked.

Ainsley laughed, again seeming amused by all of this. "Heavens no. I was the housekeeper for the Castle for the better part of two hundred years."

Quiet mumbled something, his eyes intently on the covered dish with steam seeping out the side, like begging to be let loose.

Ainsley nodded at him. "I was a great housekeeper because I knew how to handle you and your moods. A bit like how I can handle the angry leader of the Dragon Elite." She glanced at Gen. "And before I lost my memory and my mind and was reduced to menial labor and babysitting a grumpy man and his dirty crew of dragonriders, I was a diplomat for the Elfin Council. I've since returned to that job, but only part time since the Dragon Elite has evolved under the encouragement of S. Beaufont, also known as Sophia. If it were up to my husband, we'd still be living in the dark ages."

Quiet spoke, his mouth moving but no sounds coming out.

Ainsley nodded. "It is because of Soph that we have electricity in the Castle. That woman brought us into the twenty-first century." The elf glanced at Gen. "Speaking of which, I understand you're from the medieval era. When's about?"

"If you can believe it, I left there last week and it was 1426," Gen answered.

"I can believe it," Ainsley sang good naturedly. "Time is a funny, little thing with doors all over the place."

"Right," Gen said, glad that this wasn't confusing to the woman. "Anyway, I was born in 1406."

Ainsley nodded. "A bit before my time. I, like Hiker, was born in the 16th century. I'm from Ireland, of course. He's from, well, the wrong side of the bed." She laughed again.

"Oh, I don't mean to pry, but that makes you both well over five hundred years old—"

"Five hundred and fifty something to be exact," Ainsley interrupted Gen with a snicker.

"Right," Gen said, drawing out the word, thinking that the housekeeper sniffed too many chemicals during her time cleaning the Castle. She knew about these pungent chemical cleaning aids since her time living in the shiny and squeaky clean Beaufont condominium.

"You're wondering why they look so young for their age," Mahkah offered, a thoughtful expression on his face.

Gen nodded.

"Mahkah Tomahawk, here, is pretty old too. He's pushing up to four hundred," Ainsley said proudly.

Gen couldn't believe that, looking at the man's smooth skin and dark hair, devoid of a single gray. "Wow, give me all your secrets."

"You don't need them," Mahkah stated. "It's mostly the chi of the dragon that keeps riders so young. We are offered a lifespan as long as our dragon's, which can be thousands of years."

"The thing about dragonriders and their steeds is they usually die young from battles," Ainsley offered, a morbid tone in her voice suddenly. "Quiet and I, although not riders, enjoy the chi of the dragon since it lives and breathes in the Gullington. But also, just having magic keeps most young."

Mahkah nodded. "Magicians have double the lifespan of mortals. Elves and fairies live much longer than them due to their relaxed manners. But I realize that although you're new to this world, you aren't new to the world of magic. You were a

Founder of the House of Fourteen, meaning you understood the magical world better than most."

"Well, my father and I understood it well enough to know that it needed laws," Gen stated. "He was a visionary and saw that problems were brewing between the magical races. The gnomes and giants were fighting for land and resources. The elves were warring with the fairies for wellsprings. The magicians were stuck in the middle and so, we created the governing body that would be strict yet fair known as the House of Fourteen."

Ainsley nodded. "And it is still going strong, bossing everyone about. It has the structure you created with seven councilors and seven warriors from seven magical families, but now there are also the Mortal Seven to keep things balanced. Great vision you and William had. You did good, Ms. Genevieve Beaufont."

"Just Gen," she said with a smile. "My sister apparently was Genevieve."

Ainsley frowned. "How very confusing for you this must all be. We might have been trapped in the Castle for two centuries but we knew the world for hundreds of years before and then eased back into the modern ages when Sophia unlocked us from our cage. You, on the other hand, have been dropped on this strange playing board with the first egg, a brilliant reputation, a family legacy to uphold and well, a dragon who is making my husband's chest tighten with tension."

Gen leaned forward, hoping to pry some answers from the elf. "Yes, he mentioned that he knew what my dragon was, like he was something different. I know he was the first egg ever spawned and will be the last to ever hatch, but I don't get how he's special otherwise."

Ainsley cut her eyes to Mahkah, a silent message between them seeming to transpire. "And I'm not at liberty to say."

"Right," Gen groaned, sitting back in her seat again.

"You'll know when the time is right," Mahkah stated softly. "We know because Lunis told us, but you must find out because of your connection when you meet your dragon. It will be more impactful that way. And still, there's so much we don't know, like your mission and role with the Dragon Elite. That is something only you two can choose."

"That sounds overwhelming," Gen said, feeling a brand new kind of stress.

"All things happen over time," Ainsley advised in a kind voice. "And therefore, you get a chance to figure things out and adapt and grow. You don't have to eat the dinosaur in one bite."

Quiet grumbled, looking especially grumpy.

Ainsley smiled at him. "S. Beaufont is coming just now. Then we can eat. You know it's not polite to start without everyone here."

Gen turned to find Sophia striding over and although she was grateful to see her familiar face, it was covered in a very stressed expression.

CHAPTER TEN

NOT HER PROBLEM

Sophia strode over through the open double doors. She appeared extremely stressed, but that was probably because of Hiker's bad mood that she had to endure. "Is this all of the people who live in the Castle?" Gen asked, motioning to the four of them.

Ainsley shook her head. "No, no. As you've learned, all our dragon's eggs have hatched. Before Sophia, there were a thousand dragon eggs, spawned when the first male rider was born. Then S. Beaufont spawned the other thousand. Your dragon appears to have been the first and completely spawned on his own."

Mahkah nodded in agreement to this. "Over the centuries, most of the first thousand riders and dragons died."

"That's because they were all men who fought too much and drank like fish," Ainsley teased, winking at Gen.

"True," Mahkah stated. "Then about forty or fifty years ago, the new eggs spawned. Half of the last batch of a thousand became Dragon Elite. The other half became Rogue Riders. It depended on whether they were deemed angel or demon drag- onriders. Anyway, as is with dragons and riders, many have died out, but our numbers are fairly strong on both sides with roughly eight hundred active still. They've all been assigned various roles in the world and therefore many are away on missions. They only return to their homes when they need rest or new orders."

"That must be why Hiker was so cross about me showing up and putting a wrench in his organization," Gen related. "He said that he'd figured out the ranks and assignments and now I was going to cause him a headache."

"Hiker was looking for a reason to complain," Ainsley offered. "He keeps asking for a vacation, but we all know that man doesn't really want one. He wants a problem so then he can gripe about it. He's probably secretly being giddy in his office that you showed up, requiring him to have to rethink the structure of the Dragon Elite."

"I didn't realize that a new member would cause such an upset," Gen muttered, glaring at her plate.

"Oh, well, you're not just any new member," Ainsley stated, giving Mahkah a knowing look. "You're something…special…"

"Come sit, S. Beaufont." Ainsley patted the seat next to hers when Sophia neared the end of the table. "Let's call Hiker various insulting names and you can tell us all about your problems."

Sophia slid into the seat with a sigh. "I don't have any prob- lems. That's just the thing. The Commissioner of Los Angeles has been murdered and it's absolutely not my problem, but Hiker wants it to be."

"Los Angeles?" Gen asked, all the places and words new to her. "That's where Clark and Liv live, right?"

"Right," Sophia chirped, watching as Quiet dove into the covered dishes, not waiting a moment longer. "It's also where the entrance to the House of Fourteen is and the Rogue Riders. It's an epicenter for magic due to many factors."

"Like show business, which is quite literally a bunch of spell work," Ainsley said, uncovering a tray of rolls and offering one to Gen.

She took it with a polite smile. "That's unfortunate about the Commissioner of Los Angeles, who I'm guessing is a high-ranking official, but why does Hiker want this person's death to be your problem?"

"Yes, the Commissioner is the head of law enforcement in Los Angeles," Sophia explained. "And this official and I had an arrangement, but that was when I was the leader of the Rogue Riders. I've since been relieved of that title by the Elders, also known as the Founders now, who make the appointments through the House of Fourteen. Things were falling apart and with the evolution of the riders, I was struggling to keep things organized. It was only right that I be replaced."

"The Founders…" Gen said, chewing on her lip.

It had recently been learned that the Founders of the House of Fourteen hadn't died. Instead, their magic sealed them into another realm so that they could observe the magical world and make appointments to the various governing agencies like the Rogue Riders, Dragon Elite, Fairy Godmother Agency, and of course, the House of Fourteen.

That meant that Gen's father and sister, William and Elizabeth Beaufont, were hanging out in this other realm, known as the Land of Chimera, watching over her—making decisions on everyone's behalf. That was one reason that Gen could never go back to her timeline. Unlike some things that can be undone with time travel, the Founders had been cemented into history when they moved to the Land of Chimera.

That would have been Gen if she hadn't gone missing. At the time that the Founders all chose, they simply moved instead of dying. But Gen reminded herself that this was how her life was supposed to go. She was always supposed to step through that time travel gate and live her life in this modern world.

"Yes, and S. Beaufont, they were right to relieve you as leader of the Rogue Riders," Ainsley cut in, ladling creamy mashed potatoes onto Gen's plate, like a mother taking care of her charges. "You were already second-in-command as the field leader for the Dragon Elite. You started the Rogue Riders but you were never meant to keep the role as their leader."

"True," Sophia said, taking a bite of the fresh-baked roll. "And it's like Ron Swanson says, 'Never half-ass two things. Whole-ass one thing.'"

Gen laughed, taking the ladle that Mahkah handed her for the brisket in the center of the table. "Is this Ron Swanson a dragonrider? He sounds smart."

"He's a fictional character on television, which I realize you don't know about," Ainsley answered. "Have S. Beaufont get you a phone and start watching YouTube and Netflix. That will give you a crash course on pop culture references."

Gen spooned juicy brisket onto her plate, nodding along. "Yes, Liv, Clark and the others have kept me sheltered, saying they didn't want to overwhelm me with too much too quickly. But at some point, I'll just have to dive forward."

"Just know that the world has changed in ways you can't even imagine in six hundred years," Ainsley advised, taking a bite of her string green beans. She held up her fork and laughed. "Like forks! We have forks now and use them at most meals."

"I've practiced." Gen winked at her before glancing back at Sophia. "It sounds like it's a good thing that you're not the leader of the Rogue Riders with this new drama in Los Angeles."

"That's the thing," Sophia began with a sigh. "Hiker thinks that it's going to cause a problem with the Rogue Riders since we had an agreement with the Commissioner and had worked with him for years. But it's not my problem. I've stepped back from the group and that's for the best. I wasn't an effective leader because I'm an angel dragonrider and the Rogue Riders are made of demon riders."

"Can you explain that to me?" Gen asked. "There are good and bad riders and dragons?"

"Life isn't black and white like that," Ainsley answered, probably because Sophia was chewing. "Bad isn't the absence of good. There is light and there is dark and both are necessary. Mother Nature made it so that there were angel riders and dragons who were self-sacrificing and altruistic. They are perfect as peacemakers for the Dragon Elite. But we can't dismiss the fact that crime will always exist, so the Rogue Riders manage the criminal world because they, as demon riders and dragons, are rebellious in nature. Each is perfectly suited for their role. And only angel magicians are attracted to angel dragons and vice versa."

"That's fascinating," Gen mused. "The idea of not eradicating crime, but keeping it organized and at bay is very unorthodox. I like that."

Sophia nodded. "When the first batch of dragon eggs hatched, all the demon riders became rogue and created problems because they had no purpose. They were deemed horrible and therefore outcast. When the second batch of eggs started to hatch, Hiker and I knew that we had to find a purpose for the demon dragonriders. So we played to their strengths."

"It was the first time the two types of dragons and riders were able to get along," Mahkah offered in a low voice. "Before that we warred over our differences. Now we realize we have separate missions."

"And the idea is to have balance both between good and bad, like with the Rogue Riders' mission to monitor criminals," Sophia added. "Crime is a pressure cooker and if we tried to squash it out, then it would explode. So we allow crime on a low level and usually those contacts with criminals gives us valuable insight into bigger rings that we can take down."

"So don't get rid of the guy selling knock-off designer purses because he can tip you off on the guy who is murdering in the back alleys," Ainsley said with a laugh.

Gen didn't know exactly what knock-off designer purses were but she could fill in the blanks. "That's really smart and realistic. Crime is inevitable but can be managed, it seems."

Sophia huffed. "It sort of was, although I was struggling with it. However, the Commissioner kept things tight in the City of Los Angeles, while also allowing the Rogue Riders to manage and supervise the crime rings. It was a good partnership. Things will be in flux when a new official takes his place, but again, that's not my problem."

"I wonder who murdered him," Ainsley said, staring off in wonder.

Sophia shook her head. "Again, not my problem. That's under the jurisdiction of the leader of the Rogue Riders—Dwayne Stone."

CHAPTER ELEVEN

BREAKING POINTS

<u>The Expanse, The Gullington, Scotland, United Kingdom</u>

The sword sliced through the cool, damp air, making a whistling sound. Gen's breath clouded before her as she faced the invisible foe on the cold, unforgiving grounds of the Expanse of the Gullington. Her boots pressed into the frost-hardened earth with each maneuver.

The wind howled around her, a wild chorus that matched the fierceness in her heart, whipping her hair and the fabric of her attire into a frenzied dance. She lunged forward, her sword slicing through the chill air, an echo of battles long past vibrating in her grip. With each thrust and parry, her movements were fluid yet sharp, honed by years of discipline and the raw emotions churning within her from her abrupt plunge through time.

The metallic trace of the blade cut through the wet scent of the Expanse, grounding her in the moment, even as her mind roiled with the dissonance of centuries. She could hear the distant clash of steel on steel from memories that clung to her like shadows, guiding her hand in a ballet of aggression and control.

Gen spun, her sword arcing gracefully yet deadly, as she imagined striking at the heart of her confusion and frustration, battling the invisible enemy that mirrored her own turmoil.

The sky above was a tumultuous canvas, reflecting her internal storm, with clouds racing across as if fleeing from unseen pursuers. Her every breath was a defiance, a claim to her strength and resilience, each exhale visible in the cold air as if casting out the specters of her dislocation.

As she halted, standing amidst the quieting winds, Gen's chest heaved, her sword lowering but her spirit undiminished, the silent moors bearing witness to her unyielding resolve.

"You can fight, but that's no surprise," Sophia said, having snuck into place around a table of weapons, giving Gen a coy smile.

With ragged breath, Gen lowered the sword and shrugged. "My father taught me when I wouldn't shut up. He said women should be pretty and I said, I'd rather cut bad men. I won in the end."

"You're a legend in the making," Sophia observed. "We just need to find you the right weapon. Which is why I've enlisted an expert to help."

"A gnome who is the breathing and beating force of this land?" Gen pretended to ask. "Or a stoic warrior who knows everything about what a dragon is feeling by looking at them?"

"My husband," Sophia answered with a sly smile, holding up her hand to the grounds where a dashing tall and dark-haired gentleman dressed in armor strode out. He was both modern and old-world in appearance. "His name is Wilder and you've met his boss, Subner, the Protector of Weapons, who lives with Father Time. And, of course, he's also a rider for the Dragon Elite."

"Of course," Gen agreed with a nod. "And I have met Subner. He is the unhappy type."

Sophia chuckled. "He'd wear that like a badge of honor. And

yes, Subner presides over all weapons and my husband, Wilder, is his assistant."

"Pleased to make your acquaintance," the man with piercing blue eyes full of old wisdom said when he neared Gen, wringing her hand.

"So what does it mean that you're the assistant to the Protector of Weapons?" Gen asked, watching as the dragonrider, with a grace to impress, pivoted, making his way over to the table of weapons.

He withdrew a sword, testing the balance in his hands and then turned around, smirking. "It means that I feel and know every experience every weapon has ever been through just by touching it. This is a blessing and a curse. I can see through time, to histories not told. I can see death when I touch a blade. But I also know the strengths and weaknesses of every weapon and how they failed the one who wielded them, or rather, how the one who held them failed."

"That's chilling," Gen said, when Wilder handed her the sword he'd picked. She exchanged it for the one she'd been exercising with. "So what would you have me do?"

"Practice," he answered. "We're going to find the weapon that matches you. The one that will play to your strengths while minimizing your weaknesses. I'm sure, as a Beaufont, this won't be hard. They all seem to magnetize to weapons, about like how you and Sophia magnetized to unhatched dragon eggs, which I shouldn't have to tell you is quite rare."

"I'm glad you did tell me," Gen said, giving Sophia a pointed look. She swung the sword through the air a bit, testing the blade's weight, deciding how she'd like to use it. Then she neared the wooden post meant for sparring and wheeled around in a full circle and brought the sword across the wooden pole. The beam didn't give, the metal blade did, shattering in two, ricocheting through the air.

Everyone froze, looking around at the aftermath of what had

just happened there. Then Wilder threw up his hands, a wide grin on his face as he laughed with surprise.

"Did you just break the sword?" Wilder asked, a look of shock and amazement on his face as he regarded Gen.

Her gaze jerked down to the sliver of the sword that had broken off the top of the weapon. "I'm sorry. Maybe the metal is brittle from age."

"It's a giant-made sword," he pointed out. "They only get stronger with age."

He leaned over and picked up the piece of the sword, inspecting it. Then he glanced back over his shoulder at Sophia, grinning as he held up the piece of broken metal. "She broke the sword."

"It happens," Sophia said with a laugh. "Maybe that just means a sword isn't the right weapon for her."

"I think you're correct," Wilder stated, trotting over to the table of weapons and grabbing a bow and a single arrow. "Let's try this. It's a great weapon for riding on the back of a dragon. I happen to love a bow and arrow and it suits this whole Robin Hood look you've got going on."

"Oh, finally a reference I can understand," Gen said, taking the bow and arrow. "I quite like the idea of being like Robin Hood. Maybe I can be the new, modern version."

"Yes!" Wilder cheered, pointing at the target in the distance. "Now let's see how your aim is, Miss Robin Hood."

Gen gripped the bow in her hands, nocking the arrow into place and pulling back the string. She had shot with many a bow in her day, hunting and policing the streets, as she often took upon herself to do, against her father's insistence. But that was the spirit that won her the role of warrior—a position she never wanted.

If Gen was honest, since finding that dragon's egg and hearing his voice in her head, she only ever wanted to be a dragonrider. But that wasn't an option that existed in her mind until the first dragonrider arose and then it's all she could think about. Now, she was being given that chance, in a brand new world, with a vast field of possibilities.

Feeling a hope like she'd never experienced before blossoming in her heart, Gen stretched back the string even more, lining the arrow up with the target. Then, just as she was about to let it go, she felt a snap, followed by a zinging noise and then an assault as something broke.

"Did you just break the bow?" Wilder asked her, rushing forward, not mad, but utterly confused.

Gen glanced at the bow in her hands with a broken string and the arrow that had faltered to the ground below. "I'm so sorry. I don't know what happened. I was just concentrating and… Maybe the string was weak."

"Maybe the string was brand new," Wilder countered with a laugh. "I put it on myself this morning." He glanced back at Sophia with an amused expression. "She broke the bow."

"I saw," Sophia said, patting the curled elfin-made sword on her hip fondly. "It's because Beaufonts like blades. I have Inexorabilis, Liv has Bellator and Rose has Paternus. Give her something with some teeth."

"What about a javelin?" Wilder offered, trotting back off to the weapon table. He picked up a long wooden spear with a sharp tip, spinning around and facing Gen. "I feel like I know how this is going to go, but hey, humor me and try it. Can you throw this at the target?"

Gen took the spear, finding it sturdy in her hand. She nodded, glaring across the grounds at the bullseye in the distance. Then she raised her arm over her head, pulled it back and flung the javelin with a grace to impress.

It spiraled through the air, whirling like an acrobat before it connected with the center of the target. On impact, the handle of the spear splintered and broke in half. The tip of the blade pierced through the target, breaking it into pieces, sending bits of the board ricocheting and then falling to the ground. The whole thing landed in a total mess on the grass, broken javelin handle, target and separated spear tip.

Wilder gave Gen a muted stare. "Did you just break the javelin?"

"I think that the handle was splintered," she said with an apologetic look.

He shook his head, glancing at Sophia. "She broke the javelin." In a mock display of annoyance, he marched over to the wreckage and looked down at it. "And this is why we can't have nice things, isn't it?"

Sophia laughed. "So we haven't found Gen's weapon. It's just going to take a bit more practice. She is magnetizing to her dragon and we both know how complicated that can be. Her strength will be coming and going until she gets a handle on it."

"I didn't break a single thing while magnetizing to Simi, my dragon," Wilder said with a laugh. "Just so you know, Soph, you're her sparring partner. I'm sitting out on this training. I don't like having my bones broken."

Gen gave Sophia an apologetic look. "You don't have to spar with me. Maybe I am a bit angsty right now."

"Of course you are," Sophia said, smiling thoughtfully at her. "And you can spar with Lunis. He'll be a good match for you. But first, I've got another training exercise for you that's a little less hands-on and a bit more mental focus."

"Do I have to think?" Gen asked, giving her a worried expression.

"Worse," Sophia answered with a wink. "You have to feel."

CHAPTER TWELVE

IN STILLNESS, STRENGTH AWAKENS

<u>Falconer Cave, The Expanse, The Gullington, Scotland, United Kingdom</u>

After hiking for ten miles, Gen and Sophia arrived at a hidden cave, its entrance cloaked by moss and stone. Sophia had said the next part of Gen's training with the Dragon Elite involved a mental exercise. After hours of combat training with a massive dragon, Gen was more than happy to use her mind over her body, especially after the long hike up the hills.

Stepping inside, she was greeted by the cool kiss of air, a soothing balm to her weary spirit. The gentle drip of water echoed like a serene melody, inviting her to release the burdens of her past. The walls, adorned with crystalline formations, shimmered in the dim light. They cast dancing shadows that played with her imagination, reminding her that beauty often lies in the unseen.

The earthy scent of damp moss and the mineral tang of stone filled Gen's lungs, grounding her in the present. Beneath her feet, the smooth rock offered a stable foundation, encouraging her to plant herself firmly in this new world. As they ventured deeper, the cave seemed to embrace her, its narrow passages widening into a spacious chamber that hummed with a quiet energy.

Here, in this sanctum, surrounded by the whispers of the earth, Gen found a space for introspection, a place where the external noise of her life in the 1400s and the overwhelming stimuli of the twenty-first century could not reach her. The cave, with its ancient stillness, seemed to mirror her own quest for identity and belonging, offering solace and a reminder that, like its enduring walls, she too could withstand the ravages of time and change.

The cavernous space was dark and cold, like most caves. However, there was something unique about the stillness in the space, although Gen couldn't put her finger on why exactly.

"So what are we supposed to do?" Gen asked, looking around as her eyes adjusted to the dark.

"I'll tell you how I was told when I was brought here by Hiker Wallace, 'Sit and be quiet,'" Sophia said with a sneaky grin.

Gen sighed. "Oh, good, I could use a nap."

"Sorry, but if you snooze, I'm obligated to kick you back awake," Sophia said, and then her grin dropped. "However, after seeing the way you wrestled Lunis, I'll probably just gently prod you back awake."

"What's the purpose of this exercise?" Gen asked, looking around at the strange place known as Falconer Cave.

"To meditate and find something deep within yourself," Sophia answered.

Gen gave her an expression that said, "Are you kidding me?"

Sophia offered her a look of understanding. "It is through meditation that we come to understand ourselves, receive insights on problems, and become one with the universe."

Gen frowned. "You sound like one of those hippies that Liv is always making fun of."

Sophia nodded. "You will make fun of them too. It's a Beaufont family tradition."

"So what do I do?" Gen asked. "I've never really meditated and don't know what to expect. What's my purpose?"

Sophia smiled thoughtfully. "Your experience meditating will be unique to you and what you need to know. But I will offer this bit of advice: to connect with yourself, you must first connect with the world around you. Falconer Cave is ideal for that because it's isolated from everything around it. An anomaly that is unique on the outside and bare on the inside."

"Okay," Gen said, drawing out the word. "When do I know that I've achieved the training goal?"

"You will know," Sophia said simply, with a sly grin now.

"Will you stop overwhelming me with information?" Gen joked.

Sophia looked around the cave. "Do you hear that?"

Gen paused. Listened. Shook her head. "What? I don't hear anything."

"Exactly," she stated. "When you hear the voice of the angels and all their messages, that's when you're done. When you no longer have questions and intuitively know answers to things yet to be asked, then you're done. When you can hear the spirit of the universe within you, then you can go."

This had to be the strangest training exercise. How did she connect with herself or the universe? And how did she know when she achieved it? Would the messages from the angels sound different from the random ramblings in her head?

"Okay, I'll go talk to angels then," Gen said, settling down. "Sounds a bit like song lyrics."

Sophia laughed, the noise echoing in the cave. "You're very intuitive and that's before even meditating. There is a song called She Talks to Angels by The Black Crowes. I'll play it for you sometime, along with the last hundred years of music."

"What about music before that, like in the 19th century?" Gen asked.

Sophia shook her head. "It's not worth the time."

"Are you staying?" Gen asked, settling herself down on the hard, cold rock.

"I will be outside waiting," Sophia replied, motioning to the way they'd come. "I'll wait as long as it takes. Just try and connect to the angels. They will tell you what you need to know. They always do, but you have to establish a communication with them first, through silence."

Gen nodded, feeling like she'd rather break a few dozen weapons again than do this task. However, she wanted to be a dragonrider more than anything else, so she settled her mind, or at least tried to.

Her mind began to wander. Taking a breath, she tried to stop the thoughts which were like a contagious disease, spreading fast. It seemed strange to stop thinking. That was about as easy as stopping breathing.

However, it was actually breathing that helped the most. When she focused on her breath, the thoughts slowed down, becoming less intense. After a bit, Gen noticed that her breath had elongated and her thoughts had followed suit, only passing through her brain slowly and then drifting away. Whereas before she had judged every thought as good or bad, soon she found that she was simply an observer, taking notice of the ideas without coloring them one way or another.

Soon her focus shifted to the area around her in the cave. She suddenly felt outside of herself in a very distinctive way. The temperature, she knew without knowing how, was exactly fifty degrees. There were sixteen different species that called Falconer Cave home. Of those, three were magical and unclassified. Of those, one was crawling on Gen's boot presently.

She didn't feel the little creature, but instinctively she knew it was there. Usually upon such knowledge she would have jumped up and brushed the bug off. However, Gen didn't even think of it as something else on her. She was the bug and the bug was her. They were the cave and the cave was them. They were the Gullington and the Gullington was them. They were Scotland and Scotland was them. They were the universe and the universe was them. Everything was one. Everything was connected in this world.

These observations were followed by a strange silence that seemed to stretch on for eternity. It was the silence that preceded Mother Nature. That spawned a creature so powerful she could construct a world that was strong and also vulnerable. It was the silence that filled the void before time was created. Before Papa Creola constructed how events moved on a continuum. The silence was the beginning and it was everywhere still.

Gen didn't know how long she sat in the cave, witnessing the birth of the universe in her mind. It could have been a minute or a hundred years. However, if it had been more than a day, she didn't feel hungry or tired or thirsty. She had hooked into the nourishment of the universe and she realized as long as she was connected to it that all her needs were instantly fulfilled.

From that place of knowingness, Gen realized that she could heal the world's problems. She could erase pain. She could become whatever she wanted. The idea of never leaving Falconer Cave was very tempting. She could fix everything just by maintaining her connection to the all-powerful source.

Inside that safe place of serenity, Gen could be at one with the universe. She could feel everything that she missed. She could hide away from the world that was so vastly different from the one she once knew. She could avoid the confusion of trying to understand the modern age. Gen could forget that she'd left her world behind, never to see or feel or experience it again.

"Your purpose is to change the new world in an old way," a voice said so clearly and loudly in her head.

Gen startled, her eyes opening suddenly. She looked around

the cave, thinking that someone must be there standing in front of her. There was no one.

"Hello?" she said aloud in the cave.

A disembodied voice, who Gen knew instinctively belonged to the angels, sang, "Go forth, and bring your old-world elegance to the problems of the new age. Be that which you were destined —a rebel with a heart of gold."

CHAPTER THIRTEEN

THE REBEL'S RESTING PLACE

<u>Gen's Quarters, The Castle, The Gullington, Scotland, United Kingdom</u>

Gen thought that she'd really enjoy living in the Castle at the Gullington. Maybe it was her newfound peace after conquering the meditation exercise in Falconer Cave, hearing the voice of the angels. Or maybe it was because Quiet appeared to like her, although if he said so, she didn't hear him. But it was probably because the Castle, quite literally, felt like home. It was cold and damp, with drafts whistling through the corridors.

It was so different from the condo where she'd stayed with Liv and Clark. That place in West Hollywood was nice, but strangely enough, it was too nice. The running water and shiny surfaces were a bit like overload for Gen who was used to a much different way of living.

She knew that she should be happy for the modern conveniences, but so much change at once was messing with her mind in ways she'd never experienced before. The Castle seemed to instinctively know how much of the old world that Gen wanted mixed with the modern conveniences that made life better and made her room and quarters to those specs perfectly.

The room that the Castle made for Gen was rustic with stone walls and minimal furniture done in the style of medieval design. There was a high bed covered in thick covers and tons of pillows. It looked like a giant cloud that she could fall into and after the first day at the Gullington that she'd had, that's all she wanted to do. The artwork was like the kind that Gen was used to, depicting landscapes and people of her day.

But Gen scolded herself at that thought, remembering that her time was now—it didn't matter that she grew up in the 1400s. She was a woman and soon to be dragonrider of the twenty-first century. The whole notion felt weird and wild, but also wonderful, if she were honest with herself.

How's it going? A familiar voice said in her head as Gen looked out the window onto the darkened grounds of the Expanse.

"Well, according to the angels, I'm supposed to be a rebel and therefore demand that you hatch tonight rather than in two more," Gen said, feeling strange talking out loud to her dragon, but also liking the sound of her own voice in the still and quiet of her lonely room.

That's not what the angels said to you, her dragon replied. *I heard every word. They told you to use your old-world elegance to fix the modern world, which I like very much.*

"Do you know what I'd like?" Gen challenged, looking at the bathroom that the Castle had appointed for her.

A lesson in electricity and plumbing, he offered.

"Yes, I could use that." Gen said, longing to get clean. "How do you make the magic rain thing warmer?"

It's a shower and turn it to the right, the dragon answered in her head.

"How again do you know this when you've been locked in an egg for all of your life?"

I'm plugged in, much like how you did in Falconer Cave, he replied.

"What I'd like to know is what you are and why everyone is so hush-hush about it," Gen said, reaching out and turning the knob on the so-called shower.

You've been told that it's a surprise, the dragon said, a coyness in his voice.

"Fine," she said with a sigh, enjoying the steam as it started to rise up from the water. "How are you?"

I'm in an egg, he replied. *It's cramped.*

"Hatch," she offered.

I'm not ready, he answered.

"But you will be soon?"

I will, the dragon stated. *They put me in the Nest with the other dragons. I'm growing now. Much more than I was when buried for centuries. I'll be ready as they predicted in three days.*

"Good, because the curiosity is overwhelming," Gen joked. "I want to see what strange anomaly you have. Are you a backwards dragon?"

What does that even mean?

"It means your tail is on your front and your nose is on your—"

I'm not a backwards dragon, he interrupted before she could finish her joke.

Gen laughed. "Fine. Well, I'll see you in a bit. Until then, well, I don't know what. I guess you grow and I'll train."

And by train you mean break things, he teased.

"Exactly," Gen said, disrobing and stepping into the shower. "Good night, Mr. Mystery Dragon."

Good night, Weapon Slayer.

CHAPTER FOURTEEN

THE STITCHING OF TIME

<u>The Castle, The Gullington, Scotland, United Kingdom</u>

When Gen exited her room at the Gullington that morning, feeling refreshed and ready for a new day on the Expanse, training, she was greeted by Sophia hanging out casually right outside her room, waiting for her.

"So, this is weird," Gen joked, pulling on the sleeves of the same tunic she'd worn the day before. "Are you stalking me?"

"What's weird is that you look like you're from six hundred years ago and we need you to be a little more this century," Sophia said with a casual smile.

Gen gawked at her with a mock look of offense. "Are you insulting my dress?"

"I'm saying that you need to update your look," Sophia offered, leading them down the corridor to the staircase. "You don't have to look totally modern by any means, but you should find an interplay between what you were and what you're going to become. Something that is medieval and something a little modern. I love the idea of a conventional warrior for you."

Gen laughed, grateful that she had such good friends slash

family to help her navigate these strange waters of the new world. "Okay, well, what did you have in mind? Are we going dress shopping? Because I should tell you, I don't wear dresses."

Sophia gave her a knowing look. "No, because you're a Beaufont. We wear them on our wedding days and maybe an occasion in between like graduation and what not. But we aren't dress wearers. It's in our blood, which I blame you for."

"Accurately," Gen stated with a victorious wink.

"I'm taking you to the most talented and intuitive seamster in the world," Sophia offered as they made their way down the grand staircase of the Castle. "He will instinctively know you and what will be the outfit that will work best for you and your missions and your style. Are you ready to be outfitted?"

"Is this going to hurt?" Gen joked.

"Probably not, although you might accidentally get stuck with a sewing needle or two," Sophia replied.

"I can handle that," Gen remarked. "Just as long as I don't have to wear a dress."

Sophia shook her head. "No, it's got to be something that you can throw a roundhouse kick in."

"Exactly," Gen said, smiling, grateful that the modern-day Beaufonts were so tough. It was nice to know that some things hadn't changed.

A worried look crossed Sophia's face. "But I will warn you that this seamster is a bit…different."

Gen laughed. "I've been dropped into a world with magical fire lights and carriages without horses. How different can this seamster be?"

"You mean electricity and cars," Sophia said with a laugh.

"Yeah, sure…"

"And Jeremy Bearimy is something unique that most even in the modern world haven't seen," Sophia replied.

"What kind of name is Jeremy Bearimy for a man?" Gen asked with a chuckle.

"Well, he's not a man, so it's probably the most normal part of him," Sophia said, waving Gen to follow her. "Come on. Let's go and further your education of the modern world."

CHAPTER FIFTEEN

FROM MEDIEVAL GROUNDS TO MODERN STREETS

<u>Roya Lane, London, England, United Kingdom</u>

The strangeness of Gen's life was only certain to heighten as she set foot onto Roya Lane alongside Sophia. She'd been through the crazy magical lane a time or two, but never allowed to look around, always told that she should guard her vision from things she wouldn't understand and would overwhelm her.

When Gen accidentally came to this time period, Father Time had hoped to successfully put her back in 1426. In his attempts, he had urged her to not see anything from that time period, hoping it wouldn't color her. That was because Genevieve Beaufont was in the history books, having paved a critical path for the magical world. It was only now that they knew, Genevieve of 1426 was being played by Elizabeth Beaufont. This was Gen's time, she just had to understand it first.

Now, freely able to see London in the twenty-first century, Gen saw a world she'd never imagined possible. There were things beyond probable or conceivable notions, like transports on wheels and strange light things with no horses. Sophia had called them cars and said they were the new carriages of the world.

Then there was everything else, like the smells, the sounds, the feels that came from the busyness of the street. It was like something had taken her senses hostage and she was being assaulted over and over again by them.

And the noise… It was deafening with layers and layers that felt unnatural. The sounds of the city were so varied with loud drumming on the streets, echoes from the ground below, a growling in the distance and wailing all around her. Gen didn't know what was happening out in this world to make so much noise, but also, she strangely wasn't afraid of it.

For some reason, deep down, she knew that this was her time. And she also felt that her advantage in being here was that she didn't understand it. She was new to this world and therefore, uniquely created to make it better…somehow. In what way, she didn't know, but she suspected that it would have to do with her dragon and being a Beaufont.

"Are you okay?" Sophia asked, turning to look at her as they strode down the cobbled road that Gen didn't just know, but had established—Roya Lane. It was her and her father's vision that said they needed a hub where all magical people could find access to magical things.

Gen still remembered breaking actual ground on this road and now to look up and see what it became, well it was simply the thing of dreams. Most didn't live to see their visions come to fruition. Most never saw the legacy they left behind.

Her father, William, a Founder, saw it presently from another realm known as the Land of Chimeras. But Gen knew her experience was much different. She wasn't watching what they created. She was experiencing it.

"Why do you ask?" Gen questioned, looking all around at the strange things, none of them computing.

"Besides the fact that you're drooling?" Sophia asked, winking.

"Oh, well, it is a lot to take in," Gen said, gawking around at the sight of a male gnome dressed as a pretty woman in a tight red skirt and blouse, high heels and wearing fake long flowing red hair. Their makeup was strangely good, making him or her look beautiful and also weird because of his bulbous nose and boxy jaw. "I'm just not used to seeing so many things that…"

"That defy logic." Sophia offered.

"I used to think about the world ending and how that would look—"

"That's dark," Sophia interrupted with a laugh.

Gen didn't. "I know but it's because I grew up in the medieval era. It's hard to explain how that makes you hard. I'm strange in the way that I never thought life would go on. I thought that it would all end because everything was so…unestablished. And then to see that it has, to know, that what my family did, created things that helped the world. It's mind boggling to know that the world didn't end, and the sky didn't fall, and well, that's the hardest part to digest. Then, I have to deal with the next part…"

"Which is?"

Gen gave Sophia a wide smile. "How am I going to adapt to this strange world, not made for me, but that I feel for some reason needs me?"

Sophia gave her an equally impressed smile. "I think you're going to fit in perfectly. You're like the best medieval modern warrior I can think of."

"You think?" Gen asked. "How should I act? What should I do?"

"Just question everything," Sophia suggested. "Tell everyone you see who does something wrong what you think."

"Won't that get me in trouble?"

"Yeah," Sophia answered with a grin. "And you're going to stir things up and something tells me that's your purpose. I was created by Mother Nature to establish peace. Something tells me, you were meant to make things anew by getting rid of all the turmoil. So, wipe out the filth. Clean it up with your brand-new attitude and perspective."

"I sort of like that idea, but I'm not sure if I know what's right and wrong in this world," Gen related.

"Sure you do, because no matter the time period that doesn't change," Sophia offered. "You see things in a different way than the rest of us. You will not be complacent with the things that are wrong. You will put your foot down to the misdeeds that we've all turned a blind eye to."

Gen glanced around at the strange, cobbled lane, seeing it not as a foreign and new place but as a human one. Suddenly the interactions were what she saw, and they had colors. Most were white and purely good, but she saw the bad ones in dark shades and everything in between.

The array of deeds was a rainbow that spread across Roya Lane and suddenly, for the first time in her entire life, Gen felt that she had a purpose. She wasn't meant to understand this modern new world. She was meant to use her vision to spot good and evil and make this new age better.

CHAPTER SIXTEEN

CLOAKED IN LEGACY

<u>Silk Armor, Roya Lane, London, England, United Kingdom</u>

Gen had never cared for the finer things. That was something that her father valued. That her twin sister, Elizabeth, loved. But for Gen, she liked things that weathered the test of time and battle. She wanted durability over luxury.

That was one of the reasons that picking out finer clothes was strange to Gen. But she had heard from Sophia that the seamster she was taking her to would know the best for her. With all her spirit, Gen hoped that this person knew what she needed to feel like the real warrior and dragon rider that she wanted to be.

Imagine Gen's surprise when she entered the seamster's shop to find that the owner of the Silk Armor wasn't a person at all. Standing in front of her, perched on a platform was what appeared to be a man-eating monster. The seamster was a giant spider with huge hairy legs and multiple eyes and the face of nightmares. Suddenly, Gen understood the name of the shop—the Silk Armor.

Gen would have pulled her sword, but Sophia preemptively jumped in front of her, blocking the movement, apparently, knowing that's what she'd do.

"That's Jeremy Bearimy, the master seamster," Sophia assured.

Gen didn't know how to compute the idea that a beady-eyed monster with eight legs could make her clothes. But when the creature clicked his pincers and a man ran out, holding fabric, she began to take notice.

"That's his assistant, Juergen," Sophia said, affectionately pointing at the man holding different cloths in front of Gen, like giving the giant spider an idea of how it would reflect on her skin.

"And they are the best?" Gen asked. "They can help me?"

"They are going to more than help you."

"But it's just an outfit," Gen countered.

Sophia shook her head. "Everything depends on how you arrive in each situation and battle, and that's in your clothes. So, start with that. And we already know that you're going to show up with a badass attitude. But you need an outfit to match your personality. All vigilantes arrive dressed like badasses. So please, show up like you're going to save the world."

Gen gave her a serious look. "But I'm not here to save the world."

"Not dressed like that," Sophia said with a laugh, striding forward, looking up at the giant tarantula. "I think Gen needs to look modern and then like Robin Hood. Maybe you can give her a medieval style with an edge. So maybe a braided top and a half skirt but then make it so she can throw a roundhouse kick."

"I know exactly what she needs!" Jeremy Bearimy said, clicking his pincers and then hurrying off, his furry legs scurrying for the back of the shop.

Sophia brightened, looking at the man "Oh, and Jurgen."

The assistant with a long beard turned, giving Sophia his full attention. "Yeah?"

"Make her look like the most badass Beaufont yet," Sophia said. "You've dressed us all, but she's the first, so make her, well, something better and edgier than the rest of us. Make her look like she belongs in all times."

He nodded, looking to the back where the giant spider was doing…whatever.

"I can definitely do that. We have the perfect outfit for Gen Beaufont."

CHAPTER SEVENTEEN

A WEAPON FOR LIFE

<u>Fantastical Armory, Roya Lane, London, England, United Kingdom</u>

"It's absolutely perfect," Gen said, pulling the jacket snugger around her, enjoying the way it fit her like a glove. She couldn't imagine anything ever fitting her any better. It wasn't just made for her, but it was made around her, like it fit her personality. She was wearing the absolute perfect outfit that she would ever have.

The suit that the strange large spider, who was surprisingly gentle, made for Gen was all black and armored. However, it was light and flexible with a fitted top and short jacket that would keep her warm when riding her dragon. The bottom consisted of a half skirt, also ideal for flying through the air. And the pants were thick and allowed for movement.

But most importantly it was a fierce look, mixing both elements of medieval style with the modern era. Jeremy Bearimy and Juergen had designed Gen something that made her feel more than powerful and she almost felt ready for the next phase of her life. Almost—but not quite yet.

Gen knew there was one thing she needed. She could feel its absence at her essence. She needed her dragon to hatch, for sure.

But before that, she needed a weapon that would match the power of her dragon. Gen felt that his power would be ultimate, so she needed something to complement that. But so far, she hadn't found anything that fit. Actually, she'd broken pretty much everything she'd tried, almost like she was jinxed when it came to weapons.

"I've got you covered on weapons," Sophia assured her when they entered the place that Gen had first lived upon stepping into the twenty-first century—The Fantastical Armory.

"How do you mean?" Gen asked, feeling like she was entering an old memory that was strangely new at the same time.

Sophia winked at her. "Trust me. Beaufont love all the way."

Gen didn't know what that meant, but she did feel like these people from this generation were the owners of her heart. They seemed to have her back, no matter what. So therefore, feeling like a warrior but not prepared to be in battle, she entered the place she knew that Father Time and Mother Nature called home presently. It was also a shop filled with weapons and artifacts and home to a grumpy man.

"Oh, good, another Beaufont is here," Subner, the Protector of Weapons muttered when they entered the shop of oddities.

This was the place that Gen had to call home for the days when she couldn't do anything and was waiting to be put back on her timeline. What person is told to have tea and biscuits with Mother Nature and not look out the window for days? Genevieve Beaufont. That's who.

During that time, she was pretty sure that the creator of all life told her many things secretly, but dissecting them, well, that would take some time. The woman who was the creator of all things was discreet in all ways, starting with her appearance. She wore a purple velour track suit and the whitest sneakers and had bluish gray hair to impress—all curled up like a loud and outgoing woman would have it. And although she was as old as time, literally, being mated with the creator of time—

Papa Creola, she looked about seventy years old with smooth skin lined with a few wrinkles and pink lipstick and long eyelashes.

Father Time, who went by the name Papa Creola, looked like the most handsome old man one could meet. He was a silver fox with his pushed-back salt and pepper hair, sly smile and blue eyes. He was the perfect height at six feet even and the perfect build at just around one-hundred and seventy-five pounds. And he was cool with his low tone and relaxed manner to counter Mama Jamba's southern style.

Papa Creola had to regenerate his form when he reset time to try and put Gen back in the medieval era. It hadn't worked because, from what everyone could tell, she wasn't supposed to go back. This was her time. But that hard reset had caused Papa Creola to take on a new look. He went from being an elfin hippie to a halfling. Presently, he was both a magician and a fairy, having the logic of the first and the artistic and attractive style of the latter.

Gen didn't know what dictated the appearance or mannerisms of the creators of the earth or time, but she also didn't care. These two, who were the foundation of everything, did what they did because they could and who was she to question it all. If she'd been around since the beginning of everything, she'd probably have purple hair and talk in an Australian accent, just for fun. As it were, she just wanted to understand the last six hundred years and all that she'd missed.

"You don't mean that. You're not glad that we're here," Sophia said to Subner, the grumpy guy who was wearing all black with long, dark hair partially covering his face. He was a fairy in this iteration, but had his wings cut off to negate any emotional or artistic characteristics that might come with being a fairy.

The Protector of Weapons, Gen had learned, was the grouchy type. That was apparent during her time living at his shop, the Fantastical Armory, and it was almost endearing, like an old grandparent who complained about everything but secretly liked it all.

"Let me have a look at you, dear," Mama Jamba chimed in her southern accent, striding over to Gen and Sophia.

She was shorter than the two women which was saying a lot since they were both below average. Looking at her felt like staring in the mirror and then also the world at large. It was the strangest experience and Gen never thought she'd get used to it. Peering into the creator of life's eyes was more than intimidating. But then again, she didn't want to look away from the woman who was responsible for everything—quite literally.

Mama Jamba was small and spritely in her tracksuit and sneakers, with hairspray making her large hair absolutely perfect. She smiled slyly at Gen, looking at her new outfit.

"I like this new style for you," she said, a sparkle in her periwinkle blue eyes. "It suits you. It's old and new and fun and also a little rebellious."

Gen glanced down at the outfit that felt like the best thing ever and smiled. "Thanks. It feels…right."

"Remember the way this outfit makes you feel and never choose anything or anyone that doesn't measure up the same way, dear," Mama Jamba said, like she meant something really profound but was trying to be discreet.

"Okay," Gen said, drawing out the word.

"It works, for a timeless vigilante," Papa Creola said, taking the position next to Mama Jamba, making the couple look complete. He smiled and Gen felt like she was in the company of the most beautiful set of grandparents, but that wasn't the right term for them. They were that, but times a thousand.

"Vigilante makes me sound like something fierce," Gen said with a laugh.

Mama Jamba looked at Papa Creola with a knowing smile. "Wouldn't it be great if she knew…"

"It would mess up everything," he replied with a devilish grin.

"And I like it much better when they have to figure it out on their own. Watching them be confused and struggle is fun."

"Yeah, you're right. I like that part too," Mama Jamba said. The pair clasped hands and turned, walking off for the pink armchairs at the front of the Fantastical Armory where they spent most of their time, plotting and planning the universe from the shop of oddities.

"You all are sadistic, and we love you dearly," Sophia said, waving to the pair's back.

"They are sly little devils, if you ask me," a woman Gen knew little about but loved dearly said, joining them.

It was one of the women who she'd followed through the time gate in 1426. When Gen had met Liv and Rose Beaufont in her timeline, she instinctively knew that something was wrong about them. Therefore, she followed the two women, stepping through a time gate to the twenty-first century, not realizing that she'd entered a world that she could never leave. And here she was, living a life with her relatives, six hundred years in the future, with the dragon's egg she'd buried all that time ago. Things sort of worked out, after all, Gen believed.

Rose Beaufont, Clark's daughter, was a Mortal Seven for the House of Fourteen. When Gen and her father, William, created the magical organization, it was composed of seven magician families, involving one councilor and one warrior from each for a total of fourteen. But over time, they realized that mortals needed to be involved for balance.

Then something horrid happened and mortals in the world wanted magic and sacrificed their souls for it—becoming witches and warlocks. That's when things turned really dark on the globe, but Rose and her husband, London Carraway, fixed all that, eradicating witchcraft for good.

Presently, Rose was pregnant with the key to fixing the balance. As the first and only half magicians and half mortals in the world, Rose and London had created what Mama Jamba called the perfect race. Their children's blood would allow all races to blend. It was the antidote to the separateness that had caused wars and divides since the beginning of time. Since Gen had been born there had always been battles between the races, but Rose and London's children were prophesied to fix all that—finally.

"Good to see you," Gen said, hugging the woman who she knew little about and loved dearly, like a sister.

"You too, Time Traveler," Rose replied, her long blonde hair flowing over her shoulders. She was only a month or so pregnant and therefore still working as a Mortal Seven, wearing her black armored suit and looking as beautiful as ever. But what was really remarkable about her was the red Chinese dragon who always floated by her shoulder.

Elvis was like a flying comedian but also the reason that Gen knew her father and sister, as Founders, watched from the Land of Chimera. That's what Elvis actually was—a chimera. However, he was disguised in tiny dragon form.

It was a strange arrangement but apparently, the Founders of the House of Fourteen decided that the Mortal Seven who usually didn't have magic, needed a way to protect themselves, so they were given chimeras. At will, these creatures disguised in animal form could transform into giant lions with a serpent as a tail and a goat's head on their back. They were fierce protectors of the Mortal Sevens they were assigned to by the Founders.

Rose, of course, as a halfling had magic, but she also had her chimera and because of her powers, Elvis could talk and was the strangest chimera in the world.

He communicated with the Elders, or rather Founders of the House of Fourteen, in the Land of Chimera and had confirmed that William and Elizabeth were there, looking down on them all and making appointments to the various organizations like the House of Fourteen, Dragon Elite, FGA and Rogue Riders.

"Did it hurt?" the floating red dragon asked Gen, looking over Rose's shoulder.

"What?" Gen asked, wondering if she missed something.

"Did it hurt?" Elvis repeated. "You know, when you fell from heaven."

Rose groaned. "I'm sorry. His thing right now is pick up lines. It's his gimmick and it's killing my spirit."

"Pick up lines," Gen mused. "So do you mean ways that men make themselves more presentable to women?"

"I like the way you put things," Sophia said, smiling. "And yes, that's right."

"I like the way you put things too," Elvis said, floating over closer to Gen, batting his eyes at her. "Also, are you a magician?"

Gen's brow furrowed with confusion. "Well, yeah, I'm a Beaufont."

"I thought so," Elvis replied, wiggling in the air like a flying snake. "Because you make everyone disappear."

Gen and the other women laughed. Subner grunted, flipping the page of his book. He always sat behind the glass counter at the back, pretending to read a book and eavesdropping on the conversation, usually making snide remarks under his breath.

"Are you the plague?" Subner asked, not looking up from the yellowed page. "Because you're killing me."

"Oh, you're feeling left out, aren't you?" Elvis sang, zooming over in the Protector of Weapon's direction. "I've got a line for you."

"Did you bring me here to meet with Subner?" Gen asked, pointing at the grouchy man, but looking at Sophia. "Is he going to help me find a weapon?"

Sophia shook her head. "I brought you here to see Rose. She has your weapon."

"She has *my* weapon," Subner muttered, flipping the page as Elvis settled down on the counter next to him, uninvited. The Chinese dragon didn't seem to care that he was making a mess, scattering papers and objects as he got comfortable, like a cat taking their space up high.

Gen blinked at Rose, confused. "What? What does he mean?"

Rose waved at the man, dismissively. "He's just mad because I was given Bellumferrum and I won't let him have it. I was told by its previous owner that it was to be given to a magician who was pure of heart. I didn't know who that was but now I realize that must be you."

"Oh, Bellumferrum," Gen said, enjoying the way the word rolled off her tongue. "That's a nice name…"

Rose nodded, pulling something small from her pocket. "It means Weapon of War. And it's probably the most powerful tool in existence."

"Which is why it should be mine," Subner murmured as Elvis continued to roll around on the counter, making a real mess.

"Do you have a name?" the red dragon asked, looking up at the Protector of Weapons, his long mustache unfurling. "Or can I call you mine?"

Subner ignored him, turning the page of his book.

Rose also ignored Subner, opening her hand to reveal a small obsidian cube with intricate symbols carved all around it. The object was two inches on each side and radiated a strange magic that Gen had never seen. But it was also a bit underwhelming.

Pointing at the cube, Gen said, "That's the most powerful weapon in existence?"

Rose nodded eagerly. "The way it works is that Bellumferrum only bonds to one person at a time. When needed, in battle, the person makes an intention to use the weapon and it reads their thoughts plus the needs of the situation and becomes whatever will help them. Apparently, it's a pretty big trip because you don't know what you're going to get and have a limited amount of time to figure out what it is and how to use it. But it can become anything, and therefore makes it so you are always prepared for any situation and fight."

"It's the most brilliant weapon to ever exist," Subner muttered with zero inflection in his voice. "It quite literally has a consciousness and formally bonds to the person who wields it."

This was all a bit baffling for Gen. "And it only can be used by one person?"

Rose nodded. "And currently it doesn't have an owner, but I think it should be you."

"What happened to the last person?" Gen dared to ask.

"They died in battle," Rose replied.

"But if Bellumferrum is so good, then how?" Gen questioned.

"Nothing is foolproof," Subner said, irritation in his voice as he flipped a page of his book.

Rose nodded to this. "Bellumferrum can be tricked, and it was in this situation. It became something that hindered Porthos Galopin in battle, becoming his ultimate downfall. But I firmly believe this weapon was meant for you. You're a dragonrider and this is a weapon that can adapt to all the various situations you'll find yourself in."

"And you can't break it," Sophia said with a smile.

Gen eyed the strange object, still resting in Rose's outstretched hand. "So, it can become a sword or a bow?"

"It can become anything," Subner said, sounding even more annoyed.

Gen glanced at him. "As the Protector of Weapons, if you really don't think I should have this then I'll respect it."

He actually glanced up from his book, a scowl deep on his face. "As the Protector of Weapons, I want the most powerful tools in the world. But as a citizen of this planet, I want what's best and that means, you should have it. You will need it. And the world needs you to be prepared for what's ahead or otherwise, we're all screwed."

CHAPTER EIGHTEEN

PILLOW TALK AND BATTLE PLANS

<u>Chimerick's Bar and Grill, Roya Lane, London, England, United Kingdom</u>

Gen stared at the small black cube in her hand, feeling the weight of it like a sledgehammer on her shoulders. Apparently, that's what it had become when it was the downfall of its last wielder, Porthos Galopin. The witch who had killed him, tricked Bellumferrum into becoming a giant war hammer. Porthos had exhausted himself carrying it into battle and then was too depleted to fight. The witch, Mefora Payne, had intimate knowledge of the weapon of war and knew how to feed it the wrong information.

So, it was a unique situation, but proved that the weapon wasn't foolproof. It had many downsides, the first being that one never knew what it was going to become and had to be prepared for anything. If Gen didn't know how to use a spear, then she'd have to adapt really fast in the blink of an eye. Also, because Bellumferrum relied on connecting to both the consciousness of the person who wielded it and their enemy, it could be tricked. So there were many factors at play.

The weapon was kind of a head trip for Gen, and she wasn't

sure that she wanted it as her main defense. But it felt like she had been given an honor, taking it when it could only be passed after the death of the last user.

"I don't really understand how to use this," Gen finally said, pulling her gaze away from the small black object and looking across the bar table at Sophia, Rose and Elvis.

Elvis laughed quite loudly as he took a sip of beer. "That's what she said."

Rose shook her head. "Gen won't get the reference. She hasn't seen The Office or anything else from this…millennium."

"She has to start somewhere," Elvis said, guzzling down another sip.

"Will you take it easy there?" Rose asked the Chinese dragon. "That's like your third beer."

"I'm drinking for two," he argued.

"No, you're not," she replied, pursing her lips and glancing at Gen. "I hope that your dragon isn't as weird as mine."

Sophia laughed loudly at this, taking a sip of her own beer. "Fat chance of that. She's a Beaufont. Lunis is about as nutty as a Reese's peanut butter cup."

"That's true," Rose said, nodding along, taking a sip of her water as she glanced at Gen. "You're screwed. What's His Name is going to be insane."

Gen chuckled, wiping her own drink from her mouth. "I don't know what his name is yet or what his deal is and why everyone seems so peculiar about him. I'm really anxious to know what's wrong with my dragon. I've joked to him that he's a runt." She looked directly at Sophia, hoping she'd give something away.

Sophia held up her hands in surrender. "I don't know what Quiet, Mahkah and Hiker know. They won't tell me. But it's apparently a big deal. Maybe he's the king of comedy and will really annoy the older dragons with his puns."

Everyone at the table laughed, all of them taking the chance to sip their drinks.

"I just don't get how this cube-thing works." Gen laid Bellumferrum on the table. "Like, does it only work in battle? Or what if I need a tool in a non-dangerous situation? Can I use it then?"

"I could use a bowl of pretzels right now," Elvis said and then burped. "See if it will make those."

"I think that you should drink less," Rose muttered at the dragon before giving her attention to Gen. "And from what I understand, it's to be used when you need it. So you simply hold it and make a request. But I'm sure that with practice, you'll figure it out."

"So, if I held it right now and said, give me what I need, what would happen?" Gen mused.

"Only one way to find out." Sophia waved at the cube, encouragingly. "See what it does."

"Well, do you think that's safe?" Gen asked, looking around the busy bar, which was full of strange types like giants, gnomes and fairies. She wasn't used to seeing them all mixing, since in her day, the races stayed separate.

"I think that you have to experiment with it, or you won't know how it works," Rose offered.

"Okay, well, I guess this will tell me if it works when I'm not in danger, since this place is relatively safe." Gen reached out and picked up Bellumferrum.

"I don't know," Elvis muttered, cutting his eyes to two guys across the bar. "Those types look pretty sketchy and like they might try and steal my girls."

"We're not your girls," Rose said, rolling her eyes at the red dragon, floating next to her.

"Really?" he countered. "Because your name must be Google, because you have everything that I've been searching for."

Rose groaned. "Wow, I don't think I can take it anymore." She smiled at Gen. "Please, indulge us. Ask Bellumferrum to help you. Let's see how it does."

"Okay," Gen said, wrapping her fingers around the cube.

Apparently, once Rose gave it to her, it was hers to do as she wished. Rose had made the choice of who it went to and that was set in stone at this point.

Closing her eyes, Gen concentrated, feeling the object in her grasp pulse, like it was coming alive. She felt it beat, as if it was a heart in her palm. There was an echo in her mind. A vibration in her chest. And then she saw the light even with her eyes closed.

Her hand moved as something grew in it. But the morphing was so natural, like she knew how to conform to make space for the change. And then both her hands were around something soft. Something supple. Something that she needed.

With her eyes open, Gen looked at the object that Bellumferrum had become—amazed. She glanced at Rose, Sophia and Elvis. Laughed. And pressed the object to her.

"It knows how exhausted I am," she said, squeezing the pillow that was Bellumferrum to her. "It's telling me to sleep."

"It will serve you well for all of your life," Rose said, with a smile. "I knew you were the right person to give this to."

Sophia nodded in agreement. "It's the perfect weapon for the woman who will need it all. You have the one thing you can never destroy and will help you in all situations."

Gen smiled at the soft white pillow, realizing that she simultaneously had the hardest and most useful weapon in the world to use. She'd always have to think to employ Bellumferrum. But for a woman such as Gen, she would have it no other way. It was a weapon she couldn't break because it was fit for her.

CHAPTER NINETEEN

STEPPING INTO THE UNKNOWN

<u>The Castle, The Gullington, Scotland, United Kingdom</u>

Gen awoke feeling the strangest sense of home that she'd ever known. She sat up in her bed in the Castle at the Gullington, with a sense of awe and wonder that she wasn't prone to. Placing her hands by her side and feeling the warm bed covers, she felt a deep connection to something and firmly believed that she'd found the place where she belonged. She was a Dragon Elite, and this was where her purpose resided.

As the sun started to peek out over the hills through the window, Gen remembered what day it was almost too much at once. She wanted to run toward the future of possibilities but also felt a foreboding unlike ever before. Something felt really off about what was happening next and Gen had no idea how or why.

Today was when her dragon would hatch.

Feeling a strange urgency, Gen hurriedly dressed, putting on the suit that Jeremy Bearimy and Juergen had made for her. She slipped Bellumferrum into her pocket, again accosted by the fact that something so small could be so powerful. It was a tiny black cube, but it could become a cannon if she needed it. Right then,

Gen wondered if she would ever need that—the future again was full of possibilities and uncertainties.

When Gen exited her room, she was surprised and also relieved to find Sophia waiting there for her. She was holding what appeared to be a shot of whiskey and she was wearing what looked to be an apprehensive expression.

"We have to stop meeting like this," Gen joked, brushing her hands down her armored suit. "You do have your own room in the Castle, right? You don't just live outside of mine?"

Sophia laughed. "I have my own wing because the Castle, also known as Quiet, adores me so. But because of that connection, he also threw me out of bed early and brought me here with this." She held up the shot glass of auburn-colored liquid. "Apparently, he knew you needed me and also a drink."

"But the sun is still rising, and I haven't had anything to eat," Gen remarked, still taking the shot glass from Sophia.

"I don't think it matters what you've had in your stomach when you're a dragonrider," Sophia stated. "You drink when you need to and apparently, you're going to have one of those days that demand you drink early."

"Cheers then." Gen held up the shot glass and threw back her head, taking the drink in one gulp. It burned but was also nice and warming, seeming to coat her stomach and strengthen her fortitude. Shaking her head, she blinked at Sophia. "So, what kind of day am I having that I need to start with a glass of whiskey?"

Sophia shrugged. "Hard to know for certain, but something tells me that meeting your dragon is going to be quite the occasion."

"Because he has a deep, dark secret that will surprise me?" Gen asked.

Sophia nodded. "And also, because everyone has turned out for the affair. Get ready to put your social hat on because I haven't seen this many people on the Expanse since..." She thought for a moment. "Well, since ever. Every dragon and rider for the Dragon Elite and everyone of interest has turned out for the hatching."

"Why?" Gen asked, stiffening and strangely glad for the whiskey first thing in the morning.

"Well, I'm not sure, actually," Sophia replied honestly. "I don't know what's so unique about your dragon, besides the obvious. He was the first egg spawned and will be the very last to ever hatch. That in itself is something remarkable. But Quiet, Mahkah and Hiker all know what makes him even more extraordinary. However, I have a feeling there's a twist that none of us saw coming."

"Why is that?" Gen questioned, having had the same feeling since awakening.

"You know how you just know that something is going to whack you in the face, even though there's nothing aimed at you or in the vicinity?" Sophia asked, a quizzical expression buzzing in her eyes.

"Yes, and I've felt like that since I woke up, although it was strangely accompanied by a sense of comfort—like I was at home," Gen replied.

Sophia nodded. "I know, but there's something going on below the surface, I feel. Like we're reading things all wrong. I don't know what we're going to learn today, but I'm certain that what we think is going to happen is going to be very different than what happens."

"What do I do?" Gen asked, feeling more trepidation than ever before.

"When you have to walk through fire, do you question if you're going to get burned?"

Gen shook her head. "No, because you know you're going to."

"What do you do?" Sophia challenged.

"You remember why you're doing it," Gen stated with confidence. "And you hold your head up high and walk through the flames because you must have a reason, which is to get to the other side."

"That's right," Sophia affirmed. "And your reason is to meet your dragon. We don't know what he is, but we know he's important. So, walk forward. Feel the flames and get to the other side. It's time you learn who you've been bonded to for the rest of your life. It's time that you discover your destiny."

CHAPTER TWENTY

AWAITING THE AWAKENING

<u>The Expanse, The Gullington, Scotland, United Kingdom</u>

Even though Gen had been warned, the number of people and dragons gathered on the Expanse of the Gullington was simply overwhelming. She stepped out of the Castle and every part of her body was vibrating with tension. As her boots sank into the soft but firm grass of the Expanse, Gen wondered if she was ready for what came next—something told her that she was born ready…

In front of her was a sprawling canvas of untamed wilderness in the heart of the Scottish Highlands, under a sky awash with hues of blue. The air was thick with anticipation. It carried the scents of earth and heather, mingling with the faint, smoky aroma of distant fires. All eyes were on Gen. Everyone eerily silent, watching as the medieval woman made her way down from the Castle. Every eye was on her, every heart sharing in the weight of the moment that lay before her.

Around her, the Expanse was filled with a congregation of magical beings. Dragonriders stood proudly beside their magnificent beasts. Most of them were men and women whom Gen had never met. They were dressed in rugged clothes and armor, weapons strapped to their backs or sides. In their eyes, they wore relentless expressions that seemed to speak of their courage and spirit for fighting for justice as one of the Dragon Elite.

Beside each of the riders were dragons of every hue and size, their scales glittering like jewels under the setting sun. Most were massive with long tails and horns on their backs. But they were all like statues, simply watching Gen as she soundlessly made her way through the crowd. Why a few hundred dragons and their riders had showed up for this hatching, Gen didn't know, but with much certainty, she knew she was about to find out.

There were also a couple of giants who stood tall in the crowd, almost even with the heads of the dragons. Then there were faces whom Gen recognized like Wilder, Sophia's husband. Beside him was Mahkah, Hiker, Ainsley and of course, Quiet, who looked very unassuming.

Then, of course, there were the faces of Gen's family, greeting her with warmth. Sophia stood next to her sister, Liv who was smiling mischievously as she waved casually, like daring to break the stillness of the crowd. Alongside her was the stoic Clark Beaufont, looking professional as ever in his starched black suit. Rose, his daughter, stood elegantly with Elvis floating in the air over her left shoulder. Paris Beaufont, who was also the head of the Fairy Godmother Agency and held the title of Saint Valentine, stood next to her cousin.

The Beaufonts were a family to impress, all holding roles fitting of royalty. That would have made William, Gen's father proud. She looked up to the heavens, where she pictured the Land of Chimera was and realized that William, the Founder of the House of Fourteen, already knew what his family had done. He was watching her right then and she hoped that she was about to make him proud. She hoped that she knew the name of her dragon—bonding him to her forever.

Standing next to the Beaufonts were two faces whom Gen never got tired of seeing, but always surprised her. Mama Jamba stood casually next to Papa Creola, who appeared quite amused and as if he was teeming with a secret. The pair would know what was so important about her dragon. They would know just about everything. However, they had informed her that they had blind spots, for no one could ever know everything, no matter how powerful because the future simply wasn't written until it happened.

At the center of it all, nestled within a circle of ancient stones that had witnessed countless such ceremonies, lay Gen's dragon egg. During the time it had lain in the Nest where the other dragons lived, it had grown massively. She simply couldn't believe it. The egg was the size of a small house, its surface shimmering with iridescent scales of purple that seemed to capture the very essence of the morning sky. Gen approached, her steps uncertain, her heart a tumult of emotions. Pride, fear, wonder and a deep, unspoken trepidation drumming inside her.

She had dreamed of this moment. Imagined it in a hundred different ways, but now that it was here, doubt crept into her heart like a shadow. What kind of dragon lay within that majestic egg? Would she be worthy of him? And the question that haunted her most: would she know his name, the name that would bind them together for eternity?

The air grew still as she reached the circle, the crowd fading and freezing even more with a hushed reverence. She could feel the eyes of every being upon her, their collective breaths held in a moment of shared suspense. The ground underfoot, a tapestry of moss and stone, seemed to pulse with the heartbeat of the earth, a reminder of the life that was about to burst forth.

Gen stood before the egg, her gaze locked on its surface, searching for any sign of the life within. A wind whistled through the air, stirring her long braid, but having no effect on the giant egg. Gen glanced up at the light blue sky to pay respect to her father and sister who were witnessing from another realm the miracle that was about to occur. The wind carried whispers of encouragement, and somewhere in the distance, a lone piper began to play a melody that seemed to echo the rhythm of her racing heart.

In that moment, Gen felt a connection to everything around her. She sensed a thread of unity that wove through her soul, linking her to the past, present and future. She was a part of this land, part of its magic and mystery. Whatever emerged from the egg would be a reflection of the world that had shaped her.

And then, without warning, it began.

CHAPTER TWENTY-ONE

THE NAME THAT CHANGED EVERYTHING

<u>The Expanse, The Gullington, Scotland, United Kingdom</u>

A faint crack appeared on the surface of the egg. It was a hairline fracture that quickly spread, webbing out across the shimmering scales. The crowd drew in a collective breath, their sounds merging with the crackling energy that now filled the air. Gen's heart hammered in her chest, every fear, every doubt silenced by the overwhelming awe of the moment.

The egg trembled. The cracks widened. Fragments of shell began to fall away. Light, pure and radiant, spilled from the openings, bathing Gen in a glow that felt as though it emanated from the very heart of the Earth. Her dragon was coming, breaking free from his prison of a shell—about to take his first breath. This would be his initial sight of the real world through his own eyes.

Gen, standing alone yet surrounded by a host of witnesses, found herself on the precipice of the unknown. Her life was intertwined with that of a creature of legend. As the egg continued to crack, revealing glimpses of the being within, she realized that this was not just the hatching of a dragon but the birth of a new chapter in her own story. It was a chapter filled with adventures and challenges, with bonds that would transcend time.

Her dragon was coming. And with his arrival, everything would change.

When the massive dragon egg started to fall away from the being within, Gen backed up, so as not to be crushed by the casing. She saw a wing. A horn. A deep purple that reflected the outside of the shell.

No one said a word. No one made a sound. Gen simply stared, unblinking as the majestic beast freed himself from his confines.

Like with all creatures in this world, we arrive alone — forging our own path and she simply knew that there was no breaking her dragon free. He must do that on his own.

When the last of the shell had fallen to the ground, the dragon was revealed and then not really. His form could be seen, but he was hunched over, exactly as he'd been in the shell. With his head down and his wings folded into his body, he looked so small to Gen. But still, he was over ten feet tall, all bundled up.

Holding her breath, Gen took a step forward. The dragon stirred, like waking from a long dream. For a moment, Gen thought that more of his shell was breaking away because a loud crack rang through the air. But all of the shell lay around the dragon. And the sound was from a bolt of lightning that shot through the sky as clouds moved in, blanketing the sky in darkness.

In a matter of seconds, like it was a solar eclipse, the Expanse was covered in darkness. It was the strangest thing that Gen had ever experienced, to have the heavens turn black in a matter of seconds and storm clouds brew overhead. The foreboding essence of that stirred all around her as the crowd tensed with an energy that was palpable. Gen, in the darkness, could make out the worried expressions of those around her as they looked up to the darkened sky. But she wasn't sure how she could see so well or why her hearing had suddenly heightened or why everything about her was abruptly intensified.

And then, the dragon brought his massive head up and looked straight into her eyes and Gen knew. She looked into the golden eyes of the magical creature before her, and she saw things she never thought possible. Gen saw the dawning of the planets when Mama Jamba created the solar system. She saw the spark of time when Papa Creola started the clocks. She saw history through the ages. Gen felt the chi of the dragon and she knew that it was not just connected to her anymore, but it was a part of her. And she also knew who her dragon was.

Standing back, Gen took in the full appearance of the violet dragon before her. His wingspan was simply incredible as he extended his reach, shaking them out for the first time. He was the size of a small cottage, and his wings made him well over twenty yards wide. But he was also slender and had a grace about him as he folded the appendages back into his body and brought down his head to peer deep into Gen's eyes.

"I've known you for all of your life," the dragon spoke, both in her head, like so many times before. But he also spoke out loud, his voice echoing across the plains, making all lean forward with intense curiosity. "Are you my one true rider? Do you know *me*? If so, then you must know my name. If you do, then I will forever be bonded to you, our lives will be one for as long as we both shall live."

Gen brought her hands to her mouth, as if in prayer. Her eyes filled with tears. She wasn't on the verge of crying because of fears that she wouldn't know his name. She was overflowing with emotion because she knew it and it was beyond anything she could have imagined. She never asked for this. Never thought it was possible. And yet, she'd been awarded a destiny unimaginable.

"I know your name and it is the same as your title," she said bowing slightly to her dragon. "You are the ruler over all dragons. The very first to spawn. The last to hatch. And the most powerful one which will ever exist. You, my dragon, are known as Emperor."

And then in unison, everyone around Gen dropped down to one knee. Every rider. Every dragon. Everyone, including Mother Nature and Father Time. They all bowed to the dragon that was meant to rule over the world—Genevieve Beaufont's dragon—Emperor.

CHAPTER TWENTY-TWO

THE GNOME'S WHISPER

<u>The Expanse, The Gullington, Scotland, United Kingdom</u>

Gen hardly had a moment to process everything that had transpired when a great murmuring broke out behind her. She turned, thinking that someone was praising her dragon. To her surprise, she found Quiet hurrying in her direction. Behind him, Hiker and Mahkah were exchanging words, both of them looking stressed as they looked between Gen and her dragon.

"What is it?" Gen asked, turning to her dragon, knowing he knew what was happening.

He peered down at her with timeless wisdom. "I'm not who you thought I was…"

"What does that even mean?" Gen said as the crowd broke out in quiet muttering, all of them wondering what was happening. "I didn't know your name before I met you. I didn't know that you were the emperor of dragons. What else don't I know?"

"You think that we're here to help the world," Emperor said, his voice low and mostly in Gen's ears and in her head.

She nodded, noticing the stirring in the crowd. People were moving away. They were panicking. "Of course. I'm a Beaufont. I'm meant to do just that."

He shook his giant head, looking at her intently. "What if your purpose is to fix it… To save it…"

Confused, Gen glared up at him. "What does that even mean? Are we talking semantics?"

"Gen, you need to decide what you want," Emperor said, giving her a deadly serious look. "Because I don't just pick you. You pick me. And if this is not the life you want, then you have only now to decide."

Everything was stirring around Gen. The commotion was building. She didn't know what all this meant. And then she felt a tug on her arm. She looked down and saw Quiet standing meekly by her side.

He mouthed words she couldn't hear over all the noise. But she suspected that she wouldn't be able to hear them, anyway.

Kneeling down, Gen brought her ear closer to the gnome's face and looked straight at him. "What? What's happening, Quiet? What's wrong?"

"Nothing is wrong," he replied and for the first time she heard the man who was so much more and the protector of the Dragon Elite. "It's just that your dragon, the emperor of dragons, doesn't belong here."

"What?" Gen asked, gawking at the gnome before her. "What do you mean?"

"He is a demon dragon," Quiet replied. "You are a demon dragonrider. You don't belong here at the Gullington with the Dragon Elite. Your job is not to fight for justice. Your job is with the Rogue Riders. You aren't meant to help the world. You are not in charge of creating peace. You are meant to fix the world. You are in charge of criminals."

CHAPTER TWENTY-THREE

THE ROGUE PATH UNVEILED

<u>Hiker Wallace's Office, The Castle, The Gullington, Scotland, United Kingdom</u>

"I don't understand how this happened," Hiker voiced, thundering back and forth across his office, on the well-weathered path he took when pacing. His head was down, his hands clasped behind his back and his jaw tight with tension.

"I don't see what the problem is, son," Mama Jamba said, curled up on the sofa in his office, looking as snug as a bug in a rug with her feet tucked up underneath her. Beside the old woman was Papa Creola who seemed cool and relaxed, sitting back, waiting for his cup of tea.

"The problem is the emperor of all dragons is a demon and meant to work for the Rogue Riders and not us," Hiker argued, halting and turning around to face the woman who was his boss—well, everyone's. "How could you let something like this happen?"

She smirked. Glanced at Gen across the room. Then her periwinkle eyes flashed to Sophia, the only other person in the room besides Gen, Hiker and Papa Creola. "I didn't just let something happen like I was playing the lottery, son. I intended it. Emperor was always meant to be a demon dragon. Gen too. They were always supposed to fight on the side of the Rogue Riders."

"But why?" Hiker boomed, throwing his hands into the air. "Why when we all know that the Dragon Elite—"

"You think you're better," Papa Creola cut in coolly, his voice low and the authority in his voice absolute.

Hiker halted. Took in a breath. Considered this and then nodded. "Of course I do. We are good. They are…rebellious."

"Genevieve Beaufont has more courage in her pinky than most of your dragonriders, son," Mama Jamba explained tersely. "She knows how to stand up for what's right and sometimes that means creating the balance that comes with policing the criminal world. I'm sorry that you don't see it, but most of your riders only want good. They aren't smart enough to see that there is gray. They don't realize that if they cut off the head of a beast that ten more will sprout. Sophia got it. She created the Rogue Riders. But, just so you know, the Dragon Elite were never meant to create the balance between good and evil in this world."

She turned. Smiled at Gen. Winked. "I always intended that job to go to the Rogue Riders. It is through managing evil that the world has a chance of surviving."

"But we create peace!" Hiker argued.

"And too much peace would kill this planet," Papa Creola stated. "The people on this Earth are human. They are flawed. And if they aren't allowed to be that, then this place would spiral into a black hole. The Dragon Elite are good at ending wars. But what the world needs most are those who allow people to be people who are flawed."

Sophia nodded, stepping forward, a noble look in her eyes. "The Rogue Riders are critical in keeping a lid on the pressure cooker of humanity. As a Dragon Elite, we only seek to fix problems, but they are meant to work with them—knowing that they can't be erased. It only makes sense that the leader of dragons and his rider was a Rogue Rider."

Hiker shook his head, seeming to still wrestle with this idea. He couldn't look at Gen, probably unnerved by her presence. "I just don't get how this happened."

"She is a twin, son," Mama Jamba pointed out. "Why didn't you see this coming? You know that one is always pure and the other always rebellious. You, yourself were a Dragon Elite and Thad, your twin, was a—"

"Criminal," Hiker growled. "My brother tried to destroy this world."

"That's because there wasn't a place for him, sir," Sophia said. "We used to shun our demon dragonriders, not giving them a place. You know, as Dragon Elite, as angel riders, we have a lot to learn about tolerance. We're part of the problem. And maybe if we were a bit more accepting of those different from us, then a lot of battles wouldn't need to be fought."

Mama Jamba smiled proudly at Sophia, nudging Papa Creola beside her. "I made that one."

"You made them all, dear," he countered.

"I know, but I gave her a little something extra," Mama Jamba chimed.

"And what did you give this one?" Hiker asked, pointing at Gen, looking at her for the first time.

"I gave her something that would make her timeless and unique," Mama Jamba answered. "I gave her something that would ensure she could rule over this world, but I also gave her a challenge unlike any of you have ever had to face."

Hiker stiffened. Looked down at Mama Jamba. Clutched his fists. "What is coming, Mama?"

"The very worst," the old woman said. Then she directed a finger at Gen. "And only she can save us from it. But only if we all believe in her. You know better than anyone that a leader needs support. So, what do you say?"

Hiker gritted his teeth. Glared at Gen. Then directed his gaze to Mama Jamba. "I trust you. If this is the way you want it."

"It's the only way…" Mama Jamba said and then smiled sweetly at Gen. "So, what do you say? Are you up for what comes next?"

Gen blinked at the strange entity. "What comes next?"

"Well, you move out," Mama Jamba answered. "You like it here at the Gullington, don't you?"

"Yes," Gen answered. "It's like home, in a way. Scotland feels rustic and like what I'm used to."

"Well, that won't do at all," Mama Jamba stated. "You need to go somewhere that will shape you and Emperor. You need something that takes you out of your comfort zone and makes you into the warrior who can fix this world."

"What?" Gen asked, looking around the room at the various faces. "Where's that?"

Sophia gave her a sympathetic smile. "You're going to Beverly Hills…"

CHAPTER TWENTY-FOUR

FROM HIGHLANDS TO HIGH SOCIETY

<u>Grounds, Rogue Rider Mansion, Beverly Hills, California, United States</u>

"Why did you keep your deep, dark, dirty secret from me?" Gen asked when she and Emperor stepped through the portal Sophia had opened from the Gullington. Now she stood in a place much different from old-world Scotland. She was back in Los Angeles, California where everything was too loud and smelled strange and was manicured in unnatural ways.

The purple dragon with a hint of gold on his chest and glowing in his eyes glared down at her. He towered over the woman, but that didn't intimidate her in the least. Just as Sophia had explained, Gen felt like Emperor's equal. She felt that she knew him without knowing him. But then, of course, she was learning that there was much she didn't know.

"Being a demon dragon should have been no secret," Emperor replied, his voice low and melodic. "Nor was it deep, dark or dirty. It would have been like telling you that you have blonde hair—you should have already known it."

She rolled her eyes at the dragon. "You surprised everyone at the Gullington. No one saw it coming."

"What did you do when those boys made fun of your sister on the streets of London when you two were eight years old?" Emperor questioned.

Gen thought back to the distant memory from six hundred years ago, but only twelve years back for her, since she was essentially twenty years old. She laughed, remembering that day clearly. "I broke both of their noses."

"Then how is it that you didn't know you would be a rebellious demon dragonrider?" he asked. "Elizabeth was always the well-mannered one between the two of you."

Gen shrugged with a sigh. "I guess I was just in denial. My father and sister were so good. Noble. I was always the one getting in trouble, starting fights."

"You didn't start fights," he argued. "You put bullies in their places. You stood up for the little guy. You took from the undeserving and gave to the poor. You are good. You're just a unique sort of noble."

"Well, thanks. Let's hope that serves us here, in this place that is by far the strangest one I've seen yet."

Gen blinked, looking around at what seemed like a kingdom ripped from a fairytale, if these stories were sponsored by outrageously wealthy elves with a penchant for gardening. Topiaries were stationed all over the green, manicured grounds where they'd found themselves. It was such a different sight than the wild Scottish hills where they'd been. It was like someone had tamed this land in every way possible, ensuring everything grew in a prescribed manner.

The topiaries were twisted into shapes more suited for a chessboard of the gods than a backyard in Beverly Hills. That was the city within Los Angeles where the Rogue Riders lived. Instead of a sentient castle, they called a large mansion home.

The place sprawled lazily across the land, a giant lounging in the sun, seemingly indifferent to the small fortunes it overshadowed. High walls whispered, "Keep out, but also, don't you wish you lived here?"

Gen trotted forward across a driveway that seemed more like a runway than a pathway. The stones were laid with precision, a carpet fit for modern royalty. Around her, gardens waged a silent war against the wild, each flower a soldier in perfect formation.

The house, with its glaring windows and sun-soaked veranda, smirked like a cat that got the cream and the mouse. Patios and fire pits spoke of gatherings, where the air was thick with stories more intoxicating than the wine. And there was a pool so serene, it could have been a mirror, reflecting a life Gen could scarcely imagine, let alone live. "Welcome to the castle of the twenty-first century," the grounds seemed to say. "Where magic is money, and nature bends to the will of those who have it."

Gen's curiosity would have pulled her farther but she caught sight of Sophia and her dragon, Lunis, stepping through the still-open portal. When they were both through it, Sophia turned, closing the portal. Lunis, like a big blue dog after a bath, shook out his wings before folding them back into his body.

"What do you think of the Rogue Rider mansion?" Lunis asked. "I designed it."

"You did?" Gen asked, gawking at the modern structure. "It's…big."

"It's a gauche monstrosity," Sophia countered with a chuckle. "But it suits the Rogue Riders since they were formed in the present era."

The blue dragon huffed, cutting his eyes down to his rider. "I happen to like the Rogue Rider mansion. It may not be the heart of a timeless gnome but it also doesn't erase hallways and trap its occupants in their rooms because it gets into a bad mood."

"Well, I happen to like the Castle a lot," Gen said, unable to keep the regret out of her voice. She averted her gaze from her dragon and Sophia, looking at a colossal and elaborate fountain sitting in the middle of the circular driveway. It had huge statues of fish spitting water high into the air.

"You felt at home at the Castle," Emperor said, apparently not able to keep a secret, announcing what he read in Gen's heart and head aloud for Sophia and Lunis to know.

She chewed on her lip, wondering how she could get back at the dragon for this admission. The problem was, he could read her mind readily using his telepathy, but the opposite wasn't true, or otherwise she would have known he was the emperor of all dragons and also a demon dragon.

"I liked the rustic feel of it," Gen muttered. "It reminded me of my time."

"Your time is here and now," Emperor reminded sternly. She was going to have to work with him on his out loud voice and maybe not saying everything between them for others to hear.

"I know, it's just that the transition isn't easy and the Castle made it a bit more digestible," Gen said, narrowing her eyes at the happy, little fountain in the distance, that seemed to be mocking her with its whimsy.

"The Castle will downright spoil you if it likes you, which it did," Sophia related. "But Emperor is right and this is your time. The best way to get used to it, is to submerge yourself in it."

"And I designed a mighty fine headquarters for the Rogue Riders," Lunis said, a mischievous grin hiding in his eyes. "I think you'll like it if you give it half a chance."

"I'm sure you're right," Gen said and smiled at Sophia. "And I know you are too."

"And she's mad at me for calling her out in front of you two," Emperor stated.

She glared up at the dragon who could eat her for breakfast, but she sort of figured she could put him in a headlock too if she so decided. "You know, just because you can read my thoughts, doesn't mean that you should."

"A headlock, really?" he growled low in his throat, putting his head down low, even with hers. "I'd like to see you try."

She narrowed her eyes at him. "You know, we are going to have to learn some boundaries if this is going to work."

"Soooooo, about the Rogue Rider mansion," Lunis said in a sing-song voice, obviously trying to break the tension building between the rider and dragon.

Gen pulled her gaze away from Emperor's, not caring that he was literally breathing down her neck—his hot breath like a furnace blowing on her.

"Yeah, the mansion," Gen muttered. "I'm sure I'll love it."

"I hope so," Lunis said. "But the mansion is about like cheap, tight underwear."

She blinked at him in confusion. "What? What does that mean?"

Sophia groaned, shaking her head.

Lunis laughed. "There's no ballroom!"

CHAPTER TWENTY-FIVE

THE WHIP THAT BINDS

<u>Grounds, Rogue Rider Mansion, Beverly Hills, California, United States</u>

The scowl that Emperor shot at Lunis gave Gen an idea. She laughed, enjoying the flare of annoyance she suddenly felt in her dragon.

"So you don't like jokes, do you?" she asked the purple dragon who, strangely enough, towered over Lunis. That was saying something because he was massive and known for his super-size, especially on the night of a full moon.

But Gen reasoned that as the emperor of all dragons, hers had to be the most impressive in size and just about everything else—like skill. They'd have to get into that soon since all she knew about Emperor's skills was that he was telepathic and psychic, but with limitations. There just hadn't been much time for that kind of sharing.

"I don't like bad jokes," he seethed, looking between Gen and Lunis. "I thought you'd outgrow that childish behavior."

The blue dragon shrugged, rolling over on the grass and scratching his back on the ground. "And I thought that after six hundred years in a shell, you'd be more fun. I guess some things never change."

"I like your jokes," Gen said, laughing at Lunis' playful behavior.

"You can have him then," Sophia teased. "He's had all his shots and is neutered."

Lunis rolled over and sprang to his feet, growling at his rider. "I am not!"

She giggled, obviously enjoying the game. "Of course you aren't. Just like no one can have you because you're not up for adoption."

Gen admired the camaraderie between Sophia and Lunis. It was a fun dynamic and she suddenly wondered if she and Emperor would ever have that. Studying the purple dragon, she didn't think so since he looked as high and mighty as a peacock in mating season, strutting through the henhouse.

"I heard that," Emperor said, glaring at Gen.

"Good," she shot back, before glancing at Lunis, motioning between the dragons. "So you really all know each other? Like always and since the beginning, even before hatching? How is that?"

"It's the chi of the dragon," Lunis explained. "Our consciousnesses are all intertwined. You're a part of it in a way now. You've probably noticed that your senses have all heightened. That's a component of it."

"Unfortunately, it doesn't make us any taller," Sophia joked, her blue eyes dazzling in the California sunlight.

"That's fine." Gen shrugged. "I'm used to being short."

"You're much shorter than I thought you'd be," Emperor said, gazing down at her.

"Well, you're not the runt that I thought you'd be, but you're smellier," Gen chimed.

"I am not!" Emperor boomed.

"Have you bathed since the hatching?" Gen asked, a mock

look of seriousness on her face. "You'd been in there…well, forever."

Sophia giggled, affectionately looking up at Lunis. "Remember when we first got to know each other. They remind me of us."

"They really do," Lunis said with a smile. "How many times did I threaten to eat you?"

"Since this morning or do you mean the beginning?" she asked.

"Some things don't go away," Lunis replied, looking up to the sky. "But it looks like a few Rogue Riders are returning. That will be a good way to orient you two into this place. Just don't learn any bad habits from them."

"And don't shake their hands," Sophia said as three dragons with riders appeared from a portal in the sky and dove down toward the ground in their direction. "They usually don't wash."

"Oh, and don't be intimidated by them," Lunis said. "They aren't as well-behaved as the Dragon Elite."

Sophia smirked at Lunis. "Have you met our girl? She's already threatened to put her dragon in a headlock."

The blue dragon nodded. "And my money is actually on Gen."

Although at the Gullington, Gen had seen many a dragon, but as she studied the three flying down toward them, she noticed that these moved differently. Their riders held themselves strangely. It wasn't even something that Gen could put into words. It was more of an attitude that rider and dragon gave off, even from the distance.

There was a smaller white dragon, a bright red one, and then the largest of the three was a vibrant green. They flew in perfect formation, an impressive display vof grace and speed as they descended toward the Earth. In unison, the majestic beasts landed a short distance away, and then slowed to a fluid trot before halting right before Gen and the others.

As if they'd practiced it, all three of the magnificent creatures bowed low, their heads down and kneeling on their front legs—showing their respect to Emperor. The riders on their backs looked around at each other, like not understanding what was happening.

Sophia stepped forward, extending an arm to the giant purple dragon. "Riders, it is my honor to introduce to you the last dragon to ever hatch. Your dragons already know him and therefore they are showing their respect. This is Emperor, the ruler over all dragons."

"Oh!" a woman on the back of the white dragon yelped, her large brown eyes wide. She ducked her head, tucking her chin into her chest. "Someone should have told us."

"It was a secret," her dragon replied, lifting his own head and regaining his normal height. "There are some things we don't share with our riders. And some things that we do not know, like who the rider is who has bonded to our ruler."

Sophia smiled at Gen, holding out a presenting arm to her now. "This is Genevieve Beaufont, but you will call her Gen. She came through a time gate from the 15th century and is now here for good. She was a Founder of the House of Fourteen, a woman from the medieval era and now the rider to the emperor of dragons and the newest addition to the Rogue Riders."

If Gen expected a greeting like what her dragon got, then she'd be sorely disappointed. The dragonriders, the female and the other two both male, simply slid off the side of their dragons and landed on their feet, looking at her like she was a housefly they needed to swat out.

"Hey, Gwen," the woman said.

"Hey, you look alright for being so old," one of the men said.

Then the other simply stood, looking at her, a measured glare in his eyes as he appraised her from where he stood, next to his bright green dragon.

"Looks like we have another entitled Beaufont to deal with," the woman said, glaring at the other men.

"I bet this Genevieve has brought the plague with her," the rider next to the red dragon said, speaking again.

You're going to have to teach them to respect you, Emperor said in her head. *They feel the competition and don't want it. But you have to force your rule upon them.*

Well, it's not easy for some of us, Gen replied silently to him. *Some of us are named Emperor and all the dragons know them. And some of us go by a less conventional name and are meeting everyone for the first time.*

Just exert your dominance, Emperor implored. *Don't allow them to bully you. That's why you are my rider. No man could ever ride me because he couldn't stand up to the challenges you've seen. Use that. Be that. Shove their faces in mud.*

Gen smiled to herself as she took a step forward and Emperor lowered his head so she could stroke it like she owned him—although no rider could ever own their dragon. "I am Gen Beaufont, and you will call me that and you will not show any disrespect to me."

Then in a total act of faith, Gen withdrew Bellumferrum, not knowing what it would become. Instantly, she made her intention known to the object. Before her eyes, the cube glowed brightly and morphed in her hands into a plasma whip. Gen had never seen or heard of the bright, glowing object but Bellumferrum told her what it was at once. It had transformed into something sturdy and strong and she instinctively knew what to do with it.

If the weapon surprised Gen, then she covered it fast and as soon as the whip materialized fully, she brought it back and then around her head, slashing it through the air. With a crack, the whip shot through the space. Thankfully the riders were quick to dart away from its trajectory. Thankfully Sophia and Lunis weren't in the territory where it hit the ground. And thankfully Gen used the whip like an expert, ricocheting it through the air before pulling it back over her shoulder again and then forward once more.

It made a loud snapping sound, like a bolt of lightning through the air, followed by a bright light. Everything happened so quickly, but having leveled the playing field, Gen slowed her movements, stilling suddenly and staring at the three dragonriders before her. Two of the three cowered, shielding themselves behind their dragons.

"Do not ever call me by the name in which I used to found the House of Fourteen and do not ever refer to me as old or you will pay. My name is Gen, and I'm not old. I'm just medieval."

"Y-Y-Yeah, yeah, you got it," the man with the red dragon stuttered, nodding eagerly, a total look of fear in his eyes.

"O-O-Of course," the woman stammered, standing tensely behind her dragon.

"Yes, totally," the man with the green dragon stated, not having budged from his stoic place, but looking very entertained by this display.

CHAPTER TWENTY-SIX

THE WHIP VANISHES, THE POWER REMAINS

<u>Grounds, Rogue Rider Mansion, Beverly Hills, California, United States</u>

To Gen's surprise, the plasma whip simply disappeared as quickly as it materialized, turning back into a small, black cube. It was a product of her intentions and it had done exactly as she desired—put those challenging her in their place without hurting anyone.

Gen wanted to make a show and she'd done that. She wanted to be taken seriously, and by the look on the three dragonriders' faces, she'd accomplished her goal. But she also didn't want to harm anyone and since there were no cuts or injuries, she'd managed that. All because of the small object in her hands.

Gingerly, Gen clasped her fingers around Bellumferrum, holding it in the palm of her hand. No one questioned that it was a plasma whip moments before. The three dragonriders didn't seem shocked that the weapon had disappeared, but Gen reasoned they saw many things that were unexplainable all the time and knew how to hide their surprise.

Well done, Emperor said in her head.

Gen stayed frozen, not giving anything away. *You told me to exert my dominance. That's what I did.*

"Sooooo… Gen, you're like a strong shot of gin, aren't you," the guy next to the green dragon said. "Are you trying to knock us on our asses?"

Gen didn't give anything away. She stayed standing tall, sliding the cube that was Bellumferrum through her fingers, like a coin—a threat in the movement, as if she might use it again. And who knew what it would become next… Gen sure as hell didn't.

"Show her respect as we did to her dragon," the green dragon urged his rider.

"Yes, you unmannered jerks," the red dragon said, standing tall, shaking her head.

"We might be demon dragons policing the world, but we don't have to act like criminals," the white dragon said, the only male among them. It appeared to Gen that the dragons were always the opposite gender of their rider, like they were countering them with the balance of the male and female energy.

"Of course, my queen," the man paired to the red dragon said, bowing low, a real show of chivalry in his movements. He had mousey brown, curly hair and wore glasses. He was lanky and tall and an air of dorkiness about him but also authority—making for a strange combination. He turned to Gen and bowed again. "I apologize for my comment. We never expected the likes of you. What a surprise and privilege."

"It is an honor to meet the rider of the ruler of dragons," the other man said, bowing his head slightly. He was tall, with a strong build and had dark brown hair that was spiked and angled to the side. His blue eyes held a strong charisma that was intriguing but his smile made him look casually rugged somehow, like he was a jokester on the battlefield.

"Yeah, teach us your ways," the woman said, curtseying slightly, but Gen could tell she didn't mean it. She was tall for a woman with long flowing brown hair and big brown eyes and red lips. She was pretty and done up like one of those models that Gen had seen on what Liv had said were Hollywood billboards. If Gen wasn't trying to be the bigger person and pick her battles, she would have used Bellumferrum again on the woman, but right then wasn't the time to exert dominance. She'd already done that and very well.

"This is Sullivan Smith," Sophia said, holding her hand out to the man with curly hair next to the red dragon. "We call him Sully."

"And many other things behind his back," Lunis joked with a snicker.

The others laughed.

Sophia didn't laugh, but kept her stoic demeanor as she introduced. "Beside him, you'll meet Blaze, his dragon, who has the power of fire magic, as you might have guessed."

Gen nodded, realizing that Emperor already knew all this.

"And this is Mona Clipper. We call her Clipper," Sophia continued, motioning to the woman who looked really beautiful —too much so and like she cared to be presented in that way. "Her dragon is Glacier and has ice magic."

Again, Gen nodded.

"Lastly, this is Jack Lane," Sophia said, nodding at the handsome man who made Gen uncomfortable for some reason, probably because of his pensive stare. "His dragon is Volt and has the power of electricity."

"What do they call you?" Gen asked. "Since the others have nicknames."

"Jack," he answered simply.

"That's not what I would call you," Gen's dragon said, his chin down and gold eyes alight.

"What is your power, Emperor?" Jack dared to ask, looking directly at the dragon.

Gen expected for her dragon to speak. Everyone probably

expected this. That's why when Jack dropped to his knees suddenly, clutching his head, all were urgently shocked. The others, Sully and Clipper ran for the fallen man. He writhed on the ground, rolling around, cradling his head, screaming in pain.

"Do you want me to show you more of my powers or have you had enough?" Emperor said so loudly that it shook the ground.

Shocked and accosted by fear, Gen looked at Sophia and Lunis, absolutely baffled. The expression on Sophia's face said it all. She was also stunned by this display. Lunis however, simply shook his head.

"Enough," Jack cried in agony as his friends tried to help him, but the pain seemed to be inside of him. "Please make it stop! Please!"

"Okay, then don't question me or disrespect my rider again," Emperor said and lifted his head nobly.

And just like that, Jack started to quiet. His moaning slowed. His movements stilled.

Gen looked up at Emperor, wanting a moment alone to ask her question, but knowing they didn't have one. So in her head, she said, *What is your power?*

I am telepathic, as you know, he answered. *And also psychic as you've witnessed. But I also have the power of mind control. It is limited for now, but in time, I will be able to control all who dare cross my path. I nearly made his head explode.*

Then it is better that we always stay on the path of good because that is a dangerous power, Gen said to him.

Something sparkled in his eyes. *Don't you know, you were always meant to be my rider because you'll be the only one who can control me. You must keep me in check because my power is so great, it could take over the world—in all the worst ways.*

Gen realized then how much the world wasn't black and white. It was an array of grays, and she was the moral compass meant to keep her dragon of crazy hues in balance.

CHAPTER TWENTY-SEVEN

UNVEILING THE URBAN CASTLE

<u>Rogue Rider Mansion, Beverly Hills, California, United States</u>

When Gen stepped into the actual house, it was complete luxury overload. If Lunis was telling the truth about designing the Rogue Rider Mansion, then he'd gone to the extreme and had an unlimited budget.

Every surface in the shiny place seemed to scream, "I'm richer than you," in a way that would make a king blush. In the entryway, dual staircases twirled upwards like ribbons in a dance, aspiring to reach a ceiling lost in the clouds—or at least, trying hard to.

The chandelier above was the essence of gaudy as it dangled, scattering light with wild abandon. "Subtlety" had clearly been banished from this kingdom, probably exiled to a land far, far away. Modern marvels masqueraded as furniture, pieces so sleek and pristine, they had to be made from unearthly materials.

Walls hosted displays larger than Gen's old village's meeting square, flickering with images of places and people she couldn't begin to comprehend. She'd heard of televisions during her first few educational lessons into this world, but didn't know they told full-color stories of places in such bizarre and vivid ways.

The air hummed with the whispers of a hundred gadgets, each boasting of an efficiency Gen found both admirable and slightly terrifying. Everything here was a testament to excess, a museum dedicated to the art of showing off. Entering this mansion was like stepping into a future where magic was made of circuits and success was measured in square footage.

"I know the Rogue Riders seem a bit tough, but you'll warm to them," Sophia consoled after giving Gen a moment to take in the strangeness of the place they'd entered. "They really are a fun and honorable group for the most part."

Gen glanced out the huge doors that led to the front steps and grand driveway of the mansion. Through the stained-glass windows, she could see Emperor and Lunis lounging on the grounds, resting before a hunt.

"I think it's me that I'm worried about them warming to," Gen offered. "I'm not like them… I'm not like anyone here. And Emperor is about as warm as a blizzard."

"Emperor is setting the tone for a lifetime of leadership," Sophia stated. "He was right to do what he did. Jack is a great guy, but you and he can't be disrespected from the start. You may be new to this world and it might take you time to learn our ways. I don't think you should jump into any role too quickly, but I also think that you demand a reverence that others don't deserve on their first day. Emperor bent Jack's knee, as he should have."

Gen nodded. "So mind control. That's a bit of a head trip."

Sophia laughed. "Oh, wow… That was a pun to impress Lunis. And yes, I didn't see that coming, but talk about a skill. It will be tricky to manage."

"I think that will be my job, according to what Emperor told me," Gen stated.

"And you were pretty quick to set the tone," Sophia said proudly. "Pulling out Bellumferrum and showing that you couldn't be bullied was brilliant. If I didn't know for a fact that you were a Beaufont, I would have guessed it right then."

Gen grinned, feeling giddy still after that moment when she held what she inherently knew was a plasma whip, although she didn't seconds before it materialized. The things that were possible with Bellumferrum were incredible. However, much like Emperor's powers, the Weapon of War could get out of control very quickly. Too much power wasn't a blessing. It was a privilege and came with great responsibility and restraint.

"So this is where I'm going to live, then?" Gen asked, looking around at the marble columns that towered over her, holding up an elaborate ceiling.

"Yes, but I'm sure that Amanda can make your space to your liking," Sophia offered.

"Oh, is she like the Quiet of the Rogue Rider mansion?" Gen asked, studying the artwork on the walls, which was drastically different from the old-world paintings in the Castle. The images of stern and tough riders and their dragons were so surreal, they looked like the painters had used magical paint.

"She's like him, but totally different," Sophia stated. "And here she is now."

CHAPTER TWENTY-EIGHT

FROM FORKS TO PHONES

<u>Rogue Rider Mansion, Beverly Hills, California, United States</u>

A woman who reeked of strange magic but also, seemed quite normal, strode from a bright archway off to the right. The magician had shoulder-length brown hair and wore glasses and unlike the tough riders Gen had just met, she was smiling. Amanda wore yoga pants, a workout top and sneakers and looked ready to take a run. Gen only knew about these outfit details because of the quick lessons that she'd gotten from Jeremy Bearimy and Juergen when they were explaining to her options for her own clothes.

The woman was holding one of those mobile phones that everyone was obsessed with in this time period. Apparently, they did everything for them and no one could live without them. Gen expected she'd see a lot more people with them at the Rogue Rider Mansion than even at the Gullington.

Smiling, chewing gum, Amanda glanced at her phone. "Give me a five-letter word."

"What?" Gen asked, looking at Sophia for clarification.

Sophia grinned, encouraging Gen to comply. "Go on then. You know words. You can't pull the medieval card with that one."

Amanda nodded, an intrigued look in her eyes. "I overheard about that from Dwayne when he was talking on the phone to someone at the House of Fourteen. He is all sorts of flustered. It's simply amazing!" She combed a hand through the air at Gen. "I'm going to love watching the drama you'll bring to this place."

"Thanks," Gen said, drawing out the word, thinking that this woman was like the modern version of Ainsley at the Gullington—that was maybe a good thing…or really bad…

"By overheard, you mean…" Sophia trailed away, giving Amanda a pointed look.

"I was eavesdropping," Amanda replied matter-of-factly. "That man never tells me a damn thing and I'm the house manager of this place. Oh, and that reminds me I totally forgot introductions." She extended her hand, her fingernails covered in bright paint and little designs. Gen got the impression they weren't her real nails, but she didn't know how that could be the case or why someone would do such a thing, inhibiting their movement with long, fake nails. Still, Gen shook her hand.

"I'm Amanda, House Manager Extraordinaire for the Rogue Riders. I take care of…well, just about everything. This place would fall to ruin without me. I do the cleaning, the cooking, the room design, the purchasing and I work to try to make the lives of all the riders and their dragons as easy as possible. Well, besides Dwayne's. I work to make his as impossible as possible."

"Oh, because he's the boss?" Gen asked, confused by this woman's brazen nature and then also intrigued.

Amanda shook her head. "Oh, no. I loved Sophia when she was our boss. I catered to her every whim. But Dwayne is on a real power trip, so it is my mission to humble him." She winked at Sophia. "I replaced his toothpaste with hemorrhoid cream. He's about to be able to whistle really well."

Sophia giggled. "I'm not sure that was a good idea. I'm certain that Dwayne is just on edge because he was thrust into the leadership role without warning."

"He was thrust into the leadership role without merit," Amanda argued. "Whatever were the Founders of the House of Fourteen thinking when they made that appointment and fired you, Sophia? I just don't get it."

Gen stiffened at the mention of the Founders, knowing that involved her father and sister watching from the Land of Chimera. They were electing the leaders of the various organizations and had recently gotten rid of Sophia and put this Dwayne Stone in charge of the Rogue Riders. It had to be for a good reason, and Sophia seemed to support the decision, saying as an angel dragonrider, she shouldn't be leading the Rogue Riders.

"Anyway," Amanda sang, glancing back at her phone which was covered in a pink and blue unicorn on the back and appeared to have jewelry hanging from the corner. "I still need a five-letter word."

"Okay, how about 'rogue,'" Gen offered.

"Rogue," Amanda said, typing on her phone. "Not bad. The 'e' is in the right place and we know we have an 'r'."

Sophia glanced at Gen. "She's playing Wordle. It's a word game on the phone. I'll teach it to you later."

"I don't have a phone," Gen stated.

"Do you want one?" Sophia questioned.

Gen looked around at the strange, modern mansion and shook her head. "Let me get used to this thing you call electricity and plumbing first."

"Which brings me to your room," Amanda said, putting her phone away. "I do all the design and I'm sure you'll have specific needs. I simply adore that everything is brand new to you. I can't wait to introduce you to Real Housewives. You're going to hate it!"

"Great…" Gen glanced at Sophia, again for help, but she was enjoying this way too much, stifling a laugh.

"So your room," Amanda went on. "Tell me what aesthetic you

want. Cottagecore, boho, emo core, grunge, wabi-sabi or maybe fairycore?"

Gen's eyes widened. She looked at Sophia and then pointed at Amanda. "Is she still speaking English? Is my communication device suddenly broken? I don't know what she's saying…"

Sophia's eyes sparkled with amusement. "Yeah, she's speaking modern-day English but even your device can't decode those words because they are ridiculous."

"Oh, so you have a thingy that decodes what we say, huh?" Amanda asked. "That's so cool."

Sophia nodded. "Yes, and it translates what Gen is saying or otherwise, well, I'm afraid we wouldn't understand her."

"Yeah, it would be all like, 'I desire my chamber to be worthy of a queen and fetch me tea before I goeth to my dragon,'" Amanda said in a sudden refined voice.

Gen laughed at this. "I'm certain that you wouldn't understand me or me you, without the communication device."

"Amanda was asking you how you want your room designed," Sophia explained.

"Oh," Gen said, a bit stumped, looking around at the bright, shiny marble. "I don't know. Maybe something warmer and rustic. Something that reminds me of being outside and has a rugged beauty, rather than makes me feel like I'm living inside a stone."

The house manager grinned at Sophia. "I love her so much, already. She's going to shake things up." She returned her gaze to Gen. "And how about food? Do you have any food allergies?"

Gen pursed her lips, wondering what this could possibly refer to in his context. "I don't think so, but I know how to eat with a fork."

Amanda laughed loudly, the sound carrying in the large space. "You're already ten steps ahead of most of the Rogue Riders. I swear, if I can get them to wash their hands before meals, it's a miracle."

"Told you," Sophia said, winking at Gen.

"You're going to like it here," Amanda said, pulling out her phone again. "I'll see to it. Come back around and find me later and I'll take you to your room. Oh, and I can't wait to meet your dragon—Emperor. When Dwayne found out about that, the gross vein on his forehead popped out. It was simply marvelous."

"So he knows everything, then?" Sophia asked. "Hiker gave him the full rundown?"

Amanda nodded, pointing to a far hallway. "And he asked me to send Gen to him as soon as she arrived."

"Why didn't you tell us?" Sophia said, urgently taking Gen by the arm and leading her toward the long hallway behind the stairway to the right.

"Because he asked me to," Amanda said. "Oh, and Sophia…"

She paused, halting Gen too. "Dwayne wants to see Gen alone. He said, and I quote, 'Tell Mrs. Goody-Goody Beaufont that she's not invited to the meeting.'"

A worried expression crossed Sophia's face, but Gen could tell she worked quickly to cover it, nodding and pointing to a door ahead. "Fine, he's through there. And you'll be fine. I'm sure you'll be okay…"

"Why wouldn't I be?" Gen asked, sensing the tension in Sophia's reply.

"Because he's going to try and bully you," Amanda answered.

"And my advice," Sophia said in a low voice suddenly, "is let him. Just lay low and don't cause problems."

"But that's not what Emperor told me to do out there." Gen pointed to the door where the dragons were.

Sophia nodded, understandingly. "That was with other, fellow riders. This is different. Dwayne is your leader. Don't start off on the wrong foot with him. I promise you, it's for the best. You're in a better position to see things if you don't put a target on your back on day one with that man."

CHAPTER TWENTY-NINE

POWER PLAY

<u>Dwayne Stone's Office, Rogue Rider Mansion, Beverly Hills, California, United States</u>

A low, brutish voice replied, telling Gen to enter when she knocked on the door. Gen stepped into the office, a chamber that seemed to swallow light whole, much like the rumors suggested Dwayne swallowed those who crossed him. The air was thick, laced with a scent of ink and something metallic, not entirely unpleasant but certainly unnerving.

Shelves lined the walls, crammed with objects that made Gen's skin prickle. There were skulls that might have been more at home on a battlefield than a bookshelf. Alongside them were strange, angular artifacts that caught the dim light, twisting it into shadows that danced too lively for comfort.

Dwayne sat behind a desk that could have served as a barricade, its surface a clutter of parchments and odd, gleaming devices. His hulking appearance was striking. The man was bald as a polished shield and his skin was adorned with inked patterns that could have told stories of battles or dark oaths. He was dressed not in armor, but in attire that hugged his frame, emphasizing the strength within, much like the chieftains of old might have worn their status for all to see.

For a long moment, he studied Gen as she took the spot in front of his desk, rigid and standing tall. His narrowed gaze on her, she knew, was meant to disarm her. To make her squirm. He was begging her to talk, but she knew how to play this power game and would not be unnerved into speaking first.

Sophia was correct about not putting a target on our back with Dwayne Stone, Emperor said in Gen's head.

But you said—

I said to exert power with the others, Emperor cut in, interrupting Gen. *You have to be strategic in all situations and that means you play different people differently. Not all are created equally. Each person is in a unique position. For Dwayne, you are to simply observe for now.*

Very well, Gen said as Dwayne leaned forward, making the first move—the first sound.

"You're not that impressive," were the first words the leader of the Rogue Riders spoke.

Gen pinned her hands behind her back and kept her face neutral. "So I'm not."

"I've heard a lot about you from Hiker Wallace," Dwayne went on, seeming not to hear her reply. "He might think highly of you, saying that Mother Nature seems to have big plans for you, but I don't share the same fan favor as the Dragon Elite."

"Understandable," Gen said simply, unaffected by this subtle act of intimidation.

A vein throbbed on his forehead, a silent testament to the simmering temper beneath his calm exterior. The office, with its dim corners and the low, heavy air, felt like a cave of secrets, each shadow a whisper of things best left undiscovered. Dwayne's presence, commanding yet contained, hinted at depths and dangers that went far beyond mere bullying or leadership. Gen sensed that he was a man who knew power and how to wield it, his every possession a piece of a larger, darker puzzle.

"You must think that because you magnetized to the first dragon egg to ever spawn that you're a big deal," Dwayne seethed.

"I don't," Gen replied evenly.

Dwayne sneered, looking disgusted by her clipped response. "You undoubtedly believe that you're something special because your dragon is the ruler of all dragons."

"I do not," Gen said, through a measured breath, trying to keep her cool, but wanting to launch herself at the man. That's what he wanted though and she wouldn't give into him. Emperor and Sophia were right to advise her not to force her dominance on him. That's what he wanted… He was trying to rile her up.

"I bet you think that you're deserving of more privileges and a higher position because you were a Founder of the House of Fourteen," Dwayne said through clenched, crooked teeth, seeming to make himself angrier.

"Not at all," Gen said at once.

"Are you mocking me?" Dwayne yelled, the vein on his forehead seeming to pulse. "Do you think that your clipped answers are funny?"

"No," she said, and almost laughed at the way she just antagonized him.

When he stood, she realized how massive he was, towering over her. "You are and will remain at the bottom of the totem pole here. You are nobody and have come into this world with nothing but a dragon's egg. I will not have you thinking that you deserve more because of your name or your dragon's rule."

"Of course." As Gen's gaze swept the room, from the menacing glint of artifacts to the man who seemed as much a relic of a brutal past as the items he surrounded himself with, she realized this office was not just a workspace. It was a fortress, a hoard of secrets guarded by a dragon in human form, his tattoos the scales that armored him against the world. And like any dragon's lair, it promised both treasure and peril, hidden among the shadows that crept too freely in the presence of the light.

"From now on, you will train and only when I deem, will you be given a mission," he said, moving his jaw back and forth. "Is that a problem for you?"

Dwayne was testing her. Trying to get Gen to argue with him. She restrained herself and managed a nod.

"And you will not try to exert your rule and only speak to me when spoken to," he stated. "How does that sound?"

"Fine," she said, sucking in a breath, feeling like she was dying inside by allowing all this.

"You will bow to my will as your leader and not create trouble, do I make myself clear?"

Gen thought she might be sick for a moment but she pushed it down and nodded. "Yes."

"Do I make myself clear?" Dwayne asked again, like he hadn't heard her reply.

"Yes," Gen repeated.

He squared off to her, looking her dead in the eyes. "Do I make myself clear?"

Sir, Emperor said clearly in her head. *Yes, sir.*

Gen gulped. Nodded. Pulled in a breath. "Yes, sir."

"Good, now get out of my sight and get ready for the meeting."

"Meeting?" Gen questioned, not sure what he meant.

"The council at the House of Fourteen," he replied, making his way to his desk. "They want to meet this fandangle dragonrider from the 15th century. They want to talk to this supposed Founder. But remember, that you work for me. Remember your place."

Gen simply nodded and then made her way out the door, away from the man whose nose she couldn't wait to break.

CHAPTER THIRTY

THE FOUNDER'S BURDEN

<u>Chamber of the Tree, House of Fourteen, Santa Monica, California, United States</u>

It was like stepping through a door to her past as Gen entered the place she'd created with her father all those years ago. But it had changed so much over the centuries that there were only hints of the original Chamber of the Tree—which was created for meetings of the House of Fourteen. Gen had been there on a few occasions in present times, but not like this, during council proceedings. She felt the beating of adrenaline and anticipation as she entered the place known for creating justice, but also full of so much drama and argument.

At her back, she felt Dwayne ushering her forward, like he didn't want to allow her out of his sight, as if she'd misbehave. She wanted to tell him off. To teach him a lesson. But she knew at her foundation that Sophia and Emperor were correct. She had to suck it up and allow him to think he had the advantage—for now…

The Chamber of the Tree was absolutely as Gen remembered and also completely different. The high bench where the council sat was at the back of the round, domed room with the illuminated tree on the wall at their backs. There the names of the seven families presently composing the warriors and councilors could be seen. Added to this were also the names of the Mortal Seven, an addition to the House of Fourteen to create balance among the non-magical and magical races.

The rounded ceiling of the chamber twinkled with lights that represented the life of every magician out in the world. That was magic that Gen and the Founders had built into the Chamber of the Tree when they created it. Back in the 15th century, there were a fraction of the twinkling lights that she now saw dazzling overhead.

Another part of the Chamber of the Tree that hadn't changed were the regulators. The Founders wanted this place to be only for truths and therefore they imbued powerful magic into two creatures—Diabolos and Jude. The black crow and the giant white tiger represented lies and honesty.

They could spot someone lying and signaled it, so that these proceedings were never riddled with deceit. There were, of course, many loopholes for getting around their lie detection, but they were very good, having personally been programmed by Gen. She had always been excellent at telling when someone was lying. Diabolos and Jude had stood all these centuries by the bench, operating as lie detectors. And currently, they were untouched by time and continuing to serve in the role they'd been given from the very beginning.

Standing in front of the bench and dressed for adventure were a few warriors. To Gen's surprise, when she strode forward, all of the warriors turned to her and bowed low. It was the greeting that Emperor had received upon hatching. It was the welcoming that the ruler over dragons had gotten when he met the Rogue Riders' dragons. And now, for once, Gen was being acknowledged in the same way.

She halted. Tensed. And looked to the side where Dwayne

stood beside her— appearing angrier than hell by the display of respect.

Nervously, Gen looked up at the council, grateful to see a familiar face. Staring down at her was Clark Beaufont, a slight, proud smile on his face. Beside him, his fellow councilors were wearing guarded expressions, like they weren't sure about this new Beaufont with a strange story and assorted background.

"The warriors for the House of Fourteen are paying their respect to the first of them," Clark said, breaking the silence in the chamber, having sensed Gen's confusion about the display around her.

All of the armored clad warriors rose, looking straight at Gen with fierce expressions. She was grateful to see Liv, one of her closest friends and one of the people she'd followed into the twenty-first century. Gen also recognized Liv's husband, Stefan Ludwig who was a warrior as well and a demon hunter specialist. Rose was often in attendance at these meetings as a Mortal Seven, but only Warriors appeared to be there now for this special session.

"Approach the bench, Miss Genevieve Beaufont," a man with a shaved head and scruffy beard said from the council area. Sophia had given Gen a quick rundown of the names and descriptions of each of the councilors and therefore she knew this was the rude and often cynical Freek Kolman.

Like she hadn't heard the order, Dwayne ushered her forward, a pinching grip on her arm. Gen jerked her head over her shoulder, her every instinct screaming for her to backhand the man. However, she restrained herself, knowing that she couldn't allow her anger to get to her.

"We understand from reports from Councilor Beaufont and Hiker Wallace that you came through a time gate opened by Warrior Beaufont," Freek said, looking down at her when she paused in front of the bench.

"You look like a Beaufont," a woman with mousey gray hair

and a warm smile said—Hester DeVries, who was apparently a healer and had been on the council for a very long time.

"It's simply astounding to be in the presence of a Founder," the woman beside Hester said, her black hair pulled back to reveal a beautiful face. She was Raina Ludwig and sister to Liv's husband, Stefan.

"It's unsettling, is what it is," a man with long curly black hair with an air of authority said, narrowing his eyes at Gen—Armando Rosario. "When the council was made aware of this mistake by Warrior Beaufont we were very disconcerted."

"I didn't make a mistake," Liv dared to cut in. "Gen was always meant to come to this timeline. Papa Creola has confirmed that. She was meant to be a dragonrider—a Rogue Rider."

"That's yet to be determined," Dwayne Stone said at Gen's back.

All eyes swiveled to the man who was undoubtedly wearing a sour expression.

A woman with light orangey-red hair shot Dwayne a look of surprise. Her name would be Seraphine Galopin, the sister to the man who last owned Bellumferrum—Porthos. "You haven't accepted Gen Beaufont into your ranks?"

"No, I haven't!" Dwayne's voice boomed.

"And why is that?" a man with a long black beard asked. This was Haro Takahashi, the only member from the original founding families besides the Beaufonts in the House of Fourteen. He was from an ancient magical family which had the vision and fortitude to create the organization still going strong in the modern world. "She is a Founder for the House of Fourteen. To have her in the Rogue Riders is beyond an honor."

"She was supposedly a part of the beginning of the House of Fourteen," Dwayne began in a low tone. "We have no way of telling how much she actually did. But we do know that when she disappeared, her sister, Elizabeth, took her place. That woman, in my opinion, is the first warrior. She is one of the Founders looking down on us now, making appointments. She and William Beaufont and the other Founders are the ones who put me into my role and you all in yours—not this woman here."

"How can you be so obtuse?" Liv dared to ask, striding forward and turning around in front of the bench, staring back at Dwayne Stone. "She is not this 'supposed' Founder. Rose and I found her in 1426, right after the House of Fourteen started. She was a Founder. Gen is one."

"Warrior Beaufont, we will handle this," Hester said, a diplomatic tone to her voice, like she was used to corralling Liv's anger.

"Dwayne, we understand that you are new to your role as leader of the Rogue Riders," Raina began in an even tone. "But I've been a councilor for a very long time and know the history of the House of Fourteen very well. To have someone like Gen here in the present time is a gift. She built the very foundation of this organization that still exists and rules to this day."

Dwayne laughed coldly. "With all due respect—"

"Which is something people say right before showing disrespect," Liv cut in, still standing in front of the bench.

"With all due respect," Dwayne repeated through clenched teeth. "If I put a single nail into a board, are you going to give me credit for building an entire house? I simply think that the reputation of this time traveler has been blown out of proportion. From what I've learned, she trespassed into the present, stole a dragon's egg in the past and has now demanded to be given honors she doesn't deserve."

Gen's eyes flickered to Liv and then Clark's. They seemed to read the tension well in her gaze, both offering her sympathetic expressions.

"I think your wariness of Genevieve Beaufont is to be commended," Freek said evenly. "We shouldn't judge someone simply based on their name or a supposed history that we can't confirm."

Armando nodded, glaring down at Gen. "I agree with that sentiment. And this is not to say that you're not worthy of our respect. It is only that you are untested and will have to prove your honor and deservability of privileges that all others earn through reputation."

"I haven't asked for anything," Gen dared to finally speak. "I arrived here, losing my home and everything I've ever known. I've had to acclimate to a time and place very different from everything I have ever known." Gen pointed up to the ceiling, indicating the heavens. "Do you all think that I wouldn't rather be up there, in the Land of Chimera, judging and ruling over you than down here being treated like a common criminal?"

Clark leaned forward, offering Gen a thoughtful expression. "I know that this hasn't been easy for you. But we all know that you belong here. And although it's disconcerting for some to digest, having someone of your status among us, I think in time, we will see that your presence will make history in ways your absence would have never." His gaze shot to Dwayne Stone—an accusation in his blue eyes.

"Well put," Haro said, nodding. "Welcome to this world, Gen. There is much we hope to see from you. I expect that you and your dragon will train and go on to help the Rogue Riders. We look forward to watching your progress."

"Gen is not ready to do anything for the Rogue Riders," Dwayne cut in. "She is new to this world, inexperienced and untested. I would be a fool to put her out into the field this century."

Tensing, Gen held her breath. It took everything she had not to explode right then. Thankfully, based on the expression Liv was giving her, the modern warrior was also working hard to restrain herself. Maybe the pair could hunt down Dwayne in a dark alley and teach him a lesson later.

Seraphine cleared her throat, a pursed expression on her face. "Actually, that brings us to our next order of business, Dwayne. The Rogue Riders are failing at managing the criminal world. Under your leadership, things have only gotten worse, starting with the death of the Commissioner of Los Angeles." She leaned forward. "Do you wish to explain that?"

CHAPTER THIRTY-ONE

UNVEILING DECEPTION

<u>**Chamber of the Tree, House of Fourteen, Santa Monica, California, United States**</u>

Gen was grateful that Dwayne was at her back, or otherwise he'd see the victorious smile that sprang to her face. Now it was her turn to watch him be roasted and hopefully she'd learn some covert information. She'd heard about this Commissioner's death from Sophia. It was a big concern for Hiker because he thought that it hinted at a huge problem and upset the arrangement that the Rogue Riders had established with Los Angeles. But Sophia had said it wasn't her jurisdiction anymore. It was all on Dwayne Stone and hopefully he was about to get ripped a new one for it.

"Although Commissioner Peter Stevenson's death was unfortunate," Dwayne began in an almost amused voice. "I see this as an opportunity to take back control over the City of Los Angeles."

"You think that the death of a civil servant who has devoted his life to the City of Los Angeles is an opportunity?" Clark questioned, disgust seeping into his tone.

"I think that under the previous leadership of the Rogue Riders, the old alliances have grown stale," Dwayne replied tersely. "We all know that Los Angeles is a pivotal city in creating the balance with the criminal world. If we maintain control there and with other major cities, then we hold the power."

"Yes, we are all aware that New York and Los Angeles are the major hubs of control for power in North America," Haro stated matter-of-factly. "And our concern is that the City of Los Angeles is now in flux. Someone has murdered the highest ranking law enforcement official and that's concerning in a city already out of control."

"Well, I should point out that crime was out of control before I took my role," Dwayne stated. "I believe this murder of the Los Angeles Commissioner is a result of things not being managed by Sophia Beaufont."

Liv, who was still standing at the front, staring straight at Dwayne, growled. "Sophia had a long-standing partnership with the Commissioner that kept crime at bay. Her problem was that she couldn't manage two full-time roles and didn't belong in the Rogue Riders."

"Her list of problems were long and varied, I'm learning," Dwayne said.

"Have you determined who murdered the Commissioner?" Seraphine asked.

"I can't say," Dwayne answered.

Just then, Gen caught Jude's right eye twitch. It was so slight, but she knew at once what it meant.

"He's lying!" Gen blurted out.

"Excuse me!" Dwayne boomed, marching forward and looking down at Gen with menace. "How dare you accuse me of lying?"

She pointed to the white tiger. "Because of him, I know that you do know who murdered the Commissioner because Jude's gesture has indicated that you are withholding."

Dwayne laughed darkly, his crooked teeth flashing white in

the darkness of the chamber. "I've never heard anything so foolish."

"Can you better explain yourself, Gen?" Clark asked, blinking down at her from the high bench.

Gen spun to face the council. "Dwayne said that he can't say, but the regulator's movement has clearly indicated that he is using language techniques to cover the truth. Maybe it is that he knows but is trying to act as if he doesn't. I don't know for sure, but I can tell you that Dwayne saying he can't say who murdered the Commissioner is a form of deceit."

The leader of the Rogue Riders threw his hands up in the air with a loud protest. "Because a tiger did what? I didn't see anything."

"His right eyebrow raised, which indicates that someone is avoiding telling the truth," Gen explained.

"Is that true?" Hester asked, curiously, looking down the bench at her colleagues.

Clark tapped his fingers on his chin, thinking. "I seem to remember a rumor of this information but it has since been lost. I think that could be the micro expressions that can give detailed information on the regulators. Diabolos and Jude obviously tell us when someone is lying and to which degree, but I remember there being something about more subtleties to forms of deceit."

"It is true," Gen urged. "I know it for a fact. A raised eyebrow by Jude means that someone is withholding information by using clever phrasing."

Dwayne scoffed. "How can you possibly know what the mannerism of a tiger means?"

Gen looked up at him, defiance in her eyes. "Because my father and I programmed Jude and Diabolos as lie detectors. We imbued them with the magic that has kept them alive for centuries and made them the regulators of the House of Fourteen from the beginning."

This produced many sounds of surprise from around the

Chamber of the Tree. Murmuring broke out. This was followed by clapping by Liv, still standing at the front of the bench, like holding court.

"Yep, that's my girl!" Liv sang, looking around at the other warriors. "She's my relative!"

"Quiet down, Warrior Beaufont," Freek commanded, shaking his head. "This is very speculative information. All we have is Gen's word that a small gesture from Jude means something that calls Dwayne's character into question. I caution the council on making serious judgements about this."

Armando nodded. "Well, then, maybe we can get to the bottom of this. Dwayne, do you in fact know who murdered the Commissioner of Los Angeles?"

"Yes," the Rogue Rider replied at once. "But as I said before, I can't say."

Again, Jude's eyebrow raised. This time, everyone saw it. Many more gasps filled the chamber.

"I can't say, because it was an inside job," Dwayne said in a rush. "Disclosing that information at this stage would be dangerous."

"Dangerous for whom?" Raina asked.

"For me as the leader of the Rogue Riders," Dwayne replied, not eliciting a reaction from either of the regulators. "I'm playing a very strategic game as I lay down my rule in my new position."

He was telling the truth, but Gen knew that it was about how people disclosed things that mattered. That's why her father and she had worked to try to hone in on linguistics when programming Diabolos and Jude. However, covering all the basics was difficult since there were many loopholes.

"I need more time to put my plans as leader into action," Dwayne continued, again not lying. "I'm using this opportunity to sift through the ranks and get rid of the waste. We've put a new Commissioner into place and I'm hoping that this will help for me to be more successful as the leader of the Rogue Riders going forward."

Gen was infuriated not to see a reaction from either the black crow or the white tiger. Dwayne was telling the truth, but she knew at her core that he was choosing his words carefully. Instinctively, she knew he was up to something, but what, she had no clue.

"Yes, this new Commissioner has been making many personnel changes throughout the city already," Seraphine observed. "Do you think it wise that Los Angeles undergo such drastic changes, especially with a murderer on the loose taking down head officials?"

"I've got things covered, as is my job," Dwayne stated with conviction. He then turned and gave Gen a murderous look. "And I won't have anyone disrupting that or putting my authority into question."

CHAPTER THIRTY-TWO

MOCKERY AND MASTERY

"That dude really doesn't like you," Clipper said, leaning back and lounging on Glacier.

The rider and dragon were parked on the grass, under the setting sun, having stated they wanted a front-row seat for Gen and Emperor's first training session with riding. Really, Gen believed that Clipper wanted to see her fall off her dragon or be dragged behind him and then secretly laugh.

Gen really hoped that Clipper didn't have one of those devices that recorded information like pictures and events. She'd seen Liv and Sophia using them and they were a strange bit of magic. Those phone things everyone carried really could do just about everything—it was almost too much and the advances made Gen nervous.

"Does Dwayne really like anyone?" Jack questioned, fitting a saddle onto Emperor's back, having offered to help with outfitting the pair.

"He loves me," Sully boasted, handing Gen a thick pair of riding gloves. "He said I was his second in command."

"He said you were the assistant to the leader of the Rogue Riders," Clipper argued, not having offered to help with this first lesson. "Which if you ask me, isn't a title at all."

"Well, no one asked you, did they?" Sully spat back.

In the shadow of the sprawling Rogue Rider mansion in Beverly Hills, Gen faced her next grand challenge beneath the growing twilight. Emperor, her massive, iridescent purple dragon, stood with an air of ancient wisdom and indomitable power, his scales glittering like amethysts under the setting sun. His eyes, deep pools of psychic energy, regarded Gen with a mix of curiosity and impatience.

"Are you sure you're ready to do this?" Jack asked her, standing back after checking the saddle.

"I grew up riding horses," she stated with confidence. "And they are really dumb. I think riding a cooperative and all-knowing dragon should be easy in comparison."

"But that's where you're wrong," Jack countered, looking Emperor in the eyes. "Because they are intelligent, dragons won't just allow anyone to ride them, not even their chosen rider—not if they aren't ready or their approach is not right."

He's correct, Emperor said in Gen's head.

She cut her eyes to her dragon. *Well, are you going to allow me to ride you?*

We'll see, he replied slyly.

"Not to mention that it's about like mounting a hippo," Sully imparted. "It's not as easy as you'd think."

Clipper laughed. "How would you know what it's like to ride a hippo?"

"There was this one time I had to chase these thieves through the zoo," Sully explained, proudly. "Hippos are the most aggressive animals. You know more deaths happen from hippos each year than from shark attacks worldwide. Those massive creatures are dangerously aggressive."

"And so you rode one?" Jack asked with a laugh.

"Well, it was that or be trampled by the fatty," Sully stated. "I found myself in her enclosure and she was about to bowl me over. So I timed it perfectly and jumped into the air, landing on its back. Then I rode that girl straight into the perpetrators."

Jack and Clipper laughed, both shaking their heads as if they didn't believe the story. Gen, however, knew that he was telling the truth. Even without Jude or Diabolos around, she knew when people were lying or not. However, her focus was elsewhere as her tension rose for what she had to do next.

The first task was simple in theory, yet daunting in practice. It was to mount Emperor. As Gen advanced, the dragon's telepathic voice echoed in her mind, offering cryptic guidance that felt more like riddles.

Approach this with the care and ease you would have holding someone's hand, Emperor said in her head. *You are not exerting your control onto them, but rather enfolding your fingers equally through theirs.*

I've never held anyone's hand, Gen admitted at once. *My father held Elizabeth's hand usually, while he chased after me.*

Try and imagine, then, he offered.

Fine, she said, sidling up next to him, just then realizing how tall he was. The idea of hoisting herself onto his back seemed akin to scaling a massive, living fortress. Still, she covered her intimidation and tried to find her footing. However, the problem became immediately apparent on her first try.

Just as a knight in heavy armor might struggle to climb the slick, stone walls of a castle under siege, Gen found herself grappling with the smooth, unyielding scales of Emperor's flank. Each handhold was as precarious as a rain-slicked rampart, and every movement required the strength and determination of a seasoned warrior storming a formidable keep.

Her attempts were clumsy, her feet slipping on the sleek scales, her hands grasping at the air. Laughter trickled from behind her as the fellow riders watched—amused by these attempts.

The wind also seemed to mock her as it tangled in her hair, pushing her sideways, making her task all the more Sisyphean. But with a determined squint, Gen found a ridge on Emperor's foreleg to hoist herself up, only to slide down his side in a less-than-graceful dismount. Her pride bruised, but resolve unbroken, she finally managed to cling to his back, and ungracefully kick herself up and onto the saddle, finding a steady place on his back.

Sitting up, sweat dripping into her eyes from the efforts, Gen grabbed for the reins in front of her. She didn't want to look at Clipper rolling around and laughing on the ground or Sully who was standing close by probably recording the whole thing. Out of the corner of her eye, she caught Jack, but didn't look at him directly.

"Well, if you found that easy, then the next part will be slightly more challenging," Jack explained, an amused tone to his voice. "It's about like riding a horse, but you tell him to go with your mind and you control him with your intention."

"What are the reins for?" Gen asked.

"For holding on like hell," Sully said with a laugh.

"Right," Gen said. "So I make Emperor go with my mind…"

"Riding a dragon is about forming a connection," Jack offered. "That's part of the bond, which takes time."

"So duck and roll when you fall off," Clipper teased, doubling over on the ground with more laughter.

Gen did look over at the rider now, narrowing her eyes at her. "I'm not falling off."

"Everyone falls off on their first ride," she argued. "It's called a rite of passage. You aren't a rider unless you skin your knee on your first ride." She pointed at Sully. "Or your face, in his case."

"Blaze threw me out of spite," Sully muttered, shaking his head.

Are you going to throw me? Gen asked her dragon.

Do you want me to?

Just don't kill me, Gen replied. *I'll figure this out.*

Emperor, much like a horse, but also much stronger and majestic, took off at a sprint. The thundering of his legs under Gen was a surprising display of grace, soundlessly running across the plains.

Holding on and bearing down low, Gen held her breath. When the dragon's wings unfolded and started to beat, she released the tension in her chest, feeling a freedom start to blossom in her belly unlike she'd ever felt before.

When the pair launched into the air, Gen knew that this was the best moment of her entire life. They took off and into the sky immediately, rising higher. Everything that happened next was all instinct and a seamless communication between rider and dragon.

The flight was an exhilarating terror. Emperor had launched into the sky with a powerful leap, wind lashing at Gen as if trying to pluck her from her mount. She clung to him, her fingers threading through the reins, as they ascended above the mansion, Beverly Hills shrinking beneath them.

Emperor's mind control steadied her nerves, syncing their actions until they moved as one. Yet, every gust felt like a gale, every turn a battle against the forces of nature. Her muscles screamed in protest, her grip faltering, but she held on, mastering the rhythm of flight through sheer will.

Using her intentions, not her words, Gen urged Emperor to land. However, she really didn't want to since being in the air felt more natural than walking on two feet. To her surprise, the landing was quite hard and Gen wasn't holding on tight enough. The jolt threw her to the side, and she ducked just in time to clear her head as she rolled onto the ground, landing hard on her back.

"I told you!" Clipper exclaimed. "We always fall off!"

"Got it," Gen coughed, spitting out a mouthful of dirt as she rolled up and got to her feet.

"That was impressively smooth for your first time," Sully said, sounding proud. "You even made that fall look pretty good."

Gen brushed herself off. "I tried to fall with grace."

"Okay, we'll try that again a few times and then the final tasks if you're ready," Jack said, motioning for Emperor to come around beside Gen again.

They flew together several more times before Jack deemed that they could progress to the next tasks. The final trial was the running start. Emperor came around, standing beside Gen. The wind kicked up fiercely, as if challenging her to defy it once more. She positioned herself, watching Emperor start off at a trot. He moved ahead, then turned back to face her, his psychic push urging her to run.

She sprinted, heart racing, the ground blurring beneath her feet. As she neared Emperor, he surged forward. Gen leapt, aiming for his back. Too late, she realized her miscalculation. The world spun, the ground rushed up to meet her, and pain exploded in her shoulder as she hit the turf hard. Again, she ate dirt…

Whispers of doubt crept in. Laughter from the onlookers grew louder. The wind howled in derision. Yet, within the privacy of her mind, Emperor's voice offered calm and focus.

Get up, he said in her head. ***We try again.***

Nursing her injury, she rose, determination igniting her gaze. This time, when she ran, it was with a limping gait, but an unbreakable spirit. Emperor matched her pace, his own massive form a beacon of strength. At the perfect moment, he lowered, and with a Herculean effort, Gen launched herself onto him, her grip ironclad.

She swung her leg around as he launched into the air. While the wind rushed by, Gen secured herself into the saddle, hunching down low and holding onto her dragon with a new fierceness. She felt the movement of his wings as they took off, a surge of triumph as they ascended, leaving the jeers and the estate far below.

This time, the wind was an ally, lifting them higher, and Gen, despite her throbbing shoulder, laughed into the rush of air. She and Emperor, united in defiance and strength, soared over Beverly Hills, a testament to the power of perseverance and the unbreakable bond between rider and dragon.

When they landed, Gen was surprised to find Dwayne standing next to Clipper and her dragon, watching. She knew by the look on his face that he wasn't cheering for her progress. Actually, he looked downright annoyed about it.

"That was really great!" Sully exclaimed, rushing up and holding up a hand to Gen as she clumsily slid off the side of her dragon.

She stared up at his hand and then gave him a look of uncertainty. "Thanks…"

He sighed. "It's a high-five. You're supposed to slap my hand with your own."

"Why?" she questioned.

"Because you did a good job," he explained. "It's a thing people do."

"Okay," she said and lifted her own hand and slapped it against his before pulling it back. She wasn't sure if that was what it was like to hold someone's hand, but it still felt like a nice enough, friendly gesture.

"I'd say you're a natural flyer," Jack said proudly with a toothy grin. "You'll be doing loops in no time."

"Thanks," she said, turning to Dwayne, Gen dared to grin. "So I've made progress. Maybe I'll get a case before this century is up after all, sir?"

He shook his head. "I've assigned you three tasks that must be completed before you'll get a case. I wouldn't get your hopes up. Actually, if I were you, I'd save myself the trouble and quit now and go live off your family's fortune. You're about as likely to pass these tasks as you are of getting back to the 15th century."

CHAPTER THIRTY-THREE

THE HOUSE MANAGER'S MASTERPIECE

<u>**Gen's Quarters, Rogue Rider Mansion, Beverly Hills, California, United States**</u>

Gen stepped into her new quarters at the Rogue Rider mansion, her eyes widening at the sight before her. Amanda, the house manager with a flair for the unconventional, had truly outdone herself. The room was a stunning fusion of modern elegance and medieval charm, proof to Amanda's uncanny ability to blend the old and the new.

A rustic stone fireplace dominated one wall, its warm glow casting dancing shadows across the room. Beside it was a large, blue plush pillow that seemed to invite Gen to sink into its embrace. The walls were adorned with tapestries depicting scenes of dragons soaring through the skies, their intricate details a nod to Gen's own incredible journey.

"What do you think?" Amanda asked, an expectant look on her face.

"I actually love it," Gen said, looking around.

"Why do you say 'actually?' Did you have doubts?" Amanda asked, looking between Gen and Sophia who was studying the space, smiling brightly.

"I ate mud for dinner," Gen replied. "I have doubts about everything in my life now."

"Well, I made you a place to wash out your mouth and in a style that I thought would suit you." Amanda pointed to the corner where a washing basin stood atop a beautifully carved wooden stand, its copper basin gleaming in the soft light.

Gen couldn't help but smile at the familiar sight, a touch of home in this strange, new world. The bed, a magnificent four-poster with rich, burgundy drapes, looked like it had been plucked straight from a castle chamber.

Yet, as Gen explored further, she discovered the subtle touches of modernity that Amanda had so thoughtfully incorporated. A sleek, minimalist desk sat beneath a window, its surface bare save for a single, elegant lamp. The closet doors, a marvel of engineering, slid open to reveal a spacious interior, complete with built-in shelves and drawers.

"What's that?" Gen asked, pointing to the large pillow on the floor.

"Oh, that's something that Sophia always has in her room, so you got one too," Amanda said proudly. "That's a bean bag. You sit on it."

"Nice," Gen said, watching as Sophia strode over and plopped down in the big, plush pillow.

The floor was a warm, honey-colored hardwood and partially covered by a luxurious, intricately patterned rug that looked like it had been woven by the skilled hands of a medieval artisan. And there, nestled in the corner, was a bookshelf filled with tomes both ancient and modern, which showed Amanda's understanding of Gen's love for the written word. The house manager was very intuitive and had done her homework.

As Gen took in the room, she felt a sense of peace wash over her. Amanda had created a space that was uniquely hers—a haven that celebrated her past while embracing her future. This was a room fit for a warrior. It was a place where Gen could rest, recharge and prepare for the battles ahead, although it sounded like she'd be training for the rest of her life.

"Oh, and Dwayne left this for you," Amanda said, lifting a piece of paper off a side table and handing it to Gen. "It's your list of tasks that you have to complete for training."

Gen unfolded the parchment, taking in the strange blocked type. Her eyes widened.

Catching the look of horror on her face, Sophia sprang to her feet and strode over. "What is it?"

"I have to solve a murder," Gen said, looking at the list of tasks that Dwayne had assigned her before she could get a Rogue Rider case. "That's my first assignment on my internship for that evil man."

Amanda held up a finger. "But first you have to find a murder."

"And then I have to solve it," Gen repeated, an idea brightening in her eyes suddenly. "Maybe Dwayne is asking me to murder him. Then I'll know who did it and case closed, all done."

"I think I can actually help you shortcut some of these tasks," Sophia offered, looking over Gen's shoulder at the list.

"Really?" Gen asked, hope springing to her chest. "How? I've got to solve a murder and then…" She gasped with even more shock than before. "I have to complete six hundred hours of shadowing other Rogue Riders. Oh, that man… I get the significance of that specific number of hours that Dwayne picked."

"Because you're six hundred years off your original timeline," Amanda guessed.

Gen nodded, glancing back at the list. "And then I'm supposed to catalog and observe over fifteen hundred magical creatures."

Amanda laughed. "Because you're from the fifteenth century. Wow, I didn't think that man had a sense of humor."

Gen grimaced. "I still don't think he does."

"I know I can help you with the first one," Sophia said. "Then we just have to get clever with the other two."

"How in the world can you do that?" Amanda questioned.

"Well, I know people," Sophia answered. "And then there's this whole time travel thing that could work in our favor. I mean, I can bend a few arms, maybe make some Rogue Riders help you out with shadowing hours. Who is to say how you did this all so quickly, as long as we can prove that you did? Dwayne is trying to make it impossible. We're just going to make it look like you possibly did it, right after you solve an actual murder, of course."

"You're good and evil at the same time, Sophia," Amanda gushed, a delighted grin on her face.

"I'm strategic," Sophia countered with a wink. "And I know how to beat bad men at their own games by still playing by the rules. I win because I don't cheat. They lose because I know that they will."

CHAPTER THIRTY-FOUR

THE CASE OF THE CURSED SOAP OPERA

Stage Twenty-Six, Canoodle Lot, Fairyland Studios, Los Angeles, California, United States

Sophia managed to set Gen up with a famous and apparently immortal detective. He was a bit after her time, but she had met him recently. It was this great detective who had helped to find Gen when she'd been lost in modern-day London when Father Time attempted to put her on her timeline in 1426, but it didn't work. The man followed the clues in a huge and confusing city and found Gen, which was exactly after she'd dug up her dragon's egg in what was now known as Hyde Park.

This detective was thought to be a fictional character by most. But because the Beaufont family always knew the secrets in this world, they'd discovered that he was a real man and an immortal sleuth who was compelled to solve mysteries for all of time. It was a strange bit of magic, but there were many unexplained characters like this on the globe. Many were demi-gods who Mama Jamba had created to do various jobs.

Sherlock Holmes was notoriously known for being the greatest detective of all time. He had solved almost every case he'd ever been given. He had a mind designed to see details and deduce information in order to unravel mysteries. Currently, he was working a murder case in Los Angeles, which was perfect for Gen. Sophia had known about this since he was a family friend, constantly helping the Beaufonts, and she'd arranged for Gen to meet up with the great detective.

Many thought, based on the books written about Sherlock, that his assistant was a Dr. Watson. That *had been* true, but currently and probably for the rest of time, his assistant was strangely King Rudolfus Sweetwater. This man, who Gen had also met when lost in London, was by far the most bizarre character anyone had ever interacted with. However, that was not why he was the king of the fae or the richest man in all the world, but only an extra bonus to his over the top character.

Catching sight of the two men standing next to the large metal building, Gen hurried over, waving for them to see her, although, she was certain that they had as soon as she materialized. They were expert detectives, after all.

"Oh, did you get lost?" King Rudolf asked, jovially waving at Gen as she hurried over. "I bet Wilshire Boulevard looked totally different in your time. The Gaylord Hotel probably didn't even exist."

The king was by far one of the most attractive men Gen had ever seen with his short, blond hair and bright blue eyes. He had a timeless elegance and was probably a great resource for her since he'd been around since the 15th century. Fae weren't just gorgeous and dumb, they also lived a thousand years—well, unless they drank chemicals in an attempt to get drunk. Then they died rather young and quickly.

Sherlock Holmes cut his eyes to the man wearing a purple tunic and slacks. "America didn't exist in Gen's time…"

The great detective looked very different than his assistant in a dark brown tweed suit jacket with patches on the elbows and slacks to match. He had a flat cap covering his brown hair and pulled down over his studious eyes, which also matched his attire.

"Oh, right. Well, I forget what was where and when." Rudolf pointed to a tree that was growing out of a small patch of earth surrounded by concrete in what was apparently a movie lot. "Did we have those in the 15th century? Or are those a newer invention of Mama Jamba's?"

Gen grinned at the man, hoping that he was joking, but getting the impression that he was deadly serious. "Trees have been around from the beginning, I'm certain." She glanced at Sherlock, who seemed not bothered by the dimwittedness of his assistant. Apparently, it's what helped him to think on these cases. "Sophia said that you were working a murder case here at this…television studio, is it?"

She looked around at the strange place that was all metal and rock, like a forest had been banished from the place, except the lone tree in the distance. There were many loud vehicles of various sizes and strange equipment. This was apparently the place where those stories were made that broadcast onto the magical screens known as televisions.

"Yes, it's where the soulless come to tell the creatives how to live their lives," Rudolf said in a hushed voice.

Sherlock rolled his eyes. "He's talking about movie executives and how they create obstacles for actors and writers and whatnot."

"Okay," Gen said, drawing out the word. "Well, thanks for the education. I think between the two of you, I might get a better handle on the present day and all its strangeness."

She meant that too. Rudolf had such a different way of looking at the world and Sherlock seemed to decode it in a more logical way.

The great detective pointed at a building beside them. "And yes, we have a string of murders that you can assist with since you've been assigned to solve a case. The deaths have been happening here on the set of a popular soap opera show known as Sunset Cove. The director, cast and crew all believe that the set is cursed by a strong magic."

"Why do they think that?" Gen asked, watching as Rudolf withdrew a silver flask from his pocket and unscrewed the lid.

The fae took a swig from the container and wiped his mouth with the back of his hand. "Because the old director, when he quit, stormed off the set and yelled, 'I curse this place.'"

Sherlock nodded. "Since then, anyone who plays the love interest opposite the main character, dies tragically. There's been three fatalities. Now no one will take the part and the actress, Alexus who plays the lead is threatening to quit. The show is about to be terminated and the stage here condemned if we don't solve the case."

"So you don't think that the director actually cursed the show?" Gen asked.

"We do not," Rudolf replied, offering her the flask of liquid.

Gen shook her head.

"People kill people, not curses, usually," Sherlock explained. "Someone is behind this and we need data in order to make a deduction."

"Well, it sounds like it is the previous director," Gen offered.

"He's dead, having killed himself after leaving," Rudolf stated. "So it's probably not him, but maybe…"

"It's not him," Sherlock said, studying the building in front of them. "Also, ghosts usually don't kill people. People kill people. Someone is behind the string of murders and possibly the person who killed the director is our murderer."

"So you don't think it was a suicide?" Gen questioned.

"It's a theory," Sherlock replied. "But a theory is only as good as the evidence supporting it, which is what we must collect now."

Rudolf turned to Gen, offering his arm, like a chivalrous

gentleman. "Are you ready to solve the case of the cursed soap opera?"

Gen found herself smiling, grateful that her assignment had paired her up with these two men. She believed she would learn a lot from them and have a good time in the process. Slipping her arm around the fae's, she nodded. "Yes, teach me your ways of detecting and let's find the murderer."

CHAPTER THIRTY-FIVE

UNSCRIPTED CRIMES

<u>**Stage Twenty-Six, Canoodle Lot, Fairyland Studios, Los Angeles, California, United States**</u>

"Where are your wings?" Gen asked the fae when they entered the tall metal building.

Rudolf glanced sideways at her. "I glamour them away because they are a nuisance and don't really work. They are for show."

"Oh, back in the day, they were a sign of beauty and prestige," Gen remarked, remembering the strange interactions between the different races.

"Things have shifted and we go for more practical over esteem," Rudolf related, a look of disgust on his face. "For instance, in this day and age, people wear these awful things called cargo pants so they can carry things on their person."

"I'll keep an eye out for that," Gen said, looking around at the television studio. There were tons of strange equipment and stacks of supplies. But the weirdest part was that there was half of a living area with furniture, a partial kitchen and then a workspace.

"Observe, not just see," Sherlock advised, looking around at the large open space.

"Why does it look like someone lives here?" Gen asked, pointing to the living spaces.

"It's a set where they film the television shows," Sherlock explained.

"But someone obviously lives here too," Rudolf stated.

"How do you gather that?" Sherlock questioned his assistant.

"Because I feel the room and emotions guide the undercurrent of truth," the king answered.

Sherlock shook his head. "That's an awful way to confuse the facts."

"Doesn't this feel like someone's home to you?" Rudolf asked, holding out his hands.

Sherlock drew in a breath. "I don't operate based on feelings."

"Well, what about the fact that up there in those rafters, there's a cot, blankets and a pillow?" Rudolf pointed up to the ceiling where there indeed looked to be a makeshift bed.

Sherlock narrowed his eyes, combing his fingers over his chin. "That's very interesting. Good find, King Rudolf."

He bowed. "Thank you. I believe I've earned myself another drink." Rudolf pulled the flask out of his pocket and opened it, taking a swig.

"Let's go and question the cast and crew." Sherlock led them off toward two men standing by a strange piece of black equipment with lenses and lots of knobs and buttons.

They turned at the sight of the unlikely group, giving them quizzical glares.

"I'm the investigator for these string of murders," Sherlock said, a commanding tone to his voice. "Which one of you is the director for Sunset Cove?"

"That would be me," a short man with dark hair said. "I've told the police everything I know. I'm not sure what else you want me to tell you. This set is simply cursed. Everyone knows it. There's sufficient evidence to prove that."

"And what evidence is that?" Rudolf asked.

"Well, the murders for starters," the director answered. "Then before each one, the actor is erased from the footage that we recorded the day of."

Sherlock gave the director a scrutinizing expression, seeming to see through him. "Why did the original director leave and end his life?"

"Oh, because he and the actress who plays our main character, Alexus, were in a relationship," the director answered. "But he found love letters from her costar, the romantic lead, in her trash."

"So he quit and killed himself?" Gen asked. "That seems a bit extreme."

"It was the curse," the other man next to the director said.

"And you are?" Rudolf asked him.

"I'm the camera guy," he replied.

"The old director was the one who cursed the show, though," Sherlock stated.

The camera man shook his head. "This show has been cursed since the beginning. Every director always loses his mind, going crazy."

"Doesn't that worry you?" Rudolf asked, looking at the director.

"Yes, of course," the man replied, honestly. "But this show is a blockbuster and I would have been a fool not to take the job."

"What were you doing before this?" Sherlock questioned.

The man frowned. "Well, I was the assistant director."

"For all the other directors who went crazy?" Rudolfus asked, suspicion in his tone.

"Well, yeah…" the director answered, diverting his eyes to the side.

Sherlock gave his assistant a pointed look before glancing back at the director. "Why do you think they lost their minds?"

"It's a stressful job," the man answered. "There's a lot of pressure to get it right. Like I said, this is a money maker show."

"And you said that when the three actors had been murdered, that right before, footage from the day's shooting disappears?" Rudolf asked, taking a drink from his flask. He pointed at the camera guy. "Wouldn't that be your territory?"

"Well, yeah," the guy replied. "But how do you think I feel? I lock it up in the vault at night and then show up the next day and find out that it's missing a character. That's a whole day of shooting. Then we get the news that the actor is dead. It's very jarring. I'm telling you that this place is cursed."

"And who has access to this vault?" Gen asked, the wheels in her brain starting to spin fast.

"Well, I do," the guy replied. "And the director."

"No one else?" Sherlock questioned.

"There's an extra set of keys in the vault, but they stay in there," the director imparted. "This set is cursed and that's the only explanation. Because of all this mess, we're in jeopardy of getting canceled. We're all going to lose our jobs."

A loud clattering noise behind the men interrupted the conversation. All looked up to see a man fumbling with a box of props that were quickly spilling out onto the floor.

"Hey, what are you still doing here?" the director asked, looking back at the guy. "Weren't you supposed to be gone already?"

"Sorry, boss," the man said, shoving the box hurriedly onto the shelf in front of him. "I was just leaving."

"Good, because we're about to start shooting and you know we need the set clear," the director said, shaking his head. "And you dropped that stuff because you were moving too fast again. You have to slow down and take your time, or you drop stuff, you know that."

"I know, boss," the man said, rushing away, moving with surprising speed.

"Who is that?" Sherlock asked.

The director turned back around. "That's the janitor. He works the morning shift so the set is clean by call time. Anyway, what was I saying? Oh, right, we're all going to lose our jobs because of this curse."

Rudolf took another drink. "Does the crew and cast know the show is in jeopardy?"

"Well, yeah," the cameraman replied. "But no one wants to play Alexus' costar, so we're quickly running out of options."

"The janitor overheard you when you said that though," Rudolf pointed out. "Maybe that's why he dropped the box of stuff."

The director shook his head. "Nah. That guy is union. He'll get another job somewhere on the lot. I'm glad for that too, because he used to be a big shot writer but fell out with the execs. Now being a janitor is the best he can do."

The cameraman laughed. "If I were him, I'd vanish from showbusiness. But I guess when you've been in this place so long, it's all you know."

"And if you two lose your job if the show is canceled, what will you do?" Sherlock asked, looking between the two men.

The cameraman pointed at himself. "I'll be toast, but I'm be so tired of the politics and frustrations that I'll be happy to have a reason to leave."

The director smiled. "I'll use my success with the show to move on to bigger things." He cut his eyes to the side. "But who I really worry about is Alexus. This show is all she has and she'll be lost without it."

Gen turned to see a woman standing a short distance away. She was very beautiful with short blonde hair and a polished expression and looked like she was waiting to speak to them.

Sherlock must have sensed this and turned, making his way over to the actress. Gen and Rudolf followed.

"Alexus, I have some questions about the murders here on Sunset Cove," Sherlock said in a low voice.

The woman glanced at the director and cameraman, giving the three investigators a nervous expression. She nodded, huddling in close to them, like trying not to be overheard.

"They told you that the show is cursed, didn't they?" she asked, looking up at Sherlock with a trusting gaze.

"You don't believe that," he stated, reading into her question.

She shook her head. "My boyfriend, the director, didn't kill himself. We made up that night. I told him the truth and he believed me."

"And what was the truth?" Rudolf asked.

"I wasn't having an affair with the actor playing my love interest in the show," she answered. "I don't know where those letters came from that were in my trashcan. I'd never seen them before."

"So none of your costars were infatuated with you?" Sherlock questioned.

She shook her head. "Not a costar. But there is someone…"

Gen leaned in closer. "Who?"

Alexus cut her eyes to one of the men in the distance. The three turned, seeing that the director had walked off toward the back. The only one standing there was the camera guy.

"He has the hots for you?" Rudolf asked. "He realizes that you're a nine and he's like a six, right?"

"I've turned him down for years," Alexus explained. "But he's relentless. I wouldn't have put it past him to put the fake love letters in my trashcan to break us up. Well, it worked and now my boyfriend is dead and my show is about to be canceled."

"Because no one will play opposite of you anymore?" Gen guessed. "Because they are afraid of getting murdered?"

Alexus nodded. "I'm just hoping that the writers take my

advice and instead of giving me a costar, make me the full lead. That's the only way to save the show. But convincing those crusty old men is difficult. I've been trying for years. But it's a boys' club and they do whatever they want."

"Right," Sherlock said, glancing at his assistant. "Well, I think we need to check out this vault where the tampered footage was located."

CHAPTER THIRTY-SIX

RUDOLF'S FLASK OF WISDOM

<u>**Stage Twenty-Six, Canoodle Lot, Fairyland Studios, Los Angeles, California, United States**</u>

The cast and crew were all gathered in front of the vault as Sherlock Holmes had requested. The dozen or so people stood around in silence, watching the great detective stride back and forth, his head down and his hands clasped behind his back as he paced, thinking. Gen watched, peering nervously up at Rudolf.

"Has he solved the case?" she asked him.

The fae nodded. "Yes, but he's working out the details. He won't announce the way it happened until he knows the full motive, means and opportunity of the murderer."

"Do you know who did it?" Gen asked.

A laugh popped out of his mouth. "Of course. I told Sherlock. Now he's just trying to figure out how they did it."

"Wow, you two are quite the team," Gen admired, smiling at the fae. "How did you work it out?" She glanced around at the director, camera guy and Alexus as well as the many actors and crew, each with different motives, means and opportunities.

Rudolf pointed to his heart. "Listen with more than your ears. In detective work, use your heart. That's the reason that people commit murders, so you need to use your own to figure out who speaks the truth."

"I've deduced who murdered the previous director as well as the three other actors," Sherlock began in a low voice, commanding everyone's attention.

Rudolf grinned, pulling out a brand new flask that sounded full, swooshing with liquid. "This is my favorite part." He offered it to Gen and this time, she decided to take him up on his offer, grabbing for the silver flask and unscrewing the lid before having a sip. The amber whiskey was warm and welcoming. It reminded her of the morning that she met Emperor after he hatched.

"It makes sense that the person who is behind these crimes being disguised as a curse is someone who has access to the vault." Sherlock lifted his hand pointing at the large open door, propped wide by a chair. It had been unlocked for the detective's investigation, which didn't last long.

"It wasn't me!" the director exclaimed, all eyes looking at him.

"Well, you have access to the vault, having one of three keys," Sherlock countered, holding up a finger. "And you were the assistant director, passed over several times as others in the higher position went crazy. But you finally got your chance to be director and here you are—not going insane at all."

"This is absurd!" the director argued. "I didn't kill anyone. Why would I murder my own actors?"

"Well, you said yourself that this position will only lead to a better one," Rudolf sang, stealing the flask from Gen and taking a drink. "So it goes to reason that you'd sabotage the show so that it was canceled. Then you move on and take your good name and reputation for maintaining peace of mind while directing in a stressful, cursed show."

"I didn't do this!" The director's face flushed red.

"No, you didn't," Sherlock said, matter-of-factly. "Because although people are motivated to kill for money and positions, a crime like this was one of passion. One related to love."

Rudolf rocked forward on his toes and then back, handing the flask to Gen, sharing. "Which brings us to the camera guy."

"Me?" the other man said, his eyes wide. "I didn't do this."

"But also had access to the vault where the footage was kept and could be tampered with," Sherlock stated. "And you are in love with Alexus, who continuously turns you down. It goes to reason that you'd plant the fake love letters in her trashcan and try to break her up with her boyfriend, the previous director."

The camera man gawked. "I liked Alexus but I wasn't going to murder for her."

"And watching Alexus make out with other men and having to film it, that would be tough, wouldn't it?" Rudolf asked.

"Well, of course, but what was I supposed to do about it?" the camera guy asked.

"Nothing," Sherlock stated. "Because you were growing tired of this industry anyway and hoping to be let go, giving you a reason to get away from the woman you were obsessed with."

"But there was someone here who couldn't have the show canceled," Rudolf said, turning and looking at Alexus standing close by. "And you wanted to be the sole star, but the only way to do that would be to get in close with the directors. But you're one of those women who makes men crazy."

"I am not!" the woman yelled, her voice high-pitched.

Rudolf wagged his finger at her. "Oh, I know your type. The show wasn't cursed. It was just that there was a diva who thought she could romance her way to the top. If you had the directors on your side, then you could convince those writers to give you the lead."

"I don't know what you're talking about!" Alexus exclaimed, her fists by her side.

"So you didn't try to seduce the directors?" Rudolf asked. "You didn't make them fall in love with you and then when you didn't get what you wanted, you'd dump them, making them crazy?"

"Well… Maybe. But I'm not a murderer," Alexus said, starting to sob. "I wouldn't kill my costars just to get a role."

"No, you didn't because you didn't believe the show was cursed," Sherlock stated. "And it isn't. That was just a way for the murderer to sabotage Sunrise Cove. The person who killed the previous director and the actors and is behind all the mysterious events is someone who had access to the vault."

Rudolf suddenly peeled off to the right at once, disappearing backstage.

"It wasn't me!" the director declared.

"Or me," the camera guy stated with conviction.

Sherlock turned to the vault, opening the door wide. He then removed the chair propping it open and stood back. The door slowly started to close. "You see, the large vault door is on a mechanical slow release device due to its size and weight. That way it doesn't slam shut, hurting someone exiting. But if there was someone who wanted access to the vault, well, all they'd have to do was wait until the camera guy or director put the tapes inside. Then when they were walking away, they could slip out of their hiding place and stop the door right before it closed."

He reached for the side of the vault where there was a yardstick leaning against the wall. The detective picked it up and slid it in between the door and the frame just before it closed, blocking it from shutting completely. He looked up victoriously at the crowd. "From there, this person could go into the vault and remove the extra pair of keys, make a copy and then have access to the supposedly locked space."

"So the show isn't cursed?" the director asked, looking around in awe which quickly morphed into horror. "But that means one of you is a murderer."

"Indeed someone on the set of Sunset Cove is," Sherlock stated, glaring at the director. "But it was someone who wasn't motivated by greed." His gaze swiveled to the camera guy. "Or love." Finally he lowered his chin, looking at Alexus. "Or fame."

"Who did it?" Alexus asked, her voice shaking as she looked around at the cast and crew.

Sherlock held up a finger, his chest high with confidence. "The person who planted the love letters, murdered the director, the three actors and tampered with the tapes was someone motivated by revenge."

At once, Gen knew. Everything pieced together in her mind and she simply knew who the murderer was. It made complete sense.

Rudolf materialized, dragging a man restrained by a spell. "It was, of course, the janitor."

CHAPTER THIRTY-SEVEN

THE CUSTODIAN'S REVENGE

<u>Stage Twenty-Six, Canoodle Lot, Fairyland Studios, Los Angeles, California, United States</u>

"I can't believe it was the janitor," Gen mused, shaking her head.

She, King Rudolf and Sherlock Holmes stood outside the building for Sunset Cove. In the distance, the authorities were interviewing the cast and crew. The janitor was sitting in what was apparently a police car, which was ablaze with red and blue lights. Uniformed officers buzzed around the scene as everyone talked excitedly.

"It's always the janitor," Rudolf stated.

Sherlock shook his head. "It varies and it's always the person with the means, the motive and the opportunity."

"So how did you two work out that it was the janitor and not the other suspects?" Gen asked.

"Well, although the director, camera guy and Alexus had reasons to commit the crimes, none of them could fulfill all three of the requirements," Sherlock explained. "It wasn't until I investigated the vault, that I realized how the keys could be stolen.

Then something that they had said about the writers for the show got me thinking."

Rudolf grinned, looking down at Gen. "We did some digging and found that the janitor had been one of the original writers for Sunset Cove. However, when the show took off, the execs didn't want to give him credit. So they fired him and took over the show, not giving him the profits or prestige that he would have deserved."

Sherlock nodded. "Wanting to get revenge for what was stolen from him, the janitor got a job on the set. That gave him access to the director, who he murdered, after planting the letters in the trashcan, which he'd have access to."

"Not if he left early because he had to be off the set," Gen countered.

Rudolf's eyes sparkled with a secret knowing. "But the janitor wanted to stay close and what better way to do that than live on the set."

Gen's mouth fell open. "The cot in the rafters."

"Exactly," Sherlock stated. "That gave the janitor the access to plant the letters, get into the vault to get the keys and copy them, murder the director and then the other actors."

"And none of them would have been on guard, thinking they were on set alone, right?" Gen asked.

Sherlock nodded. "It's all about the element of surprise."

"And then the janitor spread the idea that the show was cursed," Rudolf stated. "Using the key to the vault and his full access of the set, he tampered with the tapes, giving weight to this cursed idea."

"But really, all the janitor wanted was for the show to fail since he wasn't getting credit for it," Sherlock stated.

"Wow, I can't believe you two figured all that out," Gen mused, amazed. "I had my suspicions of the others, but I never saw it being the janitor."

"The others had reasons that cast the spotlight on them," Rudolf began. "But in the end, all the facts pointed at the janitor."

"This is true," Sherlock said, looking over his shoulder at the chaos with the police and cast and crew before turning back to Gen and his assistant. "In detective work, eliminate the impossible and whatever remains, however improbable, must be the truth."

"Well said," Rudolf cheered, putting one arm around Gen's shoulder and the other around Sherlock's. "Now how about I take you two out for a drink? I haven't had one in minutes and I'm parched."

Sherlock nodded. "I always like the idea of celebrating a closed case with a nice sherry."

Gen smiled, allowing the king of the fae to lead her and the detective off down the pavement. "Yes, and I'll take a whiskey and maybe a bit more of your wisdom on sleuthing."

CHAPTER THIRTY-EIGHT

THE UNNATURAL ARRANGEMENT

<u>Grounds, Rogue Rider Mansion, Beverly Hills, California, United States</u>

Jaws snapped, threatening. Claws whipped through the crisp morning air, intimidating. Tails smacked the earth, alarming.

In the manicured sprawl of the Rogue Riders' estate, under an indifferent sky, Dwayne Stone commanded his dragon, Night. The sleek and formidable creature had been forced into a cruel contest against a Kodiak bear. Night, covered in gray, shiny scales, faced the bear, a creature of raw strength and primal ferocity.

Neither animal was a willing participant in this spectacle. Gen stood by, next to her own dragon, both forced to witness the heart-wrenching scene. This training session felt like a sick show of anger and sorrow.

The lush grounds and elegant topiaries around them mocked the brutality unfolding. In the distance, the neat mansion was an ironic backdrop to the savage display of brutality in front of Gen. Disgust curdled in her stomach and so badly did she want to intervene. Beside her Emperor felt her heartache for the bear and dragon forced to fight one another. And she knew he shared her sentiment.

The brown bear covered in fur and with a body that shook with winter reserves couldn't have looked more different alongside the gray dragon. Night was twice the bear's length, but their weight was comparable. The other thing that they shared were deep looks of trepidation, both creatures knowing that a real fight between them would leave both fatally injured. It was simply an unnatural arrangement and everyone watching silently knew it.

"This isn't right!" Gen protested, throwing her arms wide.

"It's training," Dwayne said through clenched teeth, standing a short distance away and proudly watching as the bear and the dragon circled each other—neither wanting to make the next move.

"It's sick!" Gen dared to say while the other Rogue Riders averted their gazes, their dragons stationed behind them. She motioned to the bystanders. "You all know that a bear shouldn't be forced to fight a dragon. He's an innocent creature and outmatched since Night has fire."

"But Night is slow, and the Kodiak bear is fast," Dwayne said, looking over his shoulder at her. "My dragon needs to learn to pick up the pace. Either he does, or the bear will teach him a lesson the hard way."

Gen shook with rage and revulsion. *Make this stop*, she said in her head to Emperor.

He glared down at her. *I can't use my mind control on Night. It will have repercussions that we do not want.*

Then stop the bear, Gen urged.

The animal needs to be able to defend himself if attacked, Emperor stated. *To intervene would be to take away his honor and pride. I can't do that.*

What's the point in having mind control if you don't use it to help others? she questioned.

The point is to know when to use such an absolute power and when it will only make things worse, he replied.

Infuriated, Gen stomped forward, throwing her arms wide in front of Dwayne. "Stop this! It's not who we are. This is not how we train. We may be demon riders, but we don't have to act like monsters!"

His eyes narrowed into little slits as he stared down at her. "Get out of here."

"No!" Gen yelled, whipping around to face the dragon and bear. "Don't fight! That's the exercise. Exert your own free choice. You don't have to do this."

"Gen…" Dwayne growled low behind her.

She ignored him, watching Night and the Kodiak bear continue to circle, staring deep into each other's eyes. They were watching every move—their every muscle tensed. Gen sucked in a breath when the dragon halted, making the bear freeze too.

The air crackled with tension as Night swung his claws through the air, but hesitated, right before it collided with the bear's massive head. With a low growl, the bear paused, confusion in its eyes, allowing Night a moment of clarity. In that breath, the dragon's natural instinct to dominate waned, replaced by a shared sense of survival and an unspoken bond between beasts.

The spectators, expecting a display of dominance, found themselves watching a poignant moment of defiance. As the bear ambled away, unharmed, Night simply watched, no gloating in his gaze.

A scream ripped out of Dwayne's mouth as he marched forward, swinging around in front of Gen. "You are out of line!"

"I am a human meant to protect and I won't stand idly by and watch cruelty," Gen said, standing tall, her shoulders back.

Anger buzzed in Dwayne's small eyes. He opened his mouth. Seemed to rethink his words. Shut his lips and then shook his head. "You might be a Beaufont but that doesn't mean that you're invincible. I will find a way to break you down."

She grimaced. "That sounds like a threat."

"The House of Fourteen and Hiker Wallace might be in your corner, but you work for me," he said. "And for now, it doesn't look like you're ever going to be working a case for the Rogue Riders. So, like I've said before, you might as well quit."

"I've already completed my first training assignment," she said smugly.

"What?" he hissed, that vein on his forehead throbbing. "What are you talking about?"

"I finished the first task you gave me," Gen replied, feeling giddy.

"You solved a murder?" he asked, as the other riders stirred in the background and Night sulked off.

Gen shook her head. "No, I detected the murderer behind four murders."

"How?" he asked, his vein pulsing on his head.

"Well, I worked with Sherlock Holmes," she explained. "He, and his assistant, taught me strategies for detecting and then I studied a case with them and we found a murderer. That's what you assigned me to do, right?"

"You were working with Sherlock Holmes?" he asked, hostility brimming in his gaze.

"And King Rudolfus Sweetwater," Gen sang, now smiling cheerfully, knowing that would make Dwayne even angrier. "He's the king over the—"

"I know who he is," the leader of the Rogue Riders cut in, curtly.

"Right, well, that's what you assigned me to do," she continued casually. "I can send you the details on the case if you want."

"No, I don't care," Dwayne said, spinning around. "Complete the other two tasks. Then we'll see about you having a case." He glared over his shoulder. "But something tells me that you're not going to make it long enough to fulfill your requirements..."

CHAPTER THIRTY-NINE

A WALK ON THE ROGUE SIDE

<u>Wilshire Boulevard, Los Angeles, California, United States</u>

"I can't believe you know Sherlock Holmes," Sully remarked as he, Gen and Jack strode down the busy street. The guys had taken her out on their patrols, which would fulfill her first set of hours shadowing Rogue Riders.

"I can't believe you know who Sherlock Holmes is," Jack said to the other man, slapping him playfully on the shoulder. They were dressed in their strange modern armor that was sleek and minimal but flattering in a way that medieval warrior clothes weren't for men. Jack had a small sword strapped to his side. Sully had one across his back. Gen, of course, had Bellumferrum nestled in her pocket.

"Hey," Sully said, peeling back, as if the playful slap hurt him. "I've watched the shows."

"Ha!" Jack laughed. "That makes more sense. I didn't think that you'd read the books."

"There are books with Sherlock Holmes?" Sully asked, suddenly confused.

"Yeah, by an author named Arthur Conan Doyle written in the 1800s," Jack said. "That's why I'm surprised to find out that

Sherlock Holmes is real and still alive. He was from London too, you know?"

"He told me," Gen replied, recalling the long conversation that she shared with Sherlock Holmes and King Rudolf after they solved the case. "Apparently, Doyle wrote the stories about the real, immortal detective."

Surprise sprang to Jack's face. "That's fascinating."

Gen nodded, agreeing. "Anyway, I know Sherlock Holmes and King Rudolf over the fae and they helped me with my first task, but to fulfill the next two on Dwayne's list, I'm going to need a miracle."

Sully laughed, shaking his head. "The way you stood up to him was…well, stupid. It was really careless of you. That bear could have snatched you as its hostage or Night could have scorched you for defying his rider. But really, I'd just worry about the wrath that you'll get from Dwayne now. He'll probably make you do a thousand push-ups during training exercises tomorrow morning."

Jack directed them around a corner, leading the way. "I think that push-ups are the least of Gen's problems at this point. And I don't think that Emperor would have allowed her to get hurt. But watching you get in Dwayne's face was about the most entertaining thing I've seen…in well, ever."

Sully nodded. "It was better than watching Game of Thrones."

"Game of what?" Gen asked, confused.

Jack waved her off as they negotiated around a crowd of people on the sidewalk. "Let's focus on giving you the rundown on patrols and how we keep this city in check and most importantly, the criminals in their place."

Gen and the two men strode down Wilshire Boulevard in Los Angeles. Each step carried her further into a world so starkly different from what she knew of 15th century London. The street was alive with the growls and hisses of metal beasts, making it feel like she was walking through a dragon's den...or more appropriately, a bear's.

The towering structures, gleaming in the sunlight, reminded Gen of castles built not of stone but of light and air. The people had their eyes fixed on small glowing talismans known as phones, that seemed to be enchanted by sorcerers. The air carried a mix of scents, none of which were the comforting smoke of a hearth or the damp earth around the Thames.

The clamor of voices and machines created a cacophony unfamiliar yet strangely rhythmic. Shop fronts, with their wares displayed behind clear barriers, looked to Gen like treasure chests awaiting a curious hand. Amidst this overwhelming consort of sights and sounds, Gen felt an odd sense of belonging, like a reminder that curiosity and wonder were not bound by time.

"In this area, Jack and I have a few places to check in on," Sully began, pausing on a street corner and pointing across the road. He indicated a row of buildings on the next block and then swept his arm wide to the other side of the street. "We've got the Bun and Run Bakery, The Whiskey Gargoyle Bar, Vital Flow Blood Center, Printing Prosperity Press, Pawn of the Dead and then of course, The Getaway Garage."

"Wait, all those places around here are illegal businesses?" Gen asked in shock.

Jack shook his head. "No, they are legitimate businesses that pay taxes and help the community in some small or large way."

"They just happen to also conduct illegal business in the process," Sully added, proudly pressing his hand to his chest. "But with our help and supervision, they ride the line of good and things remain kosher in the community."

Gen scratched her head, once again, baffled by how this managing the criminal world worked. "I'm struggling to under-stand how what we do is good. Maybe we should just lock up all the offenders and call it a day instead of wasting our time babysitting them."

Jack gave Sully a knowing look. "We were all like that on our first day, weren't we?"

"Yeah, I was like, why are we allowing this filth to exist?" Sully said with a laugh. "Let's bomb them and be done with it. Then we can go on vacation."

Jack sighed. "But sadly, there will be no long respite for us. It's simply unrealistic to think that we can eradicate crime altogether. It's been around for centuries, and it does serve a purpose."

Gen chewed on her lip, thinking. "Sophia called it a pressure cooker and said that it was a delicate balance."

"Sophia is so wise," Sully stated, fondly. "And she's right. If we locked up all the criminals, we'd have other problems. For starters, it would be impossible and that's because crooks are smart and will figure out how to go underground. In our world and under our management, they operate inside our confines. We monitor things and ensure it stays safe and within our parameters. Also, we guarantee that the greater good gets a benefit from crime existing, rather than big, bad guys getting bigger."

"It's sort of like communism of the criminal world," Jack interpreted.

"What's communism?" Gen asked.

Both men laughed.

Sully grinned at Jack. "She's so cute with her not knowing anything about the world and stuff."

"I know things," Gen spat, defensively.

Sully patted her shoulder, mockingly. "Sure, you do, love."

She glowered at him. "Don't make me stab you."

Jack lowered his chin, giving her a playful expression. "What have we said about dealing with your problems by stabbing people in the modern world?"

Gen sighed. "Apparently, it's wrong. I really miss the medieval era sometimes."

Both men gave her commiserating expressions, nodding understandingly to her challenges with adjusting.

"Anyway, also, as we were saying, getting rid of all crime and criminals would disrupt the whole ecosystem of society," Jack continued, regaining Gen's attention. "For instance, there was this crop in Europe that was getting overly consumed by sparrows. The farmers went in and eradicated the sparrow population. They thought they'd won the fight, but then a huge infestation of worms took over, fully destroying the entire crop."

"Great example!" Sully chimed. "You see, there's a balance that we have to maintain. If we took out one low level set of criminals, we'd surely get an influx of even more dangerous ones. Instead, we've figured out how to manage the non-harmful crooks and the best part is, they all work for us, helping to keep justice in balance."

"You mean, all these businesses that you listed are actually helping society?" Gen asked, looking around at the various places that Sully indicated to.

"Yeah, but let's take a walk and we'll show you firsthand," Jack offered, starting forward across the intersection. "It's better if you see the illegal operations with your own eyes and really get a hands-on lesson in crime rings."

CHAPTER FORTY

ARTISANAL BREADS AND ILLICIT SPREADS

<u>Wilshire Boulevard, Los Angeles, California, United States</u>

Hurrying to keep up with Jack among the crowd rushing by, going the opposite way on the path, Gen slid between people all dressed in funny clothing and talking on their devices of worship. The air was filled with a constant hum of noise, a discord of strange sounds that assaulted her ears from every direction. Every storefront she passed was a revelation, filled with wonders that she could scarcely comprehend.

When Jack halted in front of a store where beautiful freshly baked breads were on display through the clear glass window, Gen's mouth began to salivate. The whole place seemed to be filled with delectable pastries and beautiful cakes. The writing across the top of the glass read Bun and Run Bakery.

"I'll explain to our newbie what happens in there while you go and check on our bakery friends," Jack said to Sully, who was already opening the shop's door, making a bell chime.

Gen pointed at the place that seemed completely enchanting and delicious with utter confusion. "This bakery runs illegal activity? How?"

Jack nodded, seeming to understand her plight and also relish in it. "Oh, yeah. Bun and Run Bakery is one of our biggest illegal and potentially out-of-control operations that we have to keep a tight handle on. You see, they ship out their artisan breads all over the country, easily passing over state and even country borders because everyone loves their yeasty goods. However, baked into half of the breads are things that no one can eat."

He paused, seeming to wait for Gen to get it. She didn't. Jack sighed. "They smuggle illegal things across the plains of this great land."

"Oh, well, that sounds bad…"

"It could be, but we keep an eye on what it is," Jack explained. "It's things like contraband or recreational drugs. Stuff that can't really hurt anyone. We allow them to keep their racket going and in exchange, they tell us who else is running in the smuggling ring. When we get word that it's something we won't tolerate like automatic weapons or hard drugs, then we intervene—using the intel that the bakery provided."

"Wow, I'm not sure that I completely understand everything you just said, but that sounds really smart," Gen stated. "You use a pack of small dogs to take down the really big Chupacabra."

Jack arched an eyebrow at her. "You're surprisingly very intelligent about modern things…"

She blushed, not having expected this compliment. "Amanda stocked my bedroom with a lot of books. I've been devouring them as fast as I could. I read about the Chupacabra last night—they are vicious."

Jack nodded. "Much like arms dealers, who I don't have any patience for. So, the bakers here help us to sniff them out and take them down before they can put guns in the hands of children and unknowing people."

"Smart," Gen said, watching as Sully returned, looking happy with himself. "Did you do whatever it was you do?"

He nodded. "Yes, there's nothing on the no-no list for smuggling routes and the bakers gave me a list of their next several shipments."

"Wow, you seem to have things worked out," Gen mused.

"That we do," Jack said, proudly, turning around and pointing. "Over there we have The Whiskey Gargoyle Bar. They run an illegal fight club where people place bets. We review the list of fighters and only allow those who are really despicable on there."

Sully laughed loudly. "We literally ensure that the bad guys pummel each other."

Jack nodded. "The poor guy down on his luck and looking to make a buck to feed his family doesn't get to fight."

"That's right," Sully cut in cheerfully, pointing to a small shop with a blue awning. "That guy gets a donation from the Printing Prosperity Press secretly left at his door."

"What?" Gen asked, looking between the two men, bewildered and trying to keep up.

"That seemingly innocent print shop over there, run by a nice family, actually prints counterfeit money," Jack explained. "We allow it, provided that they report how much they put out into the economy and how. Also, half of it has to go to charity."

"Is counterfeit money safe?" Gen questioned.

"Believe me, there will always be counterfeit currency," Sully stated. "It's a lot better if we know about it and where it's going."

"And ensure that half of it goes to a good place," Jack added proudly.

"Okay, tell me about the other businesses," Gen said, her heart beating fast suddenly with excitement. She never knew the world could be good and bad at the same time and it be okay.

Sully put his arm around her shoulder, steering her to face a place across the street. "This one is my favorite." He glanced at Jack. "Can I have the honors?"

Jack nodded, a dimple surfacing on his cheek when he did.

"Well, over there at Vital Flow Blood Center, they take withdrawals from people," Sully explained.

"Withdrawals?" Gen asked, not sure what he meant.

"That place takes blood from humans," Jack imparted. "People have their blood tested in order to check their health in this era. Anyway, that's a lab. And they take blood, but they always take one extra vial from each patient."

Sully nodded. "That vial is then sold to hungry vampires on the black market. We allow the place to run if they give us a list of their buyers. It's better for the world if we know and can track all vampires. Most of them keep to themselves, especially if they are buying blood and not taking it. But it's good for us to know where they are in case one falls off the wagon."

"Wow, people test their blood to check their health," Gen said in awe.

Sully gave Jack a look of amusement. "Should we be concerned that the vampire thing totally didn't faze her?"

"Vampires were around in my time," Gen stated boldly.

"Yes, they are as old as dirt," Jack joked.

"What's next?" Gen asked, curious.

"Oh, this one is *my* favorite," Jack said, pulling Gen out of Sully's grasp and leading her down the sidewalk. He pointed to a place that had big open doors and loud noises emanating from it. There were also many cars with their front end opened up, like they had a problem. "That's The Getaway Garage. It's a place that repairs cars. You know those big metal things that go fast on the road."

Gen mock scowled at him. "I know what cars are…"

"Well, anyway, that place steals illegal parts off cars," Jack went on. "However, much like with the fight club, we approve the list of vehicles."

"And we ensure that they are real scoundrels," Sully boasted. "And usually, we pick a pretty bad time for them to have their cars stripped of parts, typically leaving them stranded when they need to make a quick getaway."

"Wow, that's very clever," Gen mused.

"Now, do you want to go into one of the seemingly reputable businesses and see how we keep the lawbreakers in check?" Jack asked, batting his eyelashes at her in a playful way.

Gen nodded, excited to see the patrols in action. "Yes, show me how you police these crooks. I want to see firsthand."

CHAPTER FORTY-ONE

THE LIONESS AND THE JOKERS

<u>Pawn of the Dead, Wilshire Boulevard, Los Angeles, California, United States</u>

Before entering the shop with bars on the windows, the guys explained to Gen what a pawn shop was. It sounded like something that she could finally relate to. That's how things worked in her time, trading goods for money and bartering for fair prices. Also, if someone didn't pay up, well, they paid in other ways.

When Gen stepped into the pawn shop on Wilshire Boulevard, she found the air thick with the scent of age and dust. As her eyes adjusted to the dim interior, she was surrounded by a menagerie of strange and wondrous objects, each one holding a tale of its own. She marveled at the strange, glowing boxes humming softly, artifacts of a future she'd yet to understand.

The gleam of metal and gemstones, under harsh artificial lights, appeared as treasure troves of mystical power to her medieval eyes. An ancient, tarnished pocket watch caught her eye, its intricate engravings hinting at a history that spanned centuries, much like her own. Beside it, a stack of worn leather-bound books beckoned, their pages yellowed and brittle with age, holding secrets that even her medieval mind could scarcely fathom.

The sounds of the shop were a mix of electronic beeps and distant traffic, melded into an unfamiliar symphony. Each object, from intricate timekeeping devices to painted canvases trapped in thin, glassy panes, seemed to be in a spell of preservation. The soft touch of worn leather and cold metal items left her fingertips tingling, a tactile dance of history's textures.

She caught snippets of conversation on the other side of the shop. Like usual lately, it was a language loaded with terms and phrases that felt like puzzles to be solved. The air tasted slightly metallic, mixed with the warmth of aged paper and wood. Here, amidst the chaos of the unknown, Gen found a curious sense of belonging, like she was a traveler anchored momentarily in the stream of time.

Realizing that she'd been off in thought and curiously studying the pawn shop, she jerked her attention up to find Jack and Sully grinning like fools at her.

"What?" she hissed, sensing that they were holding back laughter regarding her.

"She's like a baby seeing the world for the first time," Sully said, elbowing his friend beside him.

"If that baby had lethal weapons as hands and the temper of a raging bull," Jack countered with a soft chuckle.

"Which one of you wants to die first?" Gen threatened, narrowing her eyes at them.

Both men pointed at each other. "He does," they said in unison.

Gen sighed, hiding her own amusement. She was grateful that her first time shadowing Rogue Riders had been with these two jokers rather than someone like Clipper or one of the others who had chips on their shoulders.

"Hey, Gen, since we're teaching you all about our world," Sully began, pushing his glasses up on his nose, snorting slightly. "Will you tell me about the medieval world? Did you have to bathe in a trough next to the horses? What did it smell like? Was old age for humans like thirty years old?"

"Excuse him," Jack said, shaking his head. "He's obsessed with things related to the medieval era or so he thinks because he watches too much television."

"Question," Sully continued, like he hadn't heard the other man. "Did each family have an outhouse or were they more like public ones for the whole neighborhood? And did you really, well, you know what with corn cobs?"

Gen blinked at him, wondering if she should pull out Bellum-ferrum or simply use her fist. She decided to do neither and shrugged off the questioning. "Okay, so what's the deal here?" She motioned around the shop. "Do they buy illegal items that you allow in exchange for covert criminal information?"

Sully brought his fisted hand up to his mouth, like covering a sob. "Jacky boy, I do believe our girl is growing up. She's learning the ways of our world so fast."

Jack pointed at his friend, looking at Gen. "See, he deserves to die first. And yes, the pawn shop buys illegal items and sells them. We allow it as long as they give us a full list of the items and where they go."

"Wow, this continues to baffle me." Gen shook her head. "But I'm starting to get it. Crime can't be erased. Instead, it has to be regulated. But that only works if done by someone who is good and has pure intentions."

Sully cut his eyes to his friend. "I think she's complimenting us. Is this right before the lioness pounces and tears out our throats?"

"I told you he had a death wish," Jack stated, continuing forward, waving for Gen to follow him. "There's another part to this pawn shop that we keep an eye on and allow. It's in the back."

CHAPTER FORTY-TWO

A GLIMPSE BEHIND THE LOCKED DOOR

Pawn of the Dead, Wilshire Boulevard, Los Angeles, California, United States

Jack led Gen to a door where a man with gray patchy hair stood, a shifty look in his eyes. The guy obviously guarding the door held up a hand as they approached, stopping the three of them.

"That's Phil," Sully said at Gen's side. "He's the owner of Pawn of the Dead and a real hoot."

"Can't you read the sign?" the shop owner asked, through a mouthful of missing and blackened teeth.

"Yeah, it says no concealed weapons," Sully argued, pointing at the handwritten sign. "And you can clearly see I have a sword, so there."

Jack shook his head at his friend, glancing back at Phil. "We're not going in. We just want to show our new Rogue Rider the operation. And what's up with the sign anyway, man? That's new. You having problems?"

"Oh, yeah," Phil howled. "I don't know if you lot have been taking it easy or what, but there are new goons popping up all over the place. Patrols by city police are down and with it, some riffraff has been circulating causing problems for me. I can't believe I'm saying this, but we could use more law enforcement in these parts. Just their presence seems to keep this kind of thing down."

Gen drew in a breath, thinking of the Commissioner of Los Angeles who was recently murdered. He would have been in charge of the police management. It seemed some of the concerns that the council had about the influx were coming to fruition.

"Man, Phil, that is alarming," Jack said, a cool and disarming tone to his voice. "We'll definitely look into it. I can plug in with some of our police contacts who we work with, but as you know, things have been shifting in the city."

"Because you lot have a new leader?" Phil asked, not seeming happy about this.

Jack and Sully exchanged tentative looks.

"It's hard to say," Jack finally replied, diplomatically.

"I bet this has to do with that Commissioner's death," Phil growled, nodding at Gen. "And this is your new Rogue Rider. She looks a whole lot better than the two of you. Can she be the one to check in with me?"

"That's a hard no, Phil," Jack said, pointing to the door. "But we would like to show her the scope of your operation. Can you open up for us?"

Phil nodded through a toothless grin at Gen, unlocking the unmarked door and opening it for them.

Through an open doorway, Gen caught a glimpse of what looked like a gambling ring. It was a stark contrast to the pawn shop's front. The room buzzed with the clinking of coins and the mechanical whirl of strange machines. Their lights flickered like fireflies captured in jars as wheels on their fronts spun.

Gamblers moved around the space, their faces illuminated intermittently by the machines' glow. Although this wasn't like the card and dice games she was used to seeing, Gen recognized the hidden world of gambling pulsing with risk and temptation. It seemed that time changed nothing, and people still loved the thrill of taking bets and chancing their fortune on odds.

"You allow the pawn shop to run an illegal gambling ring," Gen whispered to Jack.

He nodded. "And again, in exchange, Phil tells us about the community happenings. Gamblers, strange enough, are gossipers. It's a great place to get an idea of what's going on around in the city."

"Like with the delinquent law enforcement," Gen guessed.

He nodded, darkly, sharing the look of concern she felt nagging at her.

Phil, apparently thinking they'd had enough of a glimpse, ushered them back as he shut and locked the door again. Backing away from the room filled with tobacco smoke, Gen caught the face of one of the many clocks adorning the grimy walls. "Oh, shoot. I have another meeting to get to. Sophia set it up for me to help me complete the other impossible task Dwayne assigned me."

Sully shook his head. "You're a busy lady."

"Good luck," Jack said, offering her a tamed smile.

"Thanks for this," Gen said, backing for the door to the pawn shop. "One hour of shadowing down. Only five hundred and ninety-nine left."

Jack lowered his chin, looking her in the eyes. "Don't sweat the hours. As far as I'm concerned, if Dwayne asked, you're always by my side. Within a month you'll be done, and he will have to give you a case."

"Thanks." Gen paused, feeling a strange heat as she stared into his dark, blue eyes, like pools of ocean waters. "Well, then I better get to observing and cataloging magical animals."

Jack chuckled, pointing over his shoulder at Sully. "You can check the enchanted chimp off your list."

"Hey, I'm no monkey!" Sully complained.

"No, but you might have one's brain, dummy," Jack said, glancing over his shoulder at his friend with a grin. "Chimps aren't monkeys, you Neanderthal. They are apes."

"Yeah, whatever," Sully said, walking backwards. "Come on, let's finish up here, you gorilla. I want to get back to the Rogue Rider mansion so I can watch The Witcher."

Jack smirked, returning his gaze to Gen. "Do you see why he's obsessed with you? You're like his favorite fictional character."

"What's The Witcher?" Gen asked.

A laugh popped out of Jack's mouth. "I keep forgetting how much you don't know about this time and all. Don't worry, we'll fill in the gaps. If you ever get a free hour, then stop by my room at the Rogue Rider mansion and we'll watch some educational programming together."

Gen let out a long breath. "I'm a bit nervous about this television stuff."

Another laugh flew from Jack's mouth. "She nearly jumps between a dragon and Kodiak bear but watching TV makes her nervous." He shook his head. "You're something I've never seen before, Gen Beaufont."

She started walking backwards again, smiling at him. "Well, I am from a different time when things were…harsher."

A look of amusement sizzled in his blue eyes. "You can take the girl out of the medieval era, but you can't take the medieval out of the girl."

CHAPTER FORTY-THREE

A GIANT'S VIEW

<u>Rooftop, Downtown Los Angeles, California, United States</u>

Gen didn't know what to expect when she hurried up to the top of the building where she'd been told to meet a so-called magical creatures expert. According to Sophia, Bermuda Laurens was the person who had studied more magical creatures on the globe than anyone else besides their creator—Mama Jamba.

Of course, as with all things in Gen's life, she realized at once that Sophia forgot to mention a few things about this meeting. As she rushed out onto the rooftop that looked over Los Angeles, she was amazed by the meeting spot. It gave her amazingly contrasting views between the ones she'd seen of the city from the ground to now high above it on top of this strange, spiraling building.

Then she noticed that standing on the roof, just a few yards away and regarding her with indifference, was a giant. In her day, one didn't cross a giant's path without pulling out a sword. However, Gen simply froze, not having a sword and not knowing what Bellumferrum would become if she did yank it from her pocket.

Gen looked up at the woman with short, curly brown hair,

wearing brown pants and a button-up shirt and wondered if a tiny detail had been left out about the woman she was meeting. "You're Bermuda Laurens, aren't you?" Gen guessed.

The woman, who had quite masculine features and was very tall and wide without being obese, nodded. "Of course, I am. And based on your blonde hair and bad attitude, I can already tell that you're a Beaufont."

"My attitude…" Gen trailed away, thinking that it was best not to argue with this woman. And in all honesty, her attitude probably did come over as bad since she'd rushed over here, was a mess and was also looking at the giant with slight horror right then. "Yes, I'm Gen Beaufont."

"And, yes, I'm Bermuda Laurens," the giantess began, "The expert in magical creatures and the special consultant to the Beaufont family through the last several generations who has ensured they didn't perish from their own sarcastic natures."

"I don't remember being told that latter part," Gen said, through a measured breath.

"It's true," Bermuda assured. "The Beaufonts are both the best thing that's happened to justice and ironically their own downfall, if they aren't careful. They are a really diabolical assortment, but hopefully you're not as rebellious in nature as your relatives."

Gen simply grinned, firmly believing she was the worst behaving of them all.

"Well, then shall I show you a few of my birds while we wait for your dragon to arrive?" Bermuda asked. "He's fashionably late, like he belongs to the clan that is Liv Beaufont."

"He said that he would show up when we were ready for him," Gen imparted, never having met someone with this kind of demeanor. Bermuda was both warm and cold at the same time. She was hard and soft. She was mean and kind. Gen wasn't sure how to take her.

And then there was that whole her being a giantess which instinctively felt like someone she should run away from. But

Gen reminded herself that she'd simply grown up in a more primitive time when the races didn't mix. She'd already spent time with a gnome and a fae, two races that she never would have interacted with in the 15th century. Things were different now, and Gen needed to embrace that.

"That seems like a fitting thing for a dragon to say," Bermuda stated matter-of-factly. "And as much as I'm looking forward to meeting this ruler of dragons, I'll table my excitement and share with you other creatures of similar interest. I understand that you need to meet some magical animals to fulfill requirements, correct?"

"Yes, apparently, fifteen hundred," Gen muttered before brightening. "And that would be great. Thank you."

"This way then," the giantess led them to the far side of the rooftop where many aviaries were kept. It was an odd thing to see on the edges of one side of the building, with the many birds' voices filling the air, but it was also a delightful and welcoming surprise.

As Gen neared the edge of the building she was also greeted by another sight. Perched atop a downtown Los Angeles building, she beheld a city of contrasts. Below, the vibrant heartbeat of commerce and life, streets veined with the constant flow of cars, the air buzzing with the murmur of countless stories.

Skyscrapers pierced the sky, their glass facades reflecting the setting sun like beacons of modern ambition, while in their shadows, the forgotten corners whispered tales of grit and resilience. The scent of street food wafted up, mingling with the distant sea breeze, a reminder of nature's proximity to human endeavor.

The city stretched out before her, a mosaic of light and shadow and promise and challenge. From this vantage point, Gen could see the delicate balance of beauty and decay. It was a view that captivated and humbled, filled with the whimsy of dreams against the backdrop of reality.

CHAPTER FORTY-FOUR

BERMUDA'S AVIAN WONDERS

<u>Rooftop, Downtown Los Angeles, California, United States</u>

"As the author of the book, *Magical Creatures*, and the foremost expert on this and the last century on magical creatures, I keep an assortment of animals for study," Bermuda began, striding over to a large, enclosed aviary. She opened the door and ducked inside the compartment, looking about like…well, a giantess peeking into a tiny bird cage. When she retreated back out the way she came, she was holding a colorful bird with very large wings. The creature was composed of every shade of the rainbow scattered across its body. Its wings were long and strangely covered in flower petals as well as feathers.

"I present to you, the blooming cockatiel," Bermuda said, proudly running her eyes over the majestic and beautiful bird. "This creature will be a real answer to the problems of urban development which have overrun hillsides with concrete and manmade substances."

"How so?" Gen asked, instantly intrigued.

Bermuda gave her a knowing smile. "It's better to observe these things rather than explain them." She lifted her large hand into the air, releasing the colorful creature. It took flight, flapping its wings as it dove forward, flying over the rooftop. As it fluttered its wings, little seeds fell from its petal-like feathers, scattering to the area below, raining down.

Gen was instantly curious about this, especially since as the bird flew, more and more seeds dropped from its wings, like it had an unending supply. Then the most incredible thing occurred—from where the seeds landed, little flowers appeared on the ground below instantly. The blossoms sprang up from the concrete roof where they stood. Then as the bird progressed, the flowers sprouted on the other areas where it passed, like the balconies below and the road under that. The bird was literally instantly sprouting flowers with each beat of its wings.

Proudly, Bermuda turned to Gen. "Aren't magical creatures simply amazing?"

"They really are," she replied, smiling widely.

Bermuda gave her a look of surprise. "No sarcastic reply or joke? Are you sure you're a Beaufont?"

"I'm the first one," she answered at once. "Alongside my father. So yes."

"Well, I think I like you most so far," Bermuda said, turning and striding for another set of aviaries beside this one.

Gen followed, not sure if she should be happy for this compliment or defensive of her relatives.

"Over here, we have what's known as the hit song birds," Bermuda said, reaching into the aviary this time, not ducking into it. When she pulled back her hand, there perched on it was a single little brown bird. It was so plain in comparison to the bright and colorful blooming cockatiel that it was a little underwhelming.

"What's special about this magical creature?" Gen asked, looking at the tiny, plain animal and trying not to seem disappointed.

"This little bird gets more visitors from famous music producers and Hollywood superstars than any creature on the planet," Bermuda said proudly. "I don't think he cares for the attention, but his talent earns him it."

"You mean the people who make the music in this time period?" Gen asked, confused by these strange references.

"Exactly," Bermuda stated, holding up the bird. "You see, some birds sing nice melodies. Some have enchanting calls. But the hit song bird, well, every time she sings, it's a tune that will stop thousands in their tracks. It's so compelling that it's a song that's destined to be a hit."

"So, people who make the music study this bird and take its songs for the masses?" Gen asked, trying to understand.

Bermuda shook her head. "No, they steal it. They take the hit song bird's melody and reproduce it and make millions, never looking back. But that's how the music industry goes. They take the inspiration from nature and call it their own. We can't blame the lesser talented for not knowing how to make their own music. And really, if they don't know the joy of producing art on their own, then they are truly the ones suffering."

"Wow," Gen mused, not sure what to make of this poetic lesson that she never expected from the giantess who once she would have feared. Her life had truly changed and definitely in ways she'd never expected and most likely for the better—if she could just understand the conundrum that was transportation, clogging up the streets.

"Wow, indeed," Bermuda said dryly, turning and striding for yet another aviary.

Gen followed her, enjoying a soft wind that picked up, carrying her long braid around her shoulder and tickling her skin with a nice softness. When Bermuda went to open the door to the next aviary, she turned around, checking that Gen was at her back. She halted before pulling back the door, a look of surprise on her face.

"Oh, I see you've already found the next bird I was going to show you," Bermuda said, pointing to Gen's head.

She abruptly turned, thinking she was about to be attacked by some bird of prey or something. There was nothing there.

"What?" She spun around, facing the giantess again. "I don't see anything."

The woman sternly shook her head. "No, you wouldn't since the wind bird is invisible, but it's clearly beside you, kicking up that breeze you must no doubt feel."

Just then, Gen felt something brush up against her face—like a feather. She jerked to the side, peering at nothing with annoyance. "That's a bird? There's an invisible bird beside my head?"

Bermuda held up her hand and the breeze disappeared. "Not anymore. It's presently on me. But it was beside you." She proudly looked above her arm at what appeared to be nothing. "The wind bird is responsible for changes in weather patterns, scattering seeds and ruining outside events. Its wings, which you can't see, are quite impressive and produce a wind that people can feel for miles. It is quite the incredible bird, wouldn't you say?"

"It's what is responsible for wind?" Gen asked, confused.

Bermuda shook her head. "It's one of many things. Wind is also a natural phenomenon. But wind is created by people and butterflies and events and all sorts of other factors. But yes, the wind bird is one."

"That's fascinating," Gen mused, amazed by all that she'd learned that day.

"Quite." Bermuda looked up suddenly. "Oh, and look, here is another creature responsible for creating wind with its large wingspan. And isn't he the most amazing dragon one has ever witnessed?"

Gen looked up just as Emperor glided to a smooth landing atop the roof, looking as majestic and regal as ever.

CHAPTER FORTY-FIVE

MUSEUM MYSTERIES FROM ABOVE

<u>Rooftop, Downtown Los Angeles, California, United States</u>

The ruler of all dragons looked strangely out of place on the top of the modern skyscraper roof. His shimmering purple scales and golden chest and eyes were a stark contrast to the blue skies behind him, dotted with puffy white clouds. All around him, rectangular buildings made of metal and glass were starkly different than his angular shape and rippling form.

As Emperor folded in his wings and stood tall, appraising the aviaries, Bermuda made her way over to the dragon. Awe was written on her face, as if it was the first time she'd seen a creature like this, although she'd met many a dragon. Her mouth fell open and her eyes widened in fascination as she took in the magical creature that towered over even her.

"Bermuda Laurens, your reputation precedes you," Emperor said, his deep voice carrying in the wind, most likely made by the invisible birds. "I have heard of your research through the ages and how much good and awareness it has brought to the world."

Bermuda bowed her head slightly in a show of respect. That wasn't something that Gen guessed the giantess did often. But then, she had never met or been complimented by the ruler of all dragons.

"And you, Emperor, are as incredible in form as people describe you," Bermuda stated, pausing when only a short distance from the dragon. "Your brothers and sisters knew of your existence and kept it a secret from us. They must be very grateful that you have joined them, providing the rule they have surely lacked."

Emperor cut his golden gaze to Gen, a knowing look in his eyes. "Some are happier about it than others. It was quite the shock when they learned we were demon dragon and rider."

Bermuda looked sideways at Gen. "That is simply a term to categorize. It really shouldn't have a negative connotation."

"And yet it does," Emperor stated. "Demons are soul-sucking creatures. We are associated with them."

"You manage that which angel riders and dragons would never have the audacity to control," Bermuda countered. "And under your rule, I expect that the dragons will make progress in a world that could benefit from the age-old wisdom of the dragons. Tell me, if you deem me worthy, what are your powers, Emperor?"

"I do indeed find you, Bermuda Laurens, to be qualified to know such information," Emperor replied in a dignified voice. "I have telepathy, psychic insights and mind control."

A gasp flew from the giantess's mouth. "Oh, that is very impressive."

"Oh, and I'm also incredibly strong and have fire," Emperor added, a slight lightness to his tone.

Gen laughed. "Yeah, but he can't beat me at arm wrestling."

He actually grinned at his rider. "Not yet, but I will."

Bermuda shook her head, seeming perplexed by all this new information. "Would it be permissible for me to get your measurements, Emperor?" She then added. "For research purposes, of course."

"Oh, too bad, I was hoping you were making him a pretty dress," Gen teased.

His small smile faded. "That's not funny and yes, Bermuda, you're more than welcome to do so." Emperor redirected his gaze to Gen. "I noticed some suspicious activity on the east side of this building. Why don't you make yourself useful and check it out."

"I can multitask, inspect, and think of more jokes, you know," she replied, striding over in the direction he indicated. Gen saw immediately what Emperor was referring to. There were a series of black, unmarked cars on a nearby road, next to a rather large building. The street was closed down and there was no law enforcement anywhere in sight. Actually, now that Gen thought about it, the police presence was starkly understated in the downtown area, which seemed strange for a city this size.

"This large white building here," Gen began, looking over her shoulder at the giantess next to the dragon. "What is it?"

"That's a museum," Bermuda muttered, busy with the task at hand of taking measurements of Emperor.

"Right," Gen said, returning her attention to the building. She didn't know much about this modern world. And what was going on below could be perfectly normal. But something told her by the way the men in all black next to the vehicles moved that they were doing something wrong. They had an air of paranoia about them. Also, if Emperor had noticed something, she assumed it was because his psychic intuition picked up on a disturbance.

Gen knew that as a Rogue Rider she was supposed to manage crime—allowing some of it. But there had to be a line between supervising and intervening. And something in her told her that whatever was happening below wasn't on anyone's radar and might need her involvement.

CHAPTER FORTY-SIX

JUSTICE OVER NACHOS

<u>Gracias Madre Restaurant, West Hollywood, California, United States</u>

"He said what to you?" Liv asked, taking a sip of her bright green margarita, garnished with a cucumber and a jalapeno.

Gen sipped her own drink, something orange and fruity with pineapple and berries. "Dwayne Stone said that I had to oversee over three-thousand magical creatures now. But it was only because Bermuda released all the birds while we were there for their nighttime flight and once I watched them all fly away with Emperor, she said I'd just observed over fifteen hundred species in one go. Apparently each of the exotic birds are so different that they classify as their own types. Anyway, when I told my boss I was done with that task, he was utterly pissed and assigned me more to do. He's never going to let me have a case."

Liv nodded, sitting back in her seat. "I've seen this before. He's afraid of you being in the field because as soon as you are, you're going to mess something up for him. He's hiding something. Something you'd sniff out."

Gen leaned forward, not wanting to be overheard in the busy, fancy Mexican restaurant. "I did see something today. Something that Emperor alerted me to. We think that there's a heist that's about to happen at a museum in Los Angeles."

Liv rubbed her hands together. "That's it. That's what you need to intervene on. Find out why it isn't on the Rogue Riders' radar. Because if something bad was happening of that magnitude then Sophia would have known about it. If Dwayne doesn't, then there's something sketchy about that guy. Either he's really bad at his job, or he's corrupt at it. From what I've seen of him, it's hard to say which one it could be. There's so much ego at play in Dwayne that he could be both incompetent and corrupt."

The waitress arrived with two plates of identical servings. One for Liv and one for Gen. They were apparently something called nachos, although Gen had never had them and didn't know what she was staring at presently.

They appeared to be little, thin triangles of crispy bread covered in melty cheese and an assortment of toppings. Based on the look on Liv's face, they were the best thing ever.

"Oh, and now we're in business," Liv said, settling back as the food was placed in front of them. "Get ready for your first experience of nachos. It will blow your mind."

"How do I eat these?" Gen asked, staring down at her plate as if it were a complex math equation.

"With a smile," Liv replied, picking up a piece from a non-covered edge and lifting the weighty portion to her mouth, pulling it away from its brethren. She engulfed the food, chewing with utter delight. "Go on then. I get to watch you do this. Just like a baby taking its first step."

"I'm not a baby," Gen fired.

"Then are you going to intervene on that museum heist or are you going to be a baby?" Liv fired back.

Gen thought for a moment. "I don't know. My boss pretty much hates me and will never give me a case. I'm not sure that I need more heat on me."

"Well, you are a Rogue Rider," Liv countered. "So can I give you a bit of advice?"

Gen nodded, looking between the very enticing nachos and her relative across the table. "Yeah, go for it."

"Go rogue, Gen," Liv encouraged. "Be what you are. Go out on your own. If that sorry jerk won't let you work a case, then throw down your badge and take one on your own. You never need permission to uphold justice. You only need a dragon and a weapon, and you've got both."

Gen grinned, grateful that all these centuries later, there was a Beaufont just like her. Someone so bold and good that she could feel like she wasn't alone—for once. "Okay, you're right. I'm going to do it. Emperor and I are going to. We're going to intervene in this museum heist. We're going to uphold justice."

Liv nodded, encouragingly. "But first, you're going to eat nachos. Seriously, I need to see your face. Try them."

"Right," Gen said, more afraid of the plate of chaos in front of her than armed men. She reached down with a tentative hand and peeled one of the chips away from the stack, finding that it didn't want to separate from the rest, but that it looked and smelled very appetizing as it did.

Then Gen took a bite of the vehicle full of goodness and found it to be the best thing about this time period. It was an assortment of flavors all layered upon a surface and delivered in the perfect way, atop a crispy bottom. Gen realized then that there might be other things in the modern era that would rock her world—and she welcomed it.

CHAPTER FORTY-SEVEN

DISGUISES AND DOWNTOWN DISCOVERIES

<u>Los Angeles County Museum of Art, Wilshire Boulevard, Los Angeles, California, United States</u>

From their perch atop a nearby rooftop, Gen and her dragon gazed down upon the bustling scene surrounding the Los Angeles County Museum of Art (LACMA). The striking, modernist structure complemented the urban landscape, its angular lines and gleaming facades a tribute to the city's embrace of contemporary architecture.

The exterior of the building was a patchwork of materials, with sleek metal panels interspersed with expansive glass walls that reflected the shimmering afternoon sunlight. It created a dazzling display that caught the eye of passersby.

In front of the museum, the iconic Urban Light installation commanded attention. It was a collection of restored antique streetlamps standing in perfect formation. They were like a group of glowing watchmen guarding the entrance.

Gen was immediately grateful that Liv and Sophia had given her an overview of the museum area and what she'd be seeing during this investigation. Studying the maps and getting the insights from the other two women helped give Gen references and assurances that she and Emperor could go on this rogue mission alone. She wasn't sure what they'd find, but a feeling deep at her core told her that something was askew.

The traffic on Wilshire Boulevard ebbed and flowed, a constant stream of vehicles. The cars' engines hummed and horns occasionally pierced the air, while pedestrians navigated the sidewalks, their chatter and laughter mingling with the sounds of the city.

Street vendors lined the edge of the building. Their colorful carts and savory and sweet wares tempting visitors with the scents of sizzling hot dogs, roasted nuts and fresh churros.

To the west, the Broad Contemporary Art Museum stood as a striking counterpoint to LACMA's main building. Gen didn't know what contemporary art was but Liv had described it as "trash put in a picture frame." Although Gen thought that was probably a bit of a harsh and oversimplified explanation, she sort of understood what Liv meant when she described modern art as "understated ridiculousness."

The Broad Museum, with its bold red exterior and undulating roofline, was like a visual exclamation point against the blue California sky. The Resnick Pavilion, with its elegant, glass-enclosed spaces, offered a glimpse into the museum's extensive collections. According to Sophia, who had more tolerance for different artwork, it was filled with treasures beckoning to those with a thirst for knowledge and culture.

As Gen and Emperor surveyed the scene below, they couldn't help but feel a sense of anticipation. Both shared the feeling that amidst the beauty and bustle of this cultural hub, a mystery awaited.

Gen and her dragon exchanged a knowing glance, their bond stronger than before—and growing with each day.

"Are you picking up on anything nefarious below?" she asked, looking at the purple dragon sitting by the edge of the rooftop, staring down, the same as her. However, she knew that Emperor saw the world differently than her. He felt the world through voices, hearing things people only thought to themselves. Not only that, but the ruler of dragons saw the future, but not with accuracy that could be fully trusted. It was more like shades of events that could happen, if everything went on the same path.

Emperor closed his glowing golden eyes, going within, taking a moment to sense the environment and people below. When he opened them, there was a new intensity to his gaze. "There are many outsiders below who know they don't belong. They aren't who they say they are."

"What are they doing?" Gen asked, noticing that the black, unmarked vans had all lined up at the back of the museum in a narrow alleyway, like they were hiding.

Her dragon shook his head, appearing a bit frustrated. "That I don't know. I see flashes of the future that could tell me, but sharing those visuals with you could only complicate things."

She sucked in a breath. "Seeing the future has to be very confusing."

"It really is, and especially so if I told you everything I saw about something like this," Emperor explained. "It's like me giving you a random puzzle piece but you don't have any of the other pieces to put together and then it could turn out to not even be a puzzle that involves you. It's better if you go and collect some intel. Then you can report it to me and I can see if it fits in with what I'm seeing."

Gen nodded, liking this idea of her doing a reconnaissance mission. She glanced down at her outfit. "Good thing that Sophia put this disguise on me."

Anticipating that Gen might have to go undercover, Sophia, who was apparently brilliant with disguise magic, put her in new clothes. Gen felt very strange wearing a modern linen black suit. She'd never worn such strange pants called slacks or a crisp white button-up shirt and dark blazer. Gen felt very futuristic in this outfit, but Sophia assured her that it was a plain dress that made her blend into the professional world.

"Okay, I'll go down there and investigate and then we can decide what to do next," Gen said, making her way for the edge of the building.

"Sounds good, but one piece of advice," Emperor offered, a cunning tone to his voice.

"What's that?" Gen said, peering down at the road below.

He nodded at the center of the rooftop where there was a stairwell and door. "Take the stairs. I sense you're about to scale the side of the building."

"What's wrong with that?" she challenged, her hands on her hips.

"Modern-day professionals take the elevator, not climb to work," he replied.

Gen sighed. "Fine. But can't you give me a lift?"

He shook his head. "Again, usually people arrive to work in cars or on foot and not on dragons."

"Just promise me that we'll never conform to these boring ways of the modern world, walking to work when flying and climbing are so much better."

The purple dragon grinned at her. "I promise."

CHAPTER FORTY-EIGHT

THE ART OF DECEPTION

<u>Los Angeles County Museum of Art, Wilshire Boulevard, Los Angeles, California, United States</u>

Not only had Sophia helped to disguise Gen, but she'd given her a fake identification card and called in some favors. Those had given Gen a plausible way to get behind the scenes and find out what was going on in the museum and if it was indeed truly nefarious. Thanks to Sophia's ties, Gen had the title of the Exhibitions Specialist for the Smithsonian Institute. She also had an appointment with the Los Angeles County Museum of Art's Director and Security Director.

Although going undercover really worried Gen, due to her limited knowledge of the modern world, she had been coached heavily by Liv and Sophia. Also, she had Emperor in her head and he knew more about this world than those who had been living in it for the last several decades.

What really threw Gen for a loop when she approached the museum was the banners advertising the current exhibit.

No way, she said in her head, talking to Emperor.

Life loves irony, he said with a snicker, having seen what she had using scrying—remote viewing through her eyes.

The current exhibit here is of medieval artifacts, she stated. *Is this a joke?*

At least you'll be able to tell if they're authentic items, he teased.

It's probably my damn stuff, she protested.

Don't take it, he warned. *That's stealing and that's wrong.*

Unless you're taking your stuff back, she argued. *Or if I'm taking from the rich and giving to the poor.*

Just find out what's going on in there and behave, he said.

Fine, Gen chirped, focusing on the tasks ahead.

As Gen stepped into the museum, her senses were immediately overwhelmed by the stark contrast between the sleek, modern interior and the ancient artifacts that surrounded her. The exhibit hall was a vast, open space with high ceilings and pristine white walls. It was a far cry from the stone and timber structures of her native 15th century London.

Glass display cases lined the large room, each one housing a treasure from a previous era. Their presence seemed to fill the air with the weight of history. It was almost a trick on Gen's mind, seeing things that she knew from her old life in her new one.

The time traveler's eyes were drawn to a beautifully illuminated manuscript in a case. Its pages were richly filled with vibrant colors and intricate illustrations that danced across the parchment. It was such poetic evidence of the skill and devotion of the medieval artisans.

Nearby, a set of gleaming armor stood guard. Its polished metal reflected the soft lighting and evoked memories for Gen of brave knights she once knew who wore such armor into battle. The scent of aged leather and ancient parchment mingled with the cool, conditioned air, created an atmosphere that was at once foreign and familiar to Gen's medieval sensibilities.

As she moved through the exhibit, her fingers itched to touch the relics of her own time. Desperately, she wanted to feel the rough texture of a tapestry or the smooth surface of a pottery chalice. Each item she passed felt like a tangible link to the world she had left behind. But Gen reminded herself that the medieval era was never her time—this one was. The sooner she stopped time traveling into her past, the sooner she progressed fully into her future.

The gentle hum of the museum's modern systems, the soft footfalls of other visitors, and the occasional hushed whisper all faded into the background as Gen lost herself in the wonder of these ancient objects. She marveled at the delicate beauty of a stained-glass window, its colors casting a kaleidoscope of light across the floor. The dragonrider, in disguise as a curator, paused before a carved wooden chest. Its intricate designs spoke of the pride and craftsmanship that had gone into its creation.

For a moment, Gen felt a pang of homesickness, a longing for the familiar sights and sounds of the era she once knew. However, as she looked around at the care and reverence with which these artifacts were displayed, she felt a sense of comfort knowing that the legacy of that time lived on.

Thankfully, it had been preserved and celebrated in this strange, new world. The exhibit was a bridge between the past and the present. This was a nice reminder that the human spirit, with its capacity for beauty, innovation and storytelling, endured across the centuries, connecting Gen to her roots and to the countless generations that had come before.

"Miss," a woman called at Gen's back, interrupting her reverie and the quiet in the open space.

Turning, Gen found a woman dressed similarly to her, in a navy blazer and slacks, striding in her direction. "Your tickets? You passed right through without showing one."

"Oh, right," Gen said, pulling out the identification card that Sophia had forged for her. She'd forgotten how this strange, modern world worked with all these provisions on admissions into each place. It seemed one had to show a reason to be just about anywhere public. "I have an appointment with the Director and Security Director." She flashed the badge, worried that her nervousness over the lie would betray her.

"Of course," the woman said, nodding as if expecting this information. She then lifted a microphone on a wire snaking down from her earpiece. "The Director's appointment is here."

She smiled at Gen. "They'll be here in just a moment. Please feel free to look around."

Gen nodded, turning to look at her possessions or what definitely resembled them. There was a vase in a glass case that Gen could have sworn used to sit in the corner of her bedroom. She leaned in closer, reading the placard next to the vase.

It read:

"12th Century. Venice, Italy. Used for holding holy water in religious ceremonies."

"Tanya Shaw?" a man asked at Gen's back. She tensed, knowing that was the name that she was supposed to respond to —her fake identity.

Gen turned to find two men standing behind her. They were both dressed in the same starched kind of suit as hers, although theirs were more masculine.

"I'm Scott Bernard, the Director of the Los Angeles County Museum of Art," the first man, who was short and smiled easily, said, extending a hand to her. His greeting was warm and his eyes bright with enthusiasm.

"Nice to meet you," she said, shaking his hand.

"And this is my Director of Security, Hamilton Dixon," Scott continued, indicating the man beside him. In contrast, this man seemed cold and rigid with a tight stare in his gray eyes. His black hair was pushed back and appeared wet with gel.

"Hello, thank you for meeting with me," Gen said, also shaking Hamilton Dixon's hand.

"It's a bit unorthodox for me to meet with curators," the Security Director said, sounding annoyed and impatient.

Gen had been coached on this by Liv and Sophia. "Well, I

need to be assured that all security measures are in place for the loan that we're to discuss between your museum and the Smithsonian."

"Of course, and Hamilton can definitely relieve any of your concerns," Scott said in an upbeat voice. "We take security very seriously here at the Los Angeles County Museum of Art."

Gen pursed her lips. "I hope you take it more seriously than getting your historical facts right."

Scott Bernard's mouth fell open in shock. "Whatever do you mean?"

She pointed to the vase she'd been studying. "This piece, for instance, is from the 14th century based on its craftsmanship and style."

Scott blinked in confusion. "You must be mistaken."

"I assure you that I'm not," Gen countered. "The glazing techniques on the object weren't used until that time period. Also, the vase is from Bruges, Belgium based on the clay used, which wouldn't be available in Italy."

"You know that by just studying the vase through the glass?" Hamilton Dixon asked, arching an eyebrow at her, skeptically.

"I know that because medieval artifacts are my specialty," Gen stated. "Which is how I know this vase wasn't used in religious ceremonies but rather for storing and serving wine."

"Are you sure?" Scott asked.

"I'm certain," Gen said with confidence. "How long do you plan to have this exhibit here? Maybe I can help you to fix any more inconsistencies."

"For at least three months," Scott said.

"Good, that gives us time," Gen said. "And I noticed that there were some vans around the perimeter of the building. What is happening there?"

"Oh, we're moving this exhibit down to the eastern side of the museum," Hamilton answered. "It's a more secure area."

He is lying, Gen said in her head, talking to Emperor. She worked to keep her face neutral.

You can read the lie on his face, Emperor said in her head. *But I sense it in his thoughts and can confirm, you're correct.*

But why is he lying? she said, needing more information.

"When will this move be taking place?" Gen asked and then added, "Maybe I can help."

"That won't be necessary," Hamilton said, narrowing his eyes at her. "We have all the arrangements in place and everything will be seamlessly moved tonight."

Again, Gen sensed he was holding something back. She was, after all, the one who programmed Jude and Diabolos and knew all the ways people were hiding things and being untruthful. She just didn't know what the Director of Security for the Los Angeles County Museum of Art was lying about or why. But she was definitely going to find out.

"Very well, then I'll return once the collection is in place and help with identifying false information," Gen said, diplomatically.

Scott enthusiastically clapped his hands together. "That would be lovely. Now how about we show you around and then you can hopefully consider our museum for some of the Smithsonian's prized collections in the future."

Gen clasped her hands behind her back. Nodded. And allowed the two men to lead her forward on a tour. She didn't know what was going on behind the scenes of this museum, but she was going to find out. If the medieval artifacts were moving around tonight, Gen and Emperor would be on the scene to find out exactly what was happening.

CHAPTER FORTY-NINE

WEAPONS, ARTIFACTS AND HIDDEN AGENDAS

<u>Los Angeles County Museum of Art, Wilshire Boulevard, Los Angeles, California, United States</u>

From the rooftop, Gen's eagle vision, enhanced by the chi of the dragon, made it so that she could see everything on the ground with pristine crispness. Even in the dark of the night, she easily made out the various unmarked vehicles that were lined up outside the backside of the western loading docks of the Los Angeles County Museum of Art. The men stationed around and charging into the open doors were clear in her vision. Not just them, but also the weapons they held and wore.

"Why do those men need those guns to move ancient medieval artifacts?" Gen asked, watching as the men on the ground looked around like they were moving something very sinister, rather than museum items.

"Maybe they are afraid they are going to conjure the spirits of a medieval warrior with a bad attitude who tries to chop their head off for talking out of turn," Emperor offered, looking down at her from his perch beside her on the rooftop.

"I feel like you're referring to me," she said with a growl.

"Maybe I am," the dragon said coyly, referencing a time in a bar in the 1400s when Gen got herself in a little trouble. Emperor had access to all of Gen's memories once they magnetized to each other in 1420. Since then, nothing had been a secret from the dragon and he often used it as evidence against her.

"That was one time and that guy deserved it for not having manners," Gen refuted. "And I didn't chop any heads off. Just with my words and maybe I threw some fists, but he totally deserved it."

"Did all of his mates as well?" Emperor countered, playfully.

"Well, they tried to defend him," she argued.

"Against a girl, no less," Emperor scoffed. "And when they thought they could simply hold you back and you turned it into a brawl, well things got out of hand didn't they?"

"Sort of…" she replied, cutting her eyes to the side.

"Well, so these guys below must have brought weapons, afraid the ghost of that girl was coming back for her belongings. Can you blame them?" he asked slyly.

"That's not why they have weapons," Gen sneered. "They are up to something and I'm going to figure it out." She watched, taking in every move of every man below and the cargo of medieval artifacts they were moving.

Gen stiffened when she caught sight of a man below who she recognized. "That's the Director of Security."

Emperor nodded. "Hamilton Dixon, the one you suspected of lying."

"He definitely was," Gen said. "So what did you pick up in his head or about the events going on in the Los Angeles County Museum of Art?"

"I can't say entirely since some of it is flashes of the future," Emperor answered. "But I can tell you that this Director of Security, Hamilton Dixon, is a new hire. He was recently put into place by the new Commissioner for Los Angeles and he has been making a lot of changes to security protocol at LACMA."

Gen cut her eyes to the purple dragon. "Why? And why is that what you're willing to share?"

He sighed. "I can read minds and see the future. If I told you everything I hear and see, then it would be like reading the end of a book without having read the previous chapters. You would know how things end but not how things got there. That would be very confusing for you and probably mess everything up. Also, most of what I read in people's minds is just noise and telling you everything would be a waste of your time."

"So why is it relevant that the Director of Security, this Hamilton Dixon, is new, then?" Gen questioned, watching as the man in question gave orders to the various men on the ground below.

"Because I get the impression that he works for the new Commissioner and not the City of Los Angeles," Emperor answered.

Gen's eyes widened as she rotated to look directly at Emperor. "You believe that the new Commissioner is corrupt..."

"I think so," Emperor stated. "Based on what I've read from Hamilton Dixon's thoughts."

"Which means that whoever murdered the old Commissioner for Los Angeles was behind all this," Gen said, narrowing her eyes on the scene below. "But why? What's going on in the City of Los Angeles behind the scenes? If this place is the stronghold for keeping crime at bay, then what's really happening?"

"That's what we have to figure out," Emperor said, his glowing gold eyes full of wisdom. "But I think the leads start here. I sense something about to happen in the museum that needs our attention."

Gen leaned forward, watching as the armed men loaded a crate of medieval artifacts into the back of a van. "If they are moving the exhibit down to the eastern side, then why do they need transportation?"

"And why is the van driving away?" Emperor questioned.

Gen nearly tumbled over the side of the building, leaning over the edge to keep an eye on one of the vans as it drove off the property, speeding away. "What the hell? Why are they going that way?"

"Because they are stealing the artifacts," Emperor stated, stationed beside her. "I'd felt in their minds that they were thieves, but I needed you to get on the ground before and find more information. Now this all confirms what I suspected. They aren't moving the medieval artifacts as the Director of the Los Angeles County Museum of Art believes. This is a heist."

CHAPTER FIFTY

THE ARTIFACT AVENGER

In the darkened embrace of a back alley, Gen descended like a shadow upon the thieves stealing her history. The dragonrider's form was a blur against the stark contrast of the moonlit theft. She landed from the second story of an adjacent building soundlessly, in a low crouched position.

However, the closest man in black spotted her, pulling a pistol, like the coward that he was, instead of fighting with his hands. Gen sprang up at once, throwing a roundhouse kick across the man's arm as he extended it with the gun. The clang of the metal when the weapon fell to the concrete alerted the others in the area to the disturbance—all eyes shooting straight to Gen.

The man she had just assaulted jerked his gaze to the fallen weapon in the distance, and then to the men down the long alleyway. Then deciding that he wasn't going to win this fight against this woman dressed in black, he turned and fled for the closest van, diving into the back where the doors were wide open. At once he pulled them closed, screaming to someone in the front.

Apparently, not wanting a fight either, many of the other men scattered like rats into the vans. The engines of the vehicles revved right before they peeled out, shooting exhaust onto the scene. Gen turned her attention to the other men who were backing for the museum, having been left behind by their "friends."

Facing the strange medieval warrior who appeared to have come to take back her heirlooms, they retreated. Each of the cowards darted through a large roll-up door where they'd been unloading the artifacts from the Los Angeles County Museum of Art. Gen sighed, wondering if she really seemed that intimidating. Then she caught sight of something glowing over her shoulder and turned to find that Emperor had soundlessly landed at her back, a menacing gleam in his eyes.

"I had this," she muttered over her shoulder to the dragon who had definitely been what scared the men away instead of fighting.

"And I had your back," Emperor stated in a deep voice. "Hamilton Dixon ran into the museum. He's the key to finding out who is behind this and what's really going on. Go after him."

"Fine, keep an eye on things out here and scorch any other thieves who try and escape," she ordered, taking off into the back of the museum.

In a relentless pursuit after the thieves, Gen's footsteps were a silent promise of retribution. She navigated the labyrinth of exhibits, listening for the men and the direction they'd gone. Cautiously, she approached a corner ahead, aware that someone could jump out and attack her. However, these men appeared bent on fleeing, rather than fighting.

Gen's instincts guided her through the narrow corridors and around the many walls full of empty cases. The place that had been filled with medieval artifacts that afternoon was now ransacked. Many of the items were gone or bundled up in cases in the middle of the larger halls.

Although Gen wasn't sure how many valuables had been

stolen from the museum, she was going to find them all and return them to their place. This mission just got personal. If Gen didn't get to have her family's heirlooms then the people of the world would sure as hell get to see them on display in the museum. Thieves would not profit from them.

Just as Gen had this conviction, she sped into the first main room full of glass cases, many of them half occupied. The artifacts that had been emptied were all sitting on the plastic tarps, ready to be wrapped up and transported.

"Hurry! Hurry," Hamilton Dixon yelled, waving his arms rapidly. "Grab what you can and get out the door!"

When Gen sprinted into the room, she halted, narrowing her eyes at the man on the far side of the large hall. He froze too. As did all the thieves holding various priceless objects.

"You!" he growled, his eyes full of hostility. "You don't work for the Smithsonian."

"And you don't work for Scott Bernard," Gen spat back. "Who do you work for?"

"Wouldn't you like to know," he countered, pointing a finger at her. "Get her so that we can get out of here!"

The men closest to Gen, holding artifacts, hurled the objects in her direction. She shot her hands into the air, using a freezing spell immediately, making the objects suspend in mid-air where she lowered them gently to the floor, unharmed.

"Not with the priceless artifacts, you fools!" Hamilton yelled, his face flushing furiously red. "And she's a magician! Use your guns!"

Before the men could pull their guns, Gen made a defiant sweep of her hand, magically sending a blast of wind through the air to buy herself some time. It hit them with a gale-like force, thankfully not touching the artifacts beside her but nearly knocking the men reaching for their guns off their feet.

That gave Gen the time she needed for her next move. Instantly, she grabbed for Bellumferrum, telepathically calling for the enigmatic cube's help. Like before, she didn't know what it would become, only that it would read her dangerous situation and become the thing that would help her most. For a split second, Gen worried that the Weapon of War would become a gun to combat these men—she desperately didn't want to fight fire with fire.

To her shock, Bellumferrum transformed into a metal can with a spigot on the top. Instantly, she intuitively knew it was something called an air horn. And thankfully, the Weapon of War told her how to use it which simply involved smashing the button on the top. That's where the inside knowledge stopped though and Gen had no idea what to expect when she pressed the button.

For that reason, the deafening noise that shot through the air nearly made Gen's heart jump out of her chest. Thankfully it shocked all the men too, making them freeze. The excruciatingly loud noise that cut through the air was joined by more commotion as the empty glass cases in the museum burst, shards flying all over the floors, making a cacophony of sounds. This was instantly followed by a loud siren as red lights started strobing and the alarms rang overhead.

"She's triggered the backup alarm!" Hamilton yelled, motioning toward the door. "Get out of here! The police will be called!"

All the men abandoned the fight, running for the door, Hamilton in the lead. Gen slipped Bellumferrum back into her pocket, the object already resuming its cube shape. Launching herself forward, Gen hoped to catch the men before they got away. What she really needed to do was get a hold of Hamilton Dixon—then she was going to beat him until he spilled his secrets.

As she vaulted over the obstacles in her path, Gen's gaze locked with Hamilton's. He'd turned back to look at her through the glass doors. The once-trusted Director of Security now revealed as a traitor, narrowed his gaze at her, shaking his head with fury before spinning around and taking off. She knew all too well that she'd ruined everything for him, but that was only the beginning. Gen promised to really bring that man down and whoever he was working for since it obviously wasn't the Director of LACMA.

The villains fled the museum, running for their steel chariots. They disappeared into large black vans, speeding away at once, the doors still open as they clambered in over each other. Hamilton jumped into a bright yellow sleek car that was long and low to the ground. It was much sexier than the bulky vans, its engine purring when he started it before tearing off down the road, after the other fleeing vehicles.

Gen emerged through the grand entrance, a lone warrior against the tide, her resolve as unyielding as the artifacts she vowed to protect. The night air crackled with tension as Gen looked around for her options.

From the rooftops, an elegant purple dragon as dark as the night landed with a swoosh and clatter of claws on the concrete. With his wings extended and a fierce expression of rebellion, Emperor looked back, over his shoulder at Gen. There was a glint of majesty in his gold eyes. "Need a ride?"

"I do," she said, her heart palpitating with relief and excitement. Gen launched herself forward, throwing one leg around Emperor's back as she slid easily into the saddle and hunched down low, ready for the take off and a nonstop pursuit through the streets of Los Angeles.

CHAPTER FIFTY-ONE
URBAN OBSTACLE COURSE

<u>Wilshire Boulevard, Los Angeles, California, United States</u>

As the getaway vehicles sped off into the night, Gen, using only her mind, urged Emperor to stay hot on their tail. She knew this was their only chance to catch the thieves. The City of Los Angeles, with its congested, narrow streets and many obstacles, would either serve as an ally, helping them to catch Hamilton Dixon, or it would be their very undoing.

Leaving the sirens and shattered glass of the Los Angeles County Museum of Art behind, Gen kept her eyes honed on the yellow car whipping around corners ahead. In front of Hamilton's vehicle were the black vans, their tires screeching, giving away their progress with each turn. The sights that Gen and Emperor passed were dizzying, speeding by as they flew between buildings, through the tight streets full of cars and people on the sidewalks.

Gen was all too aware of the stares and attention they were getting. Although the modern world was used to magic and crazy sights, a purple dragon racing after speeding vehicles was still quite out of the ordinary. It would be obvious to anyone on the perimeter that there was a chase happening and many held up their mobile devices of devotion and took pictures as they flew by.

The pair glided just high enough to keep the yellow car and vans ahead of it in view. However, it put them at a dangerous height, in line with many obstacles like street lights, lamp posts, and wires that traversed precariously across the road, up high. The height of objects like signs and awnings were meant to be out of pedestrian and vehicles' ways, but they were creating quite the obstacles for Emperor to navigate around.

Still, Gen didn't want to risk flying higher and not being able to catch the fleeing villains. Once she and Emperor gained on them, she planned to blast them to a full stop, trapping the thieves and getting to the bottom of what happened at the museum. Corruption was at play and it felt like something dark and sinister hiding under the surface. As a Rogue Rider, Gen policed criminals, but they could only do that if it was in their view. Whatever Hamilton Dixon was up to was definitely happening under the radar and that was simply unacceptable.

The bond between rider and dragon surged with electrifying intensity as they rocketed after their prey. The dragon's scales gleamed beneath the neon glow of Wilshire Boulevard's iconic signs, their reflections dancing across his iridescent hide like a kaleidoscope of urban magic.

"We have to get that yellow contraption," Gen urged, speaking out loud but also in Emperor's head.

It's a sports car, Emperor replied telepathically. *And it's really fast and turns more narrowly than I can.*

Ahead, Hamilton's sports car had abruptly spun to the left, swerving around a large structure that halted without warning.

"Watch out for the big metal box!" Gen yelled, ducking down, as Emperor flew up higher to avoid colliding with the obstacle.

It's a truck, Gen, Emperor replied in her head, clearing the structure and diving back down, flying low. *Can you say truck?*

Gen nearly choked on the adrenaline as soon as she realized

they hadn't crashed. She let out a breath, grateful to see that Hamilton Dixon hadn't gotten away and was up ahead, still in view. Thankfully traffic had worked in their favor, slowing the sports car's progress, giving Gen and the dragon a chance to catch up.

Emperor banked sharply, narrowly avoiding a collision with the towering glass façade of the Petersen Automotive Museum. The sports car below swerved erratically to evade capture. It nearly hit several cars in its attempts to not slow through lights. Hamilton's sports car actually trespassed onto the sidewalk, nearly mowing down several people who thankfully dove out of the way of the out-of-control vehicle's path.

The dragon's wingbeats pounded the air, echoing the relentless rhythm of Gen's heart as they dove beneath the arching streetlights. The rush of wind and adrenaline was a dizzying cocktail in her veins. Onward they surged, past the glittering storefronts of designer boutiques and the bustling energy of sidewalk cafes. The city's vibrancy was a blur of color and motion beneath them.

Hamilton's daring moves appeared to be paying off, the sports car speeding ahead, gaining distance. His tires squealed—a mocking sound to his progress, like he was rubbing it in the dragon and rider's faces.

"He's getting away!" Gen yelled, gripping the reins even tighter like that might make her dragon go faster.

In a daring maneuver, Emperor corkscrewed through the air, dodging a billboard that loomed like a colossal lookout. The sign's flickering images were a fractured mosaic of consumerism. The figures on the sign seemed offended that the pair nearly knocked into them.

The near collision sent Emperor off course slightly, nearly careening into a building. He over-corrected, dipping down low. To recover he blasted forward at super speed, making incredible progress. At that same moment, something on the road ahead slowed Hamilton Dixon's sports car, putting him straight in Emperor's path.

The dragon's tail lashed out, sending a shockwave of force that crumpled the hood of the yellow sports car. The vehicle careened into the unforgiving embrace of a lamppost. With a triumphant roar, Emperor unleashed a torrent of flames, the inferno engulfing the road before the Director of Security's sports car, trapping the vehicle in a cage of fire.

CHAPTER FIFTY-TWO

THE FRAGILITY OF MODERN MAN

<u>Downtown Los Angeles, California, United States</u>

Emperor hovered down lower over the top of the yellow sports car. That gave Gen the opportunity to pull her leg around and slide off the side. She leapt from Emperor's back, adrenaline and triumph pulsing in her veins as she landed on the hood of the sleek car.

Her eyes blazed with the righteous fury of a warrior ripped from their time and bent on protecting it from thieves. The Director of Security looked like a ghost as he peered oddly through the other side of the glass at the crazed woman, kneeling on his car and glaring at him from above.

Hamilton Dixon was strangely struggling behind a pillow of sorts that appeared to be filled with air. The thing must have shot out when the side of the car careened into the lamppost, Gen reasoned. Currently, the other side of the car was pinned against the pole, blocking that exit to the car. Gen didn't really know how these vehicles worked or opened up, but she was going to break this one in half to get to the scoundrel inside.

Pulling up her fist, Gen slammed it into the metal under her, vibrating the car. It might have hurt to smash her knuckles into the hard surface, but her gloves served as armor. Not only that, but the adrenaline filling her blood made her feel invincible.

"Get out here, you worthless coward! Face me, you son of a dung beetle. I'm going to tear you in half, you pile of horse shit!"

"No-No-No!" Hamilton Dixon stuttered, shaking his head erratically, trying to back up more in his car, but with no place to retreat to. The man's face was a mask of desperation and defeat as he found himself cornered in the car surrounded by fire and with a rage-filled warrior atop it.

Gen lifted her fist, about to smash through the glass to reach the thief and liar on the other side. A swoosh followed by a jolting wind and a change of lighting made her pause. Glancing over her shoulder, Gen realized that Emperor had extinguished the wall of flames encircling the sports car. The purple dragon stood beside the vehicle, an amused expression on his face.

Hamilton Dixon screamed from inside the car, now pushing to the far side, trying to get away from the dragon that lurked beside his window. The Director of Security seemed more like a scared child with his high-pitched yelping than a man. It was a sad sight for Gen to witness.

She pulled her gaze back to her dragon. Sensing the teasing look in Emperor's eyes, Gen lowered her fist to her side. "What? Why are you glaring at me like that?"

"Because…" he said, drawing out the word and reaching out and using his claw on the door. Nimbly, and with surprising dexterity, the purple dragon opened the car door, releasing Hamilton Dixon, or more importantly, giving Gen access to the coward.

"Oh!" Gen exclaimed, excitedly, sliding off the side of the car and speeding around the door. "That was easy."

"That's what I'm here for," the dragon said, lifting his wings and creating a wall so that the thief couldn't try and get away. "To teach you about how to use everyday things in this world."

"Thanks," Gen said, reaching into the car and yanking the man out by the collar of his shirt.

"D-D-Don't h-h-hurt meeee!" Hamilton Dixon stammered, shaking and throwing his head back and forth erratically. Gen picked him up easily and shoved him against the side of the car. The man was sweating profusely and was as soft as a feather pillow.

"You're pathetic," Gen said, bearing down on the man. However, when his eyes skirted to something over her shoulder, she knew that Emperor was there, glaring down at Hamilton. The dragon was what was really intimidating with his pensive and electrifying gold eyes.

"I-I-I can't tell you anything," the weakling said, drooling and shivering, his teeth clanging together due to fear.

Knowing that the dragon's imposing form was blocking his escape, Gen released the man and stood back, appraising the sniveling jerk. "He's not lying…"

"No, he's not," Emperor affirmed, narrowing his eyes on the man who was now crying slightly. Gen thought he might have even peed himself. It was simply sad and despicable for a man to be so weak in any day and age. However, it seemed that the modern world created more fragile people. It was strange that all the conveniences had made people feebler rather than given them the opportunity to be stronger.

"Who do you work for?" Gen asked, watching the man's face carefully for the telltale signs of deception.

Hamilton shook his head. "I can't tell you…"

Gen cut her eyes to the dragon. "What's going on? He's telling the truth. Thieves lie."

"That they do," Emperor replied. "But he really isn't allowed to say. There's a spell at work and it makes it so that he can't say the name of the person he is working for. I can't even get to the information in his mind. It's blocked."

Gen balled up her fist, about to punch the car again. However, she thought that the adrenaline had worn off enough that it might actually hurt this time. She turned her attention back on Hamilton Dixon. "Fine, then tell us where you were taking the medieval artifacts. You will know where that is and would have to have instructed your crew."

Tears actually fell down the man's face as he shook all over. "If I tell you that, they'll kill me."

"Who will?" Gen asked.

Hamilton shook his head, crazed. "I can't say. I really can't. But they will kill me if I talk."

"If you don't tell me, then *I'll* kill you," Gen promised.

"No, I can't...Please..." Hamilton sobbed.

Gen sighed, glancing up at Emperor. "Do you want a snack? You can eat this guy's arms. Or would you rather use mind control to make this joker play in the road? Maybe you can give him a bad headache? Or I could, of course, punch him until he—"

"No! No! NO!" Hamilton pleaded. "I'll tell you. But you have to let me go. You can't hurt me."

Gen pursed her lips, giving Emperor a tentative expression. "What do you think? I say we hurt him and get him to tell us. Then it's a win-win for me."

"It's better if you can get people to talk without force," Emperor advised wisely. "Save your strength and brutality for when you need it."

Gen sighed, slightly disappointed. "Fine, I won't hurt you. But tell me where they are taking the stolen artifacts. And fast. We have to stop them."

"It's too late," Hamilton Dixon said, pointing down the road. "It's down there at the Warehouse District. The address is 1600 Olympic Boulevard, Suite 100. But they'll either be done unloading by the time you get there or they're heavily armed. You won't stand a chance on your own."

Gen laughed. "For one, we won't be late. We don't have to

wait in traffic. And secondly, I don't think you know who I am or what we're capable of."

"Wh-Wh-Who are you?" Hamilton stuttered, still shaking furiously.

Gen smiled up at Emperor. "We're medieval warriors meant to protect the modern world."

"And you're not going to hurt me?" Hamilton asked, looking around for someone to help him but the street where they were was deserted.

"No, a promise is a promise," Gen said, not asking permission and reaching into the man's pockets. He screamed, backing into the car more, but not getting away. It wasn't until Gen reached into his other pocket that she found the electronic device that everyone in the modern era carried around and were obsessed with.

"What are you doing?" he asked, looking more offended that she'd taken his device than that she grabbed into his pockets without permission.

"I'm calling you a ride," Gen said, grabbing the man by the shirt again and stuffing him back into the car.

"What?!" he yelled as she slammed the door in his face.

Gen turned to her dragon, a grin on her face. "Two things. Can you tell me how to use this?" She held up the device.

He nodded dully.

"Secondly," she began, pointing at the door. "Can you lock that? I don't want him getting out until the police arrive."

The dragon nodded again and then lifted a clawed hand and smashed it into the side of the car, buckling the metal, making it impossible that it would be opened without tools. Hamilton Dixon would be locked in his wrecked sports car until the authorities were there to throw him in jail.

CHAPTER FIFTY-THREE

A DRAGON'S STRATEGY

<u>**Warehouse District, 1600 Olympic Boulevard, Suite 100, Los Angeles, California, United States**</u>

"So you just call this 9-1-1 number and they help you, no matter what?" Gen asked, turning off the device that she'd used for the first time and didn't look forward to using again anytime soon. It was strange talking to a disembodied voice—like a bizarre magic akin to telepathy. Emperor's was the only voice she wanted in her head and even then, that had taken some getting used to.

"You call them when you have an emergency and need help," Emperor stated.

"Well, I wouldn't say our situation was an emergency, but we did need someone to cart that foolish coward back there away." Gen nodded down the road where they'd left Hamilton Dixon, trapped in his sports car which was so badly damaged, even the windows wouldn't roll down. He would be fine until the authorities got there and arrested him, hoping to find all the evidence that pinned him to the robbery at the Los Angeles County Museum of Art. Now they just needed to find the stolen medieval artifacts and the person behind the big heist, who Hamilton couldn't name, due to magic.

Gen dropped the electronic device on the ground, picked up her boot and crushed it with her heel, enjoying the crunching noise it made. "But that 9-1-1 service is nice to have. Now the police can come and clean up our mess. Are we ready to go and dirty some stuff up?"

"Yes, absolutely," Emperor responded, stationed beside her in the darkened street. "And I have some ideas of how we can do that and make the best entrance possible."

Gen grinned up at him. "I'm listening. It's all about the element of surprise."

"Well, we don't want to just waltz in there, do we?" Emperor nodded his large head in the direction of the oversized metal building across the street.

Amidst the shadowed underbelly of Los Angeles, a warehouse pulsated with illicit activity, its insides filled with stolen relics of time past. The opened roll-up doors showed the activity happening within the metal walls. Men, fueled by desperation and greed, hustled beneath the skeletal beams, their shouts clashing with the clang of the crates of artifacts and treasures they'd taken from various places.

Emperor's telepathy had determined that not only was the warehouse housing some of the medieval items from LACMA. There were also items stolen from other museums all over the City of Los Angeles. It was filled to the brim with millions of dollars of valuable pieces, robbed from various sources.

The men inside the warehouse all had the same guards on their minds as Hamilton Dixon, which meant they worked for the same person. That was what Gen and Emperor had to figure out. But most importantly, they had to shut down this operation.

Crime that was controlled was one thing. Crime that could be used to benefit the community and society at large was under-standable and served a purpose. But this, well, it was an abuse to the arts, history and the people who the City of Los Angeles belonged to—the citizens.

As the vans screeched to a halt inside the warehouse, the air crackled with a frenetic energy. The armed men, their voices raw with panic, scrambled to unload their ill-gotten cargo, the fear of capture hanging heavy in the air.

Gen turned to Emperor, her chest also building with excitement similar to the villains in the warehouse in the distance. The men frantically unloading the stolen goods didn't want to get caught after their close call at the Los Angeles County Museum of Art. They thought they'd gotten away from their pursuers.

But more than anything, Gen wanted to bring down these men, making them pay for stealing that which belonged to the people. It belonged to history. It was her heritage and those of the future deserved to see it. Bad men didn't deserve to profit from the artifacts of Gen's youth.

"Right, we need to make a grand entrance," Gen agreed, returning her attention to studying the warehouse ahead. "So what's the plan? I don't want to wait until backup arrives and risk any of those thieves getting away."

"Oh, no," Emperor stated. "No one is fleeing on my watch."

"You don't wear a watch, do you?" she teased.

He cut his eyes to the top of the building, ignoring her silly joke. "We're going to ensure that we are in a position to keep all the criminals contained until they can be carted away. You wanted to climb before, so I hope you're still up for the challenge."

Gen nodded, excited for the adventure to come next as she took her place high atop her dragon, ready to soar off into the night and stop a theft that should have never happened.

CHAPTER FIFTY-FOUR

BRUISED BUT UNBROKEN

As the sound of men yelling to each other in the warehouse echoed, Gen and her dragon waited in utter silence for the perfect moment to make their entrance. The plan was simple but also riddled with potential threats. Gen had never done anything like this—and she'd done a lot of crazy, rebellious things.

But the modern world posed many unknowns. And yet, she felt secure with a dragon unlike any other beneath her and a weapon full of potential in her pocket. She might not be the average hero but she was a relentless one and refused to feel any fear right then.

As a man below declared that the last of the stolen medieval artifacts had been unloaded from the vans, Gen slid off the side of her dragon. She was careful to not make a single noise as she backed into her place. Then she nodded her confirmation to Emperor, signaling that she was ready.

From the side of the rooftop, Gen watched as Emperor moved soundlessly into place, finding a seam in the metal. Having found the perfect spot, the dragon glanced at her from several yards away—a safe distance. The night covered him in a mystery that Gen relished, knowing he was about to become a nightmare for the thieves in the warehouse below them.

The purple dragon suddenly plunged his claws into the metal rooftop below them. The steel material shrieked in protest as Emperor's mighty hooks peeled it back like the lid of a tin can. Screams and commotion ripped through the air below as chaos broke out—no one knowing what was happening above them. Like playing a rude joke on their fragile beating hearts, the dragon's head descended through the opening he'd made. Gen could just picture his golden eyes gleaming with mischief as he uttered a single, terrifying word: "Boo."

Chaos erupted. Men shouted, their voices drowning in the discord of shattering glass and toppling crates. Emperor roared with what Gen knew was pure amusement. He lifted his head from the opening he'd made into the warehouse, creating a gaping chasm into the store of stolen treasures.

The dragon's jaws parted, releasing a blistering torrent of flames that encircled the perimeter, trapping the criminals inside a searing prison of their own making. The heat was oppressive, the air thick with the acrid tang of melting metal and singed hair. The turmoil and destruction that ensued was like flute and harp music to Gen's soul. Her heart warmed at the commotion that she and her dragon caused in only a few seconds, but she knew that she couldn't relish in it for long, since she needed to act fast while they had the advantage.

Gen, nimble as a cat, slipped from the opening that Emperor had made in the rooftop of the warehouse. She landed on a towering shelf that groaned beneath her weight. She leapt from level to level, the fragile wood crates splintering under her boots as she swung herself into the fray. Knowing that she couldn't chance her balance for long on any of the structures and with the momentum she was using, Gen didn't stay in place for long, moving fast.

Yet, in her fervor, a misstep sent her crashing into a shelf of artifacts, the sound of breaking history fueling her rage. Falling with much less grace than before, Gen found three men marching toward her, weapons in their hands. She surged forward, an embodiment of fury, and her hostility more lethal than the guns they held. At once, Gen flew into action, acting faster than the men could process.

Her strikes brought most of the attackers' attention in the warehouse onto her suddenly. How she'd upstaged the dragon, she didn't know—it must have been that fall from heaven when she thought she was an angel. Whatever she'd done, it had created a whirlwind that left her surrounded, the warehouse a coliseum with her at its heart.

Thankfully there was a dragon overhead who had Gen's back. The men on the ground took aim at what they thought was the more menacing threat, pulling the trigger at once, trying to bring down the hulking dragon.

Unfazed by the attempts to destroy or harm him, Emperor continued his relentless assault. With a flick of his tail, he sent a sheet of twisted metal flying, the improvised shield deflecting a hail of bullets that ricocheted back towards their shooters. The men screamed, diving for cover amidst the labyrinth of artifacts, their bravado shattered like the priceless relics that lay in ruins around them.

Below, Gen became the storm she rode in on. Her fists found their marks with savage precision, going after the men closest to her, attacking them by sheer association with the theft of these artifacts. Each of her blows was a testament to her unyielding resolve. The only time she paused or hesitated was when she worried that her assaults would endanger one of the treasures stationed all around them in crates and on shelves. She was simply surrounded by history and treachery.

Gen fought like a woman possessed, her body a blur of motion as she dodged and weaved through the chaos. A burly man, his face contorted with rage, caught her with a glancing blow, sending her careening into a stack of ancient vases. The delicate porcelain nearly tottered off the shelf where it was stationed.

However, Gen reached out with magic, freezing the object in mid-air and carefully lowering them to the ground. She paid for the rescue though when the man punched her across the face, sending her far across the floor, nearly tumbling over another crate of artifacts. Gen caught herself, anger surging through her veins, a white-hot fury that burned away the pain.

Above, chaos unfurled like a banner as Emperor encircled the warehouse with a ring of fire. He had created a living barrier that danced with hungry flames, licking the night air with tongues of fury. Bullets, desperate attempts at defiance, rained upwards, only to be met by a shield of torn metal, hoisted by Emperor's talon. The dragon roared with vengeance as the ammunition's futile echoes ricocheted back down to the ground, making the men below scatter and take shelter from their own attacks.

Emperor enjoyed playing jailer with the flames, keeping most of the thieves at bay. The few who managed to escape were quickly plucked from their futile run for freedom and tossed back into the warehouse with a gentleness contradicting his monstrous form. Each of the dragon's actions ensured none could escape the net closing around them.

With a roar that echoed Emperor's own, on the ground below, Gen surged forward. Her attacks were a vortex of skill and savagery. She leapt and spun, her limbs a blur as she took down her opponents one by one. But even as she fought, more men emerged from the shadows, their weapons glinting in the flickering light of Emperor's flames. Gen found herself surrounded, the weight of exhaustion pulling at her bones. She used magic when she needed it for survival to throw men back or dismantle their guns.

Emperor helped her out a few times, plucking a villain from

behind her back before they knocked her out. However, they were quickly getting overrun and they both knew they couldn't hold out much longer. Hamilton Dixon might have been correct and they showed up for a fight that they couldn't win.

Just as despair began to creep into Gen's heart, the sound of sirens pierced the air. The thieves all around her froze. Their eyes widened. Fear filled every one of their faces. Fighting her was something they thought they *could* do. Defending themselves from the dragon was something they *had* to do. But fleeing the police, well, that was a brand new challenge.

Suddenly, no one was battling Gen, all of them racing for the exits. It was all too satisfying for dragon and rider when the thieves found their escape routes either blocked by fire or being intruded upon by the authorities.

The police stormed the building, their armor glinting like the scales of a great beast. They moved with practiced efficiency, their weapons trained on the criminals who cowered before them. Emperor, seeing the tide turning, ceased his assault, the flames dying away as quickly as they had come.

In the heart of the warehouse, Gen stood, bruised but unbroken, a warrior queen in a field of her conquered enemies. Around her, the remnants of battle lay scattered, the air heavy with the scent of victory and the bitter tang of damaged history. She'd protected most of the artifacts. And although they didn't know who exactly was behind this huge heist, they were much closer to answers with all these crooks being arrested. Answers would come. And then Gen and Emperor would get justice for the people of Los Angeles.

The chaos that had filled the warehouse turned to a strange bit of peace, like when the wind blows over a battlefield after the fight has been won. As the last of the thieves were handcuffed, Gen turned to Emperor. Their gazes met in silent acknowledgment of the storm they had weathered together, partners in a dance as old as time itself.

CHAPTER FIFTY-FIVE

THE UNSEEN MENACE OF THE CITY

<u>Warehouse District, 1600 Olympic Boulevard, Suite 100, Los Angeles, California, United States</u>

From the shadows, a figure in all black stood, unnoticed and uncaptured by the authorities. The man had watched from his hiding place as the medieval warrior and her dragon ruined absolutely everything. He had known, from the very moment he had learned of Gen Beaufont's existence, that she would be a formidable adversary. However, even in his darkest musings, he had grossly underestimated the sheer magnitude of the setback she would inflict upon him.

Charlie Sloane, the newly appointed Commissioner for Los Angeles, had toiled tirelessly, sacrificing more than anyone could imagine, to secure his position of power. He had worked too hard for this to have a Rogue Rider ruin everything for him.

The City of Los Angeles was his kingdom and it was supposed to bend to his every whim and desire. It was supposed to deliver treasures and powers beyond his wildest dreams. But now, it seemed, before he could lay claim to his rightful throne, he would have to contend with a meddlesome pest who dared to stand in the way of his ultimate triumph.

Crime, in all its glorious manifestations, was supposed to be his loyal servant—not a plaything to be policed by a time-traveling vigilante with a misguided sense of justice. Charlie thought that he'd prepared for any event or interruption sufficiently, arranging every piece on the chessboard of Los Angeles.

He'd put everything into place for his appointment as the Commissioner of Los Angeles. He'd set up this city so that it worked for him. However, he now realized, to his mounting fury, that he had grossly misjudged the havoc that one girl and her dragon could wreak upon his carefully laid plans. This revelation left him with no choice but to escalate his arsenal and resort to any means necessary to eliminate the threat posed by Gen Beaufont and her infernal companion, Emperor.

It didn't matter that she was a Beaufont. It didn't matter that her dragon was a ruler among his kind. They would fall just as easily as all of Charlie Sloane's opponents had. And when the dust settled, when the last embers of resistance had been extinguished, the City of Los Angeles would finally be his—a vast, pulsating mecca of crime and corruption, all engineered to elevate him to heights of power and wealth that surpassed what anyone dreamed possible.

The shadows would be his ally, the darkness his cloak and no one would get in his way as he set forth to claim his destiny—no matter the cost.

CHAPTER FIFTY-SIX

THE PRICE OF VIGILANTE JUSTICE

<u>Dwayne Stone's Office, Rogue Rider Mansion, Beverly Hills, California, United States</u>

"What were you thinking!" the leader of the Rogue Riders boomed, his voice making the many strange objects around his office vibrate on their shelves creating a sinister noise.

"I was thinking that a huge heist was going on under our noses and someone had to do something about it," Gen said, standing tall, her chest high, although she was vibrating with nerves that felt like they'd make her fall over at any moment.

Dwayne Stone narrowed his beady eyes at her, towering over her from the other side of his desk. "Do I need to remind you that you haven't finished training and weren't cleared to work a case, let alone go off on your own and make a mockery of this city?"

"Sir, I stopped a huge robbery at the Los Angeles County Museum of Art," Gen argued, feeling Emperor in her mind, trying to keep her from saying the wrong thing and getting in trouble. However, she thought she was miles past that, having done apparently a lot of things wrong that she was, presently and probably for the rest of time, going to pay the price for.

"You created a huge disturbance, breaking glass all over the museum," Dwayne argued, the vein in his head throbbing more than ever before. "You and Emperor are responsible for a ton of damage all down Wilshire Boulevard as well as destroying a warehouse."

Gen drew in a breath, her anger trying to get the best of her, but her mind owning her presence, thankfully. "I think you're missing the fact that we intervened in a major heist that would have happened if we didn't stop it. We kept the majority of those medieval artifacts at Los Angeles County Museum of Art from being stolen. We stopped Hamilton Dixon who is now under arrest. We found not just the valuables from that day's heist but also apparently from many more over the last year. We solved a huge case involving tons of museum robberies. And because we called in the authorities, we had dozens of thieves arrested."

"Did you think to call me?" he asked in a punishing low voice.

"I didn't have your number," she replied at once with a mischievous grin.

Dwayne shook his head, looking ready to reach across the desk and strike her down, he was so angry. "You aren't a Dragon Elite…"

"I know that, sir," Gen said, thrown off by the remark.

"Then why are you intervening in crimes, taking down thieves?" he questioned, his nostrils flaring. "Our job is to monitor them. To regulate. To make them work for us."

"But those men weren't working for us," she argued. "They were outside your radar."

Like he was suddenly growing bored of this conversation, Dwayne reached out, running his finger over the surface of his desk, as if checking for dust. He inspected his finger, shaking his head with disgust, either at the cleanliness of his office or at Gen. She thought it was the latter. "Yes, but you misunderstand that we are supposed to allow crime to happen to keep the world safe."

"I get that, but the crime at the museum hurt the taxpayers

who fund this city," Gen countered. "Whoever is behind all those stolen valuables in the warehouse was robbing from the citizens of Los Angeles. That crime benefited rich men who were selling things that didn't belong to them to buy exotic islands in the world. That crime was not the petty stuff that keeps the balance. It's crime that goes too far that we need to squash. Don't you see sir, that we are in the best position to regulate crime because we know what good is. If we allow bad things to happen, then we're the criminals."

He narrowed his eyes at her. Flexed his fists by his sides. Looked ready to explode with fury. "You understand nothing. You've upset a delicate balance in this city by intervening and not minding your place—"

"Is this about the Los Angeles Commissioner?" Gen dared to ask, interrupting her boss.

Dwayne froze. His gaze gripped at her for a moment, like he was trying to strangle her with his stare. His jaw tensed. "That's none of your business."

He wasn't lying, she knew. But he also knew that if he tried to, that she'd spot it. So Dwayne was avoiding answering the question.

"I know that the new Director of Security for the Los Angeles County Museum of Art was appointed by the new Commissioner," Gen said, knowing that confessing what she knew was risky, but she had to see how her boss reacted to this information.

"So?" Dwayne asked plainly, not giving anything away.

"So, why is it that there's an influx of criminals and major heists are happening in the City of Los Angeles?" Gen dared to question. "What's going on, sir?"

He threw a hand to the side, pointing at nothing at all, but meaning something specifically. "You just stepped through a freaking gate into this time period and you dare to question me on why our world and events are happening the way they are? You know nothing about this city or how it works."

"Sir, I know right from wrong," Gen cut in.

Fury swept across Dwayne's tight expression. "You are as green and uneducated as a newborn baby. But you're also as ill-behaved as a toddler, breaking rules that you don't even understand."

"Sir, we caught criminals who would have gone unchecked by you."

"You don't know that," he said, but something shifted in his gaze. He wasn't lying, but was hiding something.

"Sir, what did you know about the crimes happening at the Los Angeles museums lately?" Gen asked, realizing that she was very close to a murder attempt on her life. Still, she needed to see his eyes when he answered that question.

Dwayne cleared his throat. Swallowed. Shook his head. "It doesn't matter. This is about you..."

He was hiding something. Whether it was his own incompetence or his own treachery, Gen really didn't know, but she was definitely going to figure it out.

"You will not be acting on your own accord anymore or you will be terminated as a Rogue Rider," Dwayne Stone continued, his face suddenly slack and neutral. "You will train as I've dictated. And you won't so much as look at a criminal without my permission let alone intervene in their activity unless I deem it so. Do I make myself clear?"

Gen was absolutely grateful that she could spot liars. And she was even more relieved right then that she could lie without detection. She nodded. Held her chin high. Faked a smile. "Of course, sir. You have my word."

CHAPTER FIFTY-SEVEN

THE BEAUFONT WAY

<u>Dining Room, Beaufont Residence, West Hollywood, California, United States</u>

For a long moment, Gen simply stared at the strange food in front of her, not sure how to eat it and definitely not certain if she felt like it. The scraping of utensils on plates around the Beaufont table ground to a screeching silent halt. That's exactly when Gen realized that all of her relatives were looking straight at her from around the table.

Bringing her gaze up, Gen found Liv, Clark, and Sophia all regarding her with different expressions. Clark, per usual, seemed concerned. Sophia was offering a sensitive expression. And Liv, well, she appeared somewhat amused by Gen's melancholy demeanor.

Liv pointed to the plate of noodles in yellow sauce sitting in front of Gen. "It's called comfort food. It's supposed to make you feel better. But the way it works is that you have to put it in your mouth hole first. Even though it's the modern age, we haven't invented food consumption through osmosis yet or smell-o-vision or any other means."

Gen pursed her lips, glancing at Sophia for help. "What is she talking about?"

Sophia chuckled, waving dismissively at her sister beside her. "Liv is being…well, Liv. But she's just trying to help. You're not eating and it might help if you tried. Maybe you want some of the chicken fried steak or mashed potatoes and gravy or rolls instead of the mac-and-cheese. They are all good at filling your stomach and making you feel better."

Gen sighed, wishing that she hadn't brought her problems to her family and then grateful that they cared so much to try and make her feel better. "Thanks, but I'm just not hungry."

"I'm sure that eating will help," Clark offered. "Maybe there's something else I can prepare that will make you feel better."

Gen shook her head. "I don't think so. I'm in real trouble and it looks like I'm never going to get a case or work for the Rogue Riders. I just can't imagine eating after realizing that I've blown my chances in this world when my life here has just started."

Liv reached for one of the fresh baked rolls in a bowl in the center of the table. "Because your boss told you that you're in trouble and on probation."

"Well, yeah, he's really angry at me and told me that I've created a ton of problems for him," Gen answered.

A laugh burst from Liv's mouth. "Then it sounds like so far you're perfectly on track for being a successful Beaufont."

Gen blinked. "Wait…what?"

"She's right," Clark said, the voice of reason when it came to the group. He pointed at Liv. "She nearly got kicked out of the House of Fourteen as a warrior when she started. The councilors really didn't like her rebellious attitude and brazen way of doing things."

"Because I can sniff out corruption like a hound dog," Liv said, taking a bite of her roll and winking at Gen.

"It's true," Clark said, quite seriously. "She unearthed all the lies and deceit that others couldn't see, fixing a huge fraudulent system related to magic that had been hurting the world at large. But on the way to doing that, well, Liv was almost terminated from her role several times."

Liv nodded proudly, like this was quite the honor. She then pointed at Sophia. "And my little sister here was kicked out of the Dragon Elite when she first started. What did you do when that happened, sis?"

Sophia flushed red. "I went rogue and took down a huge corrupt magitech operation, making the Dragon Elite wake up to the problems of the modern era." She then pointed at Clark. "And our brother, well, he's constantly digging up laws, histories and facts that upend the world the council knew. It's our jobs as Beaufonts to shake things up. We upset the status quo. If you almost got fired, then it only means you're doing something right."

Gen pushed back in her chair, feeling strangely better and then a new heaviness settled on her shoulders. "So I'm supposed to break Dwayne's rules? I'm supposed to go off on my own?"

Clark leaned forward, patting the table between them. "You're supposed to follow the truth and protect this world. Unfortunately, that usually puts targets on our backs. But as Beaufonts, we've learned to accept that our fate is one as guardians over justice." He glanced up, smiling fondly at his sisters. "We've often said it is a destiny we inherited from our ancestors. Where some might see it as a curse because we never get a break, we've always seen it as an honor. We're Beaufonts. We were created to move this world forward while shepherding what is right."

"And we wouldn't have it any other way because it's who we are," Sophia said, putting her hand out too, next to her brother's on the table.

"And we share the burden, because we all do it, as a family," Liv said, extending her own hand, putting it next to her siblings.

Gen glanced at the three hands, the connection to her family.

To her past. To her present. To her future. They were like her and they made everything that she had to do next possible.

With a smile of devotion, Gen reached out, placing her hand next to the other three. In unison, all the fingers of the Beaufonts wound together, joining in a grasp, one hand on top of another.

Then all of them looked around at each other, a connectedness in their gazes.

"We've got your back, Gen," Liv said, giving her a meaningful expression. "Do what you think is right and we will support you. You're never alone."

"Never," Clark agreed. "Familia Est Sempiternum."

"Familia Est Sempiternum," all the women at the table echoed in unison.

It was then that Gen felt a bond to this family unlike she'd ever felt to any other before. She was really meant for this world. She just had to find her place in it.

CHAPTER FIFTY-EIGHT

GUARDIANS OF THE NIGHT

<u>Rogue Rider Mansion, Beverly Hills, California, United States</u>

The cheerful laughter and excited chatter from the Rogue Riders down on the lawn echoed up to where Gen and Emperor were perched up high. The sounds of partying and the firelight of the festivities below didn't make Gen feel left out. Actually, some of the others like Sully and Amanda had invited Gen to join them for that night's celebration. However, Gen wanted to be alone and therefore declined the offer. Still, for some reason, she didn't mind overhearing the happiness exuding from below.

Apparently, the Rogue Riders often cut loose like this, according to Sophia, needing to take the edge off after their stressful and dangerous jobs policing criminals. From her place sitting on the second story roof of the Rogue Rider mansion, Gen could see the others dancing around a bonfire on the lawn below. They danced and drank, cheering and playing with each other as if they'd always been friends.

Gen felt like she was in a completely different place than them as she leaned against her dragon, who lay right below the pitch of the roof. Emperor's warmth was like the fire below and kept Gen feeling secure. His quiet companionship was more than enough to make her feel safe. But she knew at some point she'd need more than her Beaufont family and her dragon. Gen would need friends—but in time, when she was ready…

"We did the right thing," Emperor said in a low voice that no one could hear but Gen, even though it was out loud and not in her head.

"I know," Gen said, drawing in a breath, looking up at the starry sky, which was much different than the one she used to stare at in 1426 London. "It's just hard…"

When the dragon snickered his belly nearly launched Gen forward. She had to press her boots into the roof to keep herself from tumbling down the slope.

"Did you think that the job of a vigilante was going to be easy or not met with resistance?" the dragon asked.

She scoffed. "I didn't know I signed up for it."

"I challenge you on that," he countered. "You always fought your father, William, telling him you weren't good enough to be a warrior for the House of Fourteen. You, at your core, believed you were made for something edgier. You thought of yourself as a rebel. And now here you are, made for policing the criminal world. How can you say you didn't sign up for it when I believe you somehow created this role for us?"

Gen drew in a breath, feeling heavy but enjoying the emotion. It felt right to be burdened right then with her emotions. Her past. What her future could hold. She relished in this moment where she was cloaked in responsibility. "You're right…"

"I think you'll find that I always am," Emperor stated, an edge of mischief in his voice.

She smiled, leaning back and snuggling into the warm belly of the dragon. "I'm not sure how or when I'll get to argue with you on that, but I'll be looking for an opportunity."

"I'm sure you will," he stated.

A long moment of silence passed between the dragon and rider, punctuated only by the laughter and sounds of the others down below on the lawn. Finally Gen said, "So what do we do now?"

"Besides whatever we want?" Emperor replied.

"I mean, in regard to Dwayne and finding out the truth behind this Commissioner business," Gen stated.

"We search for the truth," he answered. "We ask the right questions and we keep our eyes open to that which others refuse to see—the path to justice. We'll find it. I'm sure of that."

"As well as a lot of opposition," Gen added.

"Of course," he replied. "But you're not dissuaded by the fact that we'll have to break rules and most likely be defiant to our leader, are you?"

"Aren't you the leader?" she argued.

"It's complicated," he stated. "But technically, yes."

"And no," Gen imparted. "There's something not right in this city. More so than ever before. I feel that at my core. There's a reason we were put here and now in this time and place. I believe we have a job, and it's to wipe out the bigger corruptions taking advantage of this world so that we can reinstate the balance between good and evil."

"If I could see the future, then I'd say you were right."

"But you *can* see the future," she said with a chuckle.

"Oh, then let me confirm, you're right."

"So tomorrow, we get back to work," Gen said through a long yawn.

Emperor lifted one of his wings and slid it over his rider, wrapping her up like she was in a blanket, keeping her warm as the chill of the night air swept in over Beverly Hills. "Yes, tomorrow we'll get back to work."

Gen blinked out at the grounds below as the light from the bonfire started to wane. The group had settled down. Now only a few figures talked, drinking and laughing every now and then. Still, Gen was glad they were having a good time. And she felt like it was her job to watch over her would-be friends, ensuring they were safe and happy. For some reason, she felt responsible for the Rogue Riders—like protecting them was part of her birthright.

"Get some rest," Emperor said, his voice seeming to try and soothe her to sleep.

"Okay, but wake me if you need me," Gen said, her voice nearly a whisper as she trailed off.

"I always will," he hummed, his gold eyes cutting through the night. "And I'll always be here to look after you."

"Thank you, Emperor." Gen turned, cuddling up with her dragon, falling asleep fast within his protection.

The pair, curled up on the top of the roof in Beverly Hills, overlooking the modern world, had no idea the hope they represented to this day and age. They may be from another time, but they were meant to protect this one, looking after it from their high vantage point—like the true Emperor and Empress that they were.

AUTHOR'S NOTES: SARAH NOFFKE

MARCH 27, 2024

Before I start raking my fellow author and collaborator, Michael Anderle, over burning, hot coals, I'd like to start with a few thank yous. Firstly, thank you to long time readers who have been reading my books since the beginning, starting with my first one in 2014. Thank you to devoted readers who have been with the Beaufonts since the beginning starting in 2019 with Liv. And thank you to new readers, taking a chance on us—you're in for an adventure and a lot of laughs.

Okay, now lets get to raking! Oh, Michael, Michael, Michael... Why is it that you show up to a knife fight with a broken whistle? That will never get your ass out of trouble. But you get points for effort, I guess.

For those new to our books and our little dynamic, I secretly adore Mike Anderle. But for the purposes of these notes and also to give my life meaning, I've made a job of making fun and harassing him in our author notes from the beginning. What can I say, I'm good at it and he gives me unending fodder simply by being him. Also, I'm really short and have to take out my aggression in acceptable and nonlethal ways.

For those of you new to us, MAnderle coined the nickname Tiny Ninja for me because one time I showed up to a professional writing conference dressed as a ninja. Hey! They told me to dress for the job I wanted. Anyway, the name has stuck and here we are.

Also, if you're new, please know that Mike's nickname is Bird Killer. That's because he killed a bird when little and later dared to tell me about it and thought I wouldn't make fun of him for it. He's really naïve. I'm a writer. Everything you say can and will be used against you in my books. Recently, this guy at this wedding totally was rude to me and his name is Charlie. Guess who our big bad villain is in this story. Charlie! Oh, what will happen to Charlie…

Okay, back to MA. Where's that bus I'm about to throw him under? I left it around here somewhere. Anyway, I'll find it when the time is right.

So if you read the last set of books and the final author notes of The Undoubtable Rose Beaufont series, book 12, then you know that Mike tried to blame me for his health problems. He said that because I'm always writing up until the last moment, turning in books minutes before the deadline, that I give him, as the publisher, heart palpitations. Couldn't be all the soda you drink, could it, Mike?

Anyway, now I'll admit, I've written up until the 11th hour, turning in a book with minutes to spare. But have I ever been late? Not that I can remember. I get my books done and who cares if they are on the stroke of midnight? But recently, I've been ahead of schedule. This book I turned in 6 days early. Same with the last book. Sooooo I'm not taking responsibility for Bird Killer's stress. And besides, he finds out that I've turned in the book at the last possible minute after the fact. You can't have retroactive anxiety for something that already happened, can you?

Okay, there's the bus. Good! I'll just wait for the driver to gun the engine and really get rolling.

So the other day, Mike and I had a meeting on the calendar. Like the prompt little good girl that I am, I was there on Zoom on time. Where was my collaborator? Absent. Did I get mad. Oh, no, I got giddy. When half an hour later Mike is like, "OoOOOoooh shit!" I was just giggling with evil delight. I was thinking, "Oh, the ways I can hold this over your head are infinite…"

And I will.

Mike was double booked and things happen. And I'm chill and let it go. But then I told him that his mistakes become my ammunition.

I'm really, really short. Hence the aggression.

Okay, the bus is really speeding down the road so let's get to this. Lastly, Mike and I were in Sevilla, Spain recently for a conference. We were on the same flight to London on the way back. As fate would have it, Mike and his lovely wife, were two rows ahead of me and my husband. Just imagine if they had been right in front of us and all the pestering I could have done.

Anyway, you know how on every flight after the plane lands, some guy stands up before the plane comes to a complete halt. And then the flight attendants have to be like, "Everyone stay seated until the pilot has turned off the fasten seat belt sign." Well, on this flight that exact thing happened. Please, please, please tell me that you know who that guy was!

I was laughing with evil delight when Mike got reprimanded. You know he turned around and glared at me. Then he said, "You're going to use this against me in our author notes, aren't you.."

Mike, I don't do this to you. You do this to yourself 😊

This will be a fun series full of action, laughter and suspense. I'm glad you're all along for the ride. And thanks for all the laughs and more, Michael. We make a good team.

Much love and peace!
Sarah Noffke, aka Tiny Ninja

AUTHOR'S NOTES: MICHAEL ANDERLE

APRIL 19, 2024

Hello, dear friends and fellow readers on this journey we call life. Thank you for not only reading this book – but joining me here in the back!

Here is my rebuttal to my Dear Collaborator's Author Notes

Dear Esteemed Readers and the Formidable Force of Nature,

Now, to address the good-natured ribbing served up by my ~~annoying~~ esteemed co-conspirator in the written word.

Yes, I have occasionally been caught brandishing a whistle where blades might be more apropos. Perhaps it's a touch of that escapist love that drives me, or the notion that even the most off-key whistle can cut through silence to unite rather than divide. Or, it's just one of those delightful peculiarities that provide our collaboration with its unique rhythm.

Whatever, I'm just a nice guy that way.

The epithet "Tiny Ninja," a nod to my comrade's ~~short stature~~ prowess in literary agility and surprise tactics, is well earned, as is her knack for keeping the narrative ever-twisting and turning. As for my own alias, "Bird Killer," let's chalk that up to a youthful misstep—an anecdote that's since become fodder for the kind of storytelling that resonates with authenticity and character growth.

~~And expensive therapy visits.~~

When it comes to deadlines and the toll they take, I tip my hat in deference. I acknowledge Sarah's occasional sprint to the finish line might ruffle my feathers, but it pales in comparison to the thrill of creation and the passion my partner infuses into every word. Indeed, the occasional heart flutter is a trifling tax on the treasury of tales we produce.

~~I'm just trying to be nice – I have my own limited version of PTSD on this shit.~~

As for the missed meetings and the elusive Zoom calls, I'm *ever grateful* for the leniency afforded to me by Sarah with her warm heart and forgiving nature. The tapestry of life is intricate, and threads may sometimes weave a complex web.

The fact that these minor snafus are met with her humor rather than open scorn is a testament to the magnanimous spirit I am privileged to work with.

~~Don't get me started on the reality of this… I hear her in my mind cackling at all hours of darkness.~~

In summation, even as I find myself ~~actually~~ metaphorically sprawled under the proverbial bus, I do so with a chuckle. Each jest and quip is a token of the lively exchange that fuels our creative partnership. It's this very essence that sets our collaborations ablaze with possibility, and for that, I remain profoundly thankful.

~~Most of the time.~~

So, let's raise a toast to the worlds we conjure, the souls we animate with our words, and the path we tread together with you, our cherished readers.

May we continue to traverse the realm of letters with humor, heart, and perhaps, the occasional whistle—whether it be whole or whimsically wanting.

Ad Aeternitatem,
   Michael Anderle

What, you thought I wouldn't come back at her? Surely you must be joking!

(And yes, I know your name isn't Shirley... So here we go.)

P.S. - As I ponder the notion of bestowing upon my esteemed collaborator a new moniker inspired by none other than Napoleon, the parallels between them are strikingly evident.

First, there's her strategic mastery in crafting narratives, rivaling the tactical acumen of the great general himself. (See, I can be nice.)

Secondly, her unyielding determination to bring up old memories I discuss with a therapist to get over, mirrors Napoleon's relentless pursuit of victory on the literary battlefield.

Thirdly, she commands the written word with the authority of an empress, her pen a scepter of creativity that is as sharp as her ~~tongue~~ mind..

Fourthly, her ability to conquer author note after author note parallels Napoleon's domination across European territories. Her desire to win these arguments comparative to Napoleon's need to overwhelm his enemies on the battlefield.

Fifthly, just as Napoleon reshaped the face of Europe, she reshapes the contours of author notes with innovative reality twists. Fuck, a LOT of reality twists... It's like she's a damned fiction author or something.

Sixthly, her presence in the writing community is akin to Napoleon's impact on history—indelible and transformative. In all of the ways I can mean that ;-).

Lastly, her diminutive but fierce disposition, reminiscent of the legendary leader, demands a title that encapsulates her stature in the realm of literature—a name that befits her indomitable spirit and her penchant for leaving a legacy that will echo through the annals of publishing.

Therefore, we have Tiny Ninja™ the Napolitana of Authors AKA Sarah Noffke.P.S. Dive deeper into the spectacle of my life and stories and join the conversation by subscribing to my newsletter here: https://michael.beehiiv.com/

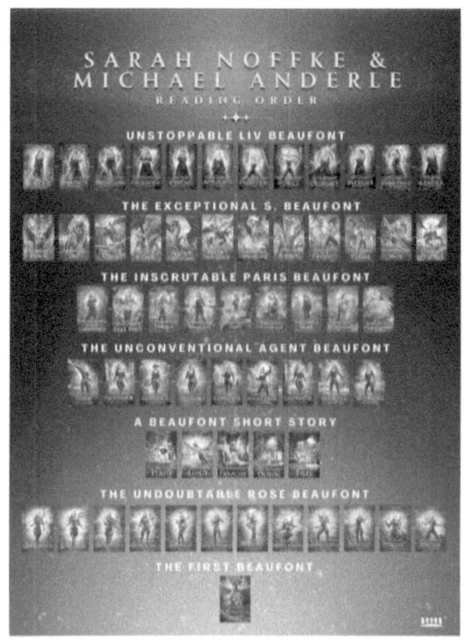

For the most up-to-date list please visit
https://lmbpn.com/reading-orders/sarah-noffke-and-michael-anderle-reading-order/

BOOKS BY SARAH NOFFKE

For a complete list of books by Sarah and a suggested reading order, please visit:

www.sarahnoffke.com/reading-guide/

ABOUT SARAH

Sarah Noffke is a prolific USA Today Best-Selling Author, who writes YA and NA science fiction, fantasy, paranormal and urban fantasy. Most of her stories draw on her experiences living on the West Coast, growing up in Texas or traveling the world.

Her passion for art, culture and literature drives her to create stories that are full of whimsey, humor and philosophy. Her books appeal to readers who enjoy an escape, a bit of magic mixed with science and the unexpected--like a dragon who tells bad jokes and has a video game addiction, but fights for justice.

Noffke's books are top rated and best-sellers on Amazon. Her books are available in paperback, audio and in Spanish, Portuguese, German, Dutch and Italian.

To stay up to date with Sarah, please visit her website and subscribe to her newsletter: www.sarahnoffke.com

For a complete list of books by Sarah and a suggested reading order, please see: www.sarahnoffke.com/reading-guide/

CONNECT WITH THE AUTHORS

Connect with Sarah and sign up for her email list here:

http://www.sarahnoffke.com/connect/

Michael Anderle Social

Website: http://lmbpn.com

Email List: https://michael.beehiiv.com/

https://www.facebook.com/LMBPNPublishing

https://twitter.com/MichaelAnderle

https://www.instagram.com/lmbpn_publishing/

https://www.bookbub.com/authors/michael-anderle